Hood Misfits Volume 3:

Carl Weber Presents

Hood Misfits Volume 3:

Carl Weber Presents

Brick & Storm

www.urbanbooks.net

Urban Books, LLC
97 N 18th Street
Wyandanch, NY 11798

Hood Misfits Volume 3: Carl Weber Presents

ISBN 13: 978-1-62286-954-1
ISBN 10: 1-62286-954-0

First Mass Market Printing January 2016
First Trade Paperback Printing September 2015
Printed in the United States of America

10 9 8 7 6 5 4 3 2 1

Distributed by Kensington Publishing Corp.
Submit Orders to:
Customer Service
400 Hahn Road
Westminster, MD 21157-4627
Phone: 1-800-733-3000
Fax: 1-800-659-2436

Acknowledgments

So here we are, book three. We never saw it coming. Thank you to all the original Misfits, the ones who were with us when this book was titled *Player*, and the original *Hood Misfits* books were still making waves on the self-publishing circuit. Jazz Nicole, Lenika, Dymetra, Laura Hughes from the U.K., Athea, 556 Book Chicks, Christina Jones, Quadir, Lizzy, Law, Jeanette James, and all the rest of our ENGA family: you guys run out and grab our books, read them, and review them as soon as we release them, and for that, we will always have love for you. To all the rest of the fam, new and old, thank you. Without you there would be no us. To Brenda Hampton, we will never be able to say thank you enough for taking a chance on us.

We hope you enjoy Enzo and Angel's story in the ENGA Series as much as you did Trigga's and Diamond's. Who knows? You may see them pop up in this book as well. You have to read it to find out. Now we're on to the next book, the next story. Let's see where it takes us.

Intro

Enzo

Prelude

I heard somewhere that you can't blame a nigga for growing up the way he did. If his environment was foul, and if he didn't have the right support around him, then what did you think he was going to be? Foul. That was just the nature of things and my world wasn't so different.

In the jungle called Atlanta, I was the newest commodity for the Atlanta Nightwings, the NFL's number one champs two times running, and I planned to make it three. Allow me introduce myself. My name is Shawn Banks, but the public and people in my past knew me as someone else. Before I got into this world, an environment that I was still learning my place in, learning what I could and could not do, I was just plain ol' Enzo, a twenty-year-old hoodlum in the streets.

Because I had been sponsored by Damien
Orlando, a well-known street king who ran the
streets of Atlanta with an iron fist, to be in
the Nightwings Football Camp for Kids, I had
a debt. The camp was a program designed to
showcase kids with potential to be the next big
thing for prospective colleges and, later, the
NFL. Damien had been the kind of street lord
who found a way to make a profit off of any- and
everything; and most of us kids in the camp
knew we had a better chance at getting scouted
by colleges if Dame had his name on us.

I found myself caught up in the hype and
promise of a better life, if only I'd do his bidding.
Shit, as a kid coming from the worst the hoods
had to offer in Chicago, better known as Chriaq
these days, Dame's offer seemed like a way out.
Dame had promised most of the world at our
feet and all we had to do was let him sponsor
us. At least, that was the lie he'd told. I had to be
a goon for one of the Trap's well-known street
demons, a nigga who many called the son of
Satan himself. The deal was I move weight and
be a killer for him, and he would ensure my spot
in college and the NFL. That nigga had pull like
that. Dame could be the illest of thugs one minute and the shrewdest of businessmen the next.
The moment I was set up into his world, my life

changed. Actually, even before that, the day I moved from the south side of Chicago, Illinois—Englewood to be exact—everything changed.

See, all my life I've had to take care of myself and my little brother. Fuck that, I also had to take care of my mom when she started losing herself to drugs. As far as I remembered she was a good woman, but she always had her dark moments where she'd lock herself in her room and leave us to take care of ourselves. It only got worse the older we got. When I was around twelve years old I was doing my usual thing. Had taken the green line L all the way to its last stop of Ashland and Halsted so I could head home and walk my block, what I called "the Wood" and others called Englewood.

Trucking over broken glass, cutting through dope boy zones and where some drugged-up homeless liked to get high near empty lots and abandoned churches and buildings, I learned how to be a fast little dude. Making sure I hit up the corner store to pick up some snacks for my four-year-old baby brother Drew and me, I also grabbed some extra stuff so we could clean the house. That day, I was stopped on the street by Drew's babysitter, an older woman who had grown up in Mississippi but moved up north long ago, Missy Charlene, as she sat on her porch watching Drew. I had thought our mom was gonna pick him up after work and after getting her hair done, but there he sat, playing with his toys with some other little kids. Just like all the times when mama had dropped Drew off, I always stopped by Missy Charlene's on my way home just to be sure Drew had been picked up.

Heading up to the porch, I could tell by Missy Charlene's face as she chewed on her tobacco and spit it on the ground that something wasn't good. She had rollers in her hair with a bathrobe on that looked more like a muumuu.

"Yo' mama ain't been by here to get this boy. Figured something must be wrong. No matter her habits, she always picks up the boy when she says," Missy Charlene said.

"How long he been here?"

"Since 'bout ten this morning. Something not right."

I nodded. It wasn't a secret that mama had a habit back then. Sometimes she could hide it well. Other times she couldn't. But I still knew Missy Charlene was right. Mama could be high as a kite and still remember to get Drew.

Packing up my baby brother, I slung my backpack on my left shoulder and snatched up his bag, taking his smaller hand in mine and heading home. Missy Charlene yelled at us to come back and visit if everything wasn't good: her code for telling us to come back to her house if we needed to. Long story short, when we got home, our moms was locked up in her room. I cleaned up my baby brother, gave him a slice of bologna and a piece of bread with a sliced apple on the side, 'cause that was all we had, and some water, then I went to check on moms like I always did.

Turning that knob to her bedroom door was the game changer that day. She lay in a fetal position, tears wetting her cheeks, as she stared off in a blank state with a needle in her arm. I knew without touching her no spirit lived in that body anymore. Remembering that day, I didn't know what to think. I wasn't sad and I wasn't mad, I just was. I was used to this, since I was old enough to remember. When I was a little shorty she'd get real mad, and throw shit around the house sometimes, yelling at me and later Drew when he was born. I used to think she hated us, but the older I got, I realized she really was running and hiding from the nigga who helped create us: our pops. I never knew the cat. Only heard whispers that he was some moneymaker down in the A, who got locked up and died in prison, so I didn't care. I just knew whenever he was in town, she'd send us to our babysitter, and then she'd go missing for a couple of days before returning home.

Thinking on my mom, I can say it was sad when all a parent left behind to look out for their kids was information in the form of a phone number and address elsewhere. That phone number and address led to my *tía* Iya, or Shy as some knew her on the streets. She came and got us days later, packing up our stuff, and moving us to her apartment in Decatur, Georgia. It was crazy for me 'cause I never really knew nothing about her.

She'd visit once a year, leaving us with clothes, gifts, and money that I'd hide. Then she'd be gone, leaving us with her hugs, kisses, and a sad look in her eyes. Back then on that day she got us, she looked at us for hours with tears in her eyes, sitting in a dingy broken chair, in her all-white linen dress and long black hair resting over her shoulder in twisted locs, before hugging us tightly and giving us kisses. That was the only day I'd ever see her that vulnerable, because after that she was hard, but loving, in a way me and Drew never had.

Tía Shy worked as a nurse, but to get extra money she'd work the weekends at the Grove Lounge where she'd spit poetry, hit some lyrical bars, and present herself as one of the hardest conscious rappers in the A. My aunt was slick with it. When she wasn't making us listen to old-school jams like Miles Davis, Public Enemy, or Pac, we were growing up listening to her outdo niggas' bars like Common and even Nas sometimes. Money was good for us. She moved us from the Trap to another fly house in Decatur positioned across the street from a sweet older lady who was taking care of her Bible and rap-quoting grandson. He was a thick, big-ass kid who was some months older than I was. My aunt would watch him sometimes when his grams needed time to herself for church or sometime his grams would watch us.

Growing up there was a'ight until the streets got turned into a war zone. He and I got recruited through our school to be a part of this football camp where Dame took an interest in us. Life was golden only for a short time, and my relationship with my aunt became hard; but she never stopped giving love and supporting my brother and me, even when she got sick and lost her baby because of the sickness. Life ain't perfect, but it is what it gives. Like I said, I always was taking care of myself or someone else, and after everything my *tía* did for us, it gave me fuel to be the best running back I could be.

The second time my life changed was when

the words "Dame's dead" was echoed around the Trap. I remember it like it was yesterday.

I sat relaxin' in the custom black-on-black rimmed-up Escalade that Dame's goons handled. I had just got done doing my rounds at the City, making sure the dimes got on stage and did what they were known to do. Pussy, ass, tits, and more pussy was all around me. I pretty much didn't give two shits 'bout it, only because it was an everyday thing for a nigga, and chicks teasing my dick in a club like this only pissed me off. I wasn't about the fantasy of pussy, more like the reality of that gushy, which, personally, wasn't that hard to get.

For a nigga like me, all I had to do was flash a smirk, and tilt my head back, and chicks seemed to rain from the skies to jump on this dick. Was I saying that in arrogance and cockiness? Naw, not really. Too many chicks would come up to me and tell me how fine, cute, and different I was because I sported a hooped nose ring, with my wavy flat top, chin beard, and, as one chick said, I was Egyptian golden honey toned. Yeah, whatever on that. I also had many chicks whispering that my dick was so good that Dame should make me a ho for broads. That shit wasn't funny to me.

I strolled through the digs, combing the place

for the standard regulars. I saw old man Scoop sitting in his cream and red suit, holding his dick and smoking on a Cuban. He watched a pretty honey with a lush fat ass, pouty lips, sparkling, silky flesh the color of curry, swish her crinkled, long black hair over her shoulder and then climb the pole to slide down it and drop into a scissor split against her girl's pussy. The whole scene had every thirsty nigga in the club standing. They spilled their drinks, clenched down hard on blunts and cigars between their teeth and made it rain in the club. Both dimes— an exotic-looking caramel treat named Angel, and Bubbles, a chocolate, thick, innocent but sultry-looking dime—were a part of Dame's mamís.

Angel was a killa in the club. Every night, niggas filled the spot up just to see her twerk. It was the same with Baby G too, but, yeah, she wasn't around anymore. Heading through the spot, I kept my eyes on everyone who wanted to be a threat to the dimes. Patrons knew not to touch unless they were uppin' the right amount of dough.

Right now, none of the major big spenders was here, so I could be real lax in how I watched the place, which was cool for me. I was tired from running the streets and training. The past couple of months seemed crazy as fuck. Dame seemed to be on some other shit with his runs and having us making trades.

Word on the street was that a lot of bosses were slowly taking their money away from him, which meant that nigga was going to be coming down hard on us soon, and blaming us for everything, when in reality it was all him. Ever since he had dipped into that young chick with the pretty doe eyes, Ray-Ray, Dame had been on planet Godzilla. Running around with an open mouth, swollen chest, and stomping on everyone that came his way. Nigga was crazy, but it wasn't my shit to worry about. I had a deal with him and he had one with me. He'd keep me trained up in football camp and I'd run his dope and be his shield while taking some classes at Georgia Tech. The negotiation was good with me anyway. I was good at zigzagging the streets and the field.

Lights stopped their flashing as the music slowed down into an island beat. I gave a nod to the dimes as I walked by with a smile heading to the back. Each dime kissed my cheek, slipping me some extra Gs for treating them right, and I strolled out to switch places with another homie, Nightmare. Nightmare was a young dude like me, all of us the same age, and he was training up for the basketball program Dame also ran to snatch up young dudes in the streets. He was a tall, lanky but swole dude.

He had tats all over his pale yellow skin with cuts that he said were tribal marks. I said he was a lying motherfucker with that shit, but he just flashed his big teeth and would always say it was true. Nightmare and me always found ways to work together. I'd call him Degrassi 'cause that nigga looked like he was ready to spit bars on "No New Friends," but in reality, I knew dude lived up to that nickname Nightmare. Whenever he touched an enemy, they never was the same.

As I opened the door, plumes of smoke slapped me on the left and right sides while I climbed into the ride. "Damn, Degrassi. You deep throat that shit enough, homie?" I teased, coughing and cracking the windows of the ride.

Nightmare sat in a Cadillac pose, his wrist resting on the steering wheel with a fat one between his fingers. A grin was on his face, making that nigga look creepy to someone who didn't know him. But me, I knew he was high as God. He passed that shit, I took a nice hit, and I slid back in my seat, relaxing.

Damn, the blaze was good.

"Eh, yuh kno' I dun play wit' mi good-good. Mi lick di shot lika mi love mi gyal up," he slurred. Nigga's eyes were so red, I thought he had pink eye and the shit was due to be crusting over anytime now.

I laughed hard at his Patois. Dude was born in the Trap but both his parents were from the islands. He was crazy by blood, which made him crazy in the streets and crazy on the court. That's why we were cool. Same agenda, same goals, used the Trap as a way to get out and get that money in the game.

We sat windin' down, shit talking about everything and nothing. Nightmare started spitting about the last moments of Doughboy, when Trigga blasted that nigga's dome out.

"Man, nigga eyes looked like two eggs sliding off a piece of toast, man!" he clowned. Dude laughed so hard that he started coughing.

Me, I had to sit back and look at him as if the nigga was crazy. "Like two eggs sliding off a piece of toast? Homie, the fuck is that? No, that cat looked like he had just found out he had swallowed acid. Nigga was goneeee."

Nightmare slapped the steering wheel hard, sounding like a horse due to holding on to the good smoke in his throat. We kept talking shit about how wack Doughboy was while passin' *our hits. Every twenty minutes, we'd change places with House, another guard for the girls, and grab whatever the dimes needed, be it food or some shit that they needed for their outfits. I had just got back in my ride when our cells started vibrating.*

The mood was quickly killed when we were told to get to the main house fast by Dame. We knew when that nigga put 187 in the texts that every nigga associated with him needed to come G'd up. So, that meant that we had to stop what we were doing, leaving the dimes at their work, and handle business.

By the time we got to the big house, a car speeding like a bat out of hell almost hit us head on, but swerved in time to miss us. I had my SIG Sauer Mosquito .22LR pistol loaded up in my hand, my other weapons of choice ready for play, when I glanced up at Nightmare and House both shouting, "Shit!"

Shock hit me hard; we all stepped out of our rides as fire kissed the skies. On the lot seemed to be the majority of Dame's goons' rides. I could name off who was in the house just by the rides that were there. But it was the blacked-out Escalade that had the familiar license plate GRIZZLY that had me feeling fucked up.

I stood in silence for a long while. After a minute, I stopped tripping and started to feel relieved as texts started hitting us with rumors about what had gone on inside. No one was sure about how everything had actually started but word was Dame was dead. There were pictures of his mutilated body hanging over his bed, a bed no one touched but that anal-ass nigga, with the words E.N.G.A. painted in blood over the carved letters DOA. All of us stood shocked.

"No way, man. That shit gotta be Photoshopped. It gotta be," House's confused voice said near me.

I said nothing. I knew the letters just like they all did. I already knew that it was time to go. My debt to that nigga, and the possibility of me not making out of the Trap, was done with the crackling of the fire in front of me. House ran forward, still surprised like we all were. I turned to look at Nightmare.

Both of our chins tilted up, we reached out to give each other our familiar handshake with a salute and both of us walked off in the Trap, going our separate ways. Trigga and Jake had done something major, I could feel it as I found my way out of the Trap, but it was the fact that they died in that fire that pushed me to do me, my agenda kicking in overdrive. Weeks later, I

kept my eyes on the news, waiting to hear any-
thing about what went on, but I got nothing,
only whispers of their death.

Back to the present day had me thinking on
the third time my life changed. It actually started
back when I walked into the Nightwings stadium, ready to train for the big game on Sunday.
Wasn't my first time walking into the stadium,
but it was my first time walking in seeing a
person from my past. Walking through the big
stadium, my eyes adjusted to the blaring lights
all around me. Music thumped while technicians
and other stadium workers bustled around setting up, cleaning, and prepping the field. To the
right of me, I saw the Bounce Girls. They were
our team's dance/cheerleading squad. I watched
as they swished their hips, bopping to "My
Homies Still" while another set of dimes stood
to the side, watching, as if learning the routine.

I looked on with my arms crossed before
heading toward my teammates. As I walked
through, I gave a glib smile when some of the
ladies called my name. Like any nigga, I drank
in the view of the ladies before me. All of them
were of varied heights, complexions, shapes, and
sizes. It was like a wonderland for the eyes and I
wasn't one who couldn't notice the morsels that
were presents. What tripped me out though was

the fact that in the group of new girls, ladies, who had just made the cut for the Bounce Girls and who were also alternatives, was a familiar face, one I wasn't expecting and one I didn't want to remember me.

She stood talking to several Bounce Girls, resting a hand on her hip to repeat specific steps to the routine. I watched her do some turn that had her spinning on the tip of her toe, lifting her leg in the air to land into a jumping split, a move I recalled she was well known for and one that always had her G-string lined with ducats. My hand rested on the back of my neck, rubbing it. I watched her sensually roll her hips as she flipped her long, dark sandy-brown hair then bit her lip, hopping back into routine to the song, showing off her plump ass through the whole thing.

Them Bounce Girls were crazy with it, but with this new addition, I knew if she kept doing what she was known for, shit, she would rise through the ranks as a star. I quickly walked by, nodding and returning the hellos to the ladies and stadium staff. Time was of the essence and we rookies had to put on a show for the sponsors who sat in their private box, watching us. We had met some of the new sponsors who were going to be keeping us all lined with deep pockets. One of them was a new guy from London.

Brotha reminded me of that cat I remembered on *The Wire;* he had the air of wisdom, and I swear a glint in his eyes that said he was a killer. It tripped me out, because the moment we shook hands, it was as if I knew the guy, and he let me know off the bat that he would be watching me closely.

Watching me was what one of the main sponsors, a cold, callous motherfucker who I tried to stay out of sight from, was doing. Micah Tems was the big man, the main nigga with all the money, the pull, the power, who not only dropped us ducats but also recruited. He was the one who made sure I was snatched up outta the Nightwings football camp I participated in after Dame was gunned down. It was his push, but he used assistants who fooled me into thinking I was clear from the residual fallback of Dame's big plan.

That day, when the entire sponsors' board checked us out and made their introductions, was the day I knew that Dame's plans was still in play. See, what most people didn't know about the NFL was the seedy underground, all the politics that went on behind the scenes. All the fans got to see was the glitz and glamour. They didn't know about the secret sponsors, men and women who put money on you as if you were a horse in the Kentucky Derby. They didn't know about the bounties put on quarterbacks, wide receivers, and running backs alike. They didn't know that if you didn't make a certain yardage a game or a certain amount of touchdowns, that the sponsors could make your life a living hell by causing bad press, or, even worse, ending your career.

All those people you saw sitting in those expensive-ass sky box seats and shit, they were the big men and women on campus. Even the owners kissed most of their asses because they kept the money coming in. From drugs to bets to prostitution, it all went on behind the scenes of the NFL. In football, teams weren't supposed to have managers. Well, they had general managers, but team managers? Nah, they didn't typically have those. But if you were a prize championship team you did.

You needed a "manager" to handle all the illegal activity going on behind the scenes. That was where Micah came in. It wasn't hard to forget someone who used to do Dame's bidding when it came to the players he sponsored, hiding bodies, and handling money. Judging by the way Micah's eyes darkened like coals as he watched me before giving me a snide smirk and a wink, I knew he was going to be a problem. That nigga was going to be a thorn in my side, one that I could not take lightly. I had to figure some things out before he figured them out for me. Had to do the one thing I was trained to do by a group of misfits back in the Trap: get my game up and develop my plan, because Every Nigga Gotta Agenda.

Dropping my bag, I laced up my kicks and jogged out into the group of my fellow rookies who greeted me with daps. Big smiles were all around. I glanced up into the stadium, locking eyes on the sponsors' box and rolled my shoulders, digging in to run my drills. I could feel that nigga watching me, and it made my skin crawl. Being in this world and not in my former one, I felt like a caged animal. Like my homie Pac once said, "I ain't a killa, but don't push me. Revenge is like the sweetest joy next to getting pussy."

There was no words truer than that shit right there. This world had me on a chessboard, one where I could feel myself being micromanaged. I had to learn how I could be me, and protect my own world, while making sure this glossy, rich one didn't get tainted in the way. It had me apprehensive and had me on guard, but one thing about me, I wasn't a sucka. I had a mind made for the game of chess. *You push me and you will get gunned down.* Those were my thoughts as I practiced that day while being watched and measured for my prowess.

That was the nature of this new world I was in and only a small scope of the ruthlessness in it. My name is Shawn "Enzo" Banks. I'm not only a playa in this game, but I'm also a killa.

Chapter 1

Shy

Weariness traveled through every nook and cranny of my body. A wretched spasm of pain cut into me, causing me to lean over in a position that was habitual for me now days. I emptied my stomach, pushing my thinning black hair from my face. I was exhausted as I sat back into the bed to get my breath. I used to have beautiful locs, but after I got stage one cancer, I chopped them off and went through my chemo. That was about two years ago. Now my frizzy mane was back and I was sick yet again, the cancer back to claim its bounty. Life had a funny way of going full circle. I guess it was karma, because my life hadn't always been perfect.

Glancing at the flat-screen TV that my nephew bought for me, in a condo I knew he stole from a nigga I despised he ever worked for, I turned up the television. A tired smile spread across my face at the thought of how much his thirteen-year-old brother looked like him. Taking care of them again had brought me joy and regret. Regret that I had been too scared to keep them with me when I knew their mother, my sister, was no good for them like I thought she was. The circumstances around her and my nephews was one of the many secrets I'd held on to, one I knew I'd have to tell them soon. The other was one I'd take to my grave.

The reason for that was because I was their true mother. When I had Shawn I was young, only eighteen, when I was violated on my way to my apartment near Decatur. Shawn was the product of that attack and I wasn't ready to take care of him like I wanted to. Sade was eager to be a mother at twenty-five, so we made an arrangement and she came to the A to pick up Shawn, and took him to Kennesaw, Georgia. She'd travel every summer so I could see Shawn growing up. My little heart was always so smart and it made me proud to watch him become so strong. Those visits were my bread and butter until I learned that my attacker had become invested in having my sister too. He'd found out where she was, attacked her, violated her, and pumped her with drugs, something I didn't know of until later in Shawn's life.

By then, my rapist had made a routine of traveling between my sister and me. He'd fuck us both and then found the means to stalk us both to the point that I got tired of running. He destroyed my sister's womb with drugs, which she continued to use to hide from the pain of him finding her and using us both. I used my gift for words to be my healing tool, even when he got me pregnant again with Drew.

He used my fear to keep me quiet. I shipped my other son off to my sister, hoping that if he hid in Chicago my attacker wouldn't find them, but I was wrong. He did, and he made her life hell. It wasn't until years later, when she was dead and police found evidence that it wasn't an overdose but foul play, that he ended up in prison, where justice found its way into his cell. He had destroyed my sister and me, and I promised he'd never lay his hands on the product of his attacks, ever.

I had kept that secret well, until my sister died. When I moved my nephews home with me, my fears became reality when Shawn was recruited by a wolf in sheep's clothing, a demon named Dame. I fought hard those days with Shawn, begging him to find a different football camp, one out of state, one away from the Trap, away from a man he had no idea was closer to him than he'd ever know, but it fell on deaf ears. He always had my and my sister's stubbornness and our ability to be fighters, loyal to family first and others second. That was our weakness, one that had been exploited well in the past, and was now being repeated.

Fear gripped me, but there was nothing I could say. I knew the devil was a lie and he was going to use my . . . my son for his own plan, and he did. Shawn became his reluctant dope boy and his prize budding star in the football camp. I watched it all, heard it all, and no matter how much Shawn tried to hide his budding predatory ways from me, it never worked, because my ears were always in the street. But like any protector, I kept it all to myself, especially the one secret he didn't want anyone to know, one that broke his soul and heart because of what Dame made him do. One that broke my own heart as well: the death of his best friend Jake's grandmother, all ordered by Dame through Shawn's trigger finger.

Those boys were close, and Dame used that knowledge to have Shawn break into Jake's grandmother's house, shoot her, then go after Jake. Sadly, it worked, but it broke my son down to his core by the act and he'd never forgiven himself for it. Even with running in the streets by that boy's side, watching Shawn have the letters E.N.G.A. tatted down the side of his ribcage, that secret ate at him deeply and broke his spirit. I hated Dame's existence before that, because of where he came from, but I hated him even more after that. There were plenty of times I tried to take him out for it all, like I had done Shawn's assistant coach, but I couldn't get close enough without jeopardizing my kids to do so.

Now I lay sick in my thoughts, karma growing in me in the form of cancer, and I prayed that the Lord would just let me stay long enough to protect my kids, because everything I ever did I did for them.

A soft, wet feel of a cloth against my forehead had me glancing up into a set of chocolate brown eyes that warmed my heart. I genuinely loved this kid as if he were also one of mine. I used to make cakes and cookies for him and his granny. I used to sit and listen to her stories she'd share with me, watching her give me recipes of dishes Jake loved, just in case she passed on in her sleep one day. I was to protect him too and I did my best; damn, I did my best. I was the one who saved him from being paralyzed; the pain of the memories always left me crying, so now I lay looking into that angel of death's face, muttering, "Forgive me."

I knew when a flash of anger and hurt spread across his face that he was really there, and the shock had me sitting up abruptly in confusion.

"You are supposed to be dead, baby boy. I . . ."

Any anger that was once in his face now faded away with wisdom I hadn't expected, and he leaned down to settle me back in bed and kissed my hot brow. "No, ma'am. Sometimes the Lord has other plans; and I see you were a part of that always, too, huh?"

Fresh hot tears trickled down and I realized I had made a confession I hadn't intended to.

"There is no vengeance in my heart for what you just told me. That nigga Dame planned it all. But he's maggot bait now. I can't kill my fam for something he had no control over. I learned that lesson awhile ago."

Head bowing, my arms wrapped around him to hold him tight, his deep voice felt like healing balm to me, and I cried.

"Besides, I see the pain in you and him changed you both, made you sick; and now from what you just told me, I want to burn that nigga's dad's grave. I got you always *Tía* Shy, that's why I'm here."

A loving smile warmed my cheeks as he wiped at my tears. I saw beside him a cake and a thick envelope. "I cried for days, baby boy. Don't you ever do that to me again, kid!"

He chuckled low, crinkles forming near his eyes, even as a smile spread across his thick, bushy beard. "Yes, ma'am, I'll make sure not to. Look what I have for you." He turned his back and showed me the cake I had spotted. "Got you this caramel cake because I remembered how you liked them. My baby girl can burn in the kitchen so she made it. I just tasted it." He chuckled as he held my hand.

"Your baby girl? Well, tell her I said thank you and next time you visit you bring her here so I can give her a hug." I chuckled. I patted the back of Jake's hand, swallowing my tears.

"Yes, ma'am. I will. I wanted to see you and give you that while I was in town," he explained.

The little boy I used to call a teddy bear was now a grown man, so changed. I could see familiar pains in his eyes. I could tell he had gone through hell, something I was familiar with.

"How did you find us?" I asked him.

"I'm always watching my fam, the ones I trained," he simply stated. "I'm set up in a way that will help you. Right now, just listen. After what you just told me, you really want to listen. There's money, a cell phone for you that connects directly to me, and a set of keys in that envelope for you and Drew. We are going to pack you up and get you outta here. For now it's best we get you in a place to heal you up and get that cancer out, *Tía* Shy, while keeping you and Drew from the fallout."

My mind immediately understood what he was trying to say. "So just because Dame is dead doesn't mean his agenda is?"

Jake gave a slight nod, cut me up a piece of cake, and watched me carefully savor it. "You're right, and y'all being in Dame's old spot ain't going to work for long but we got it covered. So Enzo can stay here do his thing so not to cause too much suspicion. We want to make sure nothing happens to you two while Enzo covers all his bases. Right now, just you and Drew will be moved to a new place, and we'll move you out in a way where watching eyes can't catch ya, trust me."

I studied his expression. His gait was in a protective position, all love and trust, and I knew he'd protect my babies, so I agreed. "Okay, whatever I have to do, I'll do it. Let us stay a little bit and we'll move there, so Shawn can get his game play ready."

"I can respect that. I'll set up some nurses you can trust. I know one who healed poison from my boy. You know him." Jake smirked.

My eyes widened and I almost choked on my cake, because I definitely did know him. He'd come to our house from time to time, too, to rest his head when he didn't trust it in Dame's setups. I asked, "Will I get to see him?"

"Yes, ma'am, if we can get you all outta here quickly and let Enzo do him in the game. We're just moving you out of here to a safe spot in Atlanta. You won't be too far, until we get you settled in your therapy," he explained.

My hand covered his again, and a knock then a peeking of Drew's head in the room let me know our conversation needed to be cut off at the pass. Drew knew some of the streets but I was proud that he still was a kid at the same time.

"Okay, baby boy, I'll explain it when I see him. He's at drill, and will be going to some party later tonight," I explained. I quickly continued, when I saw him stand, "And you're not going to kill my baby?"

Jake turned, his hands clenching before relaxing. "No. Dame did that shit to wound us both. Enzo loved my gram too, just like I love you, *Tía*. Him and me are fam, and it's all love. I just got to fuck him up later but it's all love; he's E.N.G.A. just like you used to tell us back when we were kids. You created us. I got you for life even if I ever die."

Rocko's "U.O.E.N.O." sounded from Jake's pocket. He dug into it, then gave a quick glance at his cell before looking up to give me a reassuring smile. He stepped forward to pull Drew in with a hard tug. He snaked his muscle-thick arm around my son, a boy who thought I was his aunt, and they laughed and joked.

"Your secret is mine, but I do have two people I need to tell: Trigga and my boss. They need to know that because we have someone you all need to meet," Jake said, before setting Drew down.

I didn't understand who we had to meet, but to keep us safe, I had to trust that. "Okay. No one else please."

"On my word. Love you, *Tía;* rest up or else I'll be hurt about it. We need you healthy because who else will be my seed's nana?" He gave me a gentle smile while standing in the doorway and I smiled, knowing he had found love and created life. "I got some of your stuff with me. We'll meet again."

Drew followed him out and that was the last I saw of Jake for now.

This life was karma, but eventually healing can come. That was proof in the words of a young man who always looked out for us, just as I did for them. I was the gatekeeper; that was my agenda.

Chapter 2

Angel

I recognized his face as soon as I saw him walk onto the field for practice. I didn't want to remember him. Shit, I didn't want him to remember me either. In fact, a bitch had wanted to run as far away from her old life as she could. But life didn't always work the way you wanted it to. I could tell by the way his eyes had lingered on me for just a second too long that the recognition was there for both of us.

"Best keep your eyes off the players," a feminine voice echoed in my ear.

I looked to the right of me and saw another dancer, only this one was male and he was a Bounce Girl too. I mean, you may as well have called him a girl. He was just as feminine as I was. Tino was a light-skinned slim dude who you could tell had been fucked in the ass most of his life.

I shrugged. "Was only looking."

He stood and switched over to grab some water then switched back. "Rule number one, baby girl, the players are off-limits."

"Oh, I don't want not one of those niggas. You know where my head is."

"Bitch, you better not let Micah find out you robbing these niggas dry like you do," he said then laughed.

I smirked. "The only way he'll know is if you tell him," I said then smiled.

Although I was smiling, I could tell that Tino could see the predatory look in my eyes. I could tell by the way he tilted his head and raised his brows at me. It warned him that if I even suspected he snitched me out, I would find a way to take his life.

Tino put his hands on his hips. "You know, bitch, I see that sneaky side of the game in you. You're pretty as fuck, but you got some secrets under this bad-ass body and pretty face. What's your story?" he asked.

I glanced back at the field to the player who had just happened to be glancing at me, then back to Tino and shrugged. "We all got a past, right? Do you want me to go asking why a man as fine as you is gayer than Elton John at a gay pride parade?"

A darkness overtook Tino's features for a nanosecond until he caught himself. He gave a tight-lipped smile and said, "You got that."

"I know."

"Oh, if you really wanna make bank, it's best you get your ass to that party Micah invited you to tonight."

I rolled my eyes. "The only reason Micah invited me is because he keeps trying to get me to sell my pussy."

Tino gave a girlish chuckle. "You should be used to it."

That was all he said as he smirked and walked off. I kept his smart comment in the back of my mind. Although it had made me nervous, it also told me to stay on my toes around him. Since practice was over, I started grabbing my towels and water bottle so we could head back to the locker room. Sometimes it was a hassle for me to keep my past a secret. The only way Tino found out was because he and I had been out to lunch when the manager of Magic had come through the place we had been dining. I couldn't deny that I used to be a dancer when the manager stood at our table for at least thirty minutes trying to get me to come back and shake my ass for him. The life I had led for the past four years was not one I had planned for myself.

As I walked toward the double doors, I felt
someone behind me. I didn't have to turn around
to know who it was. Although each of us played
it off as if we were headed in different direc-
tions, we both knew what was up. There were
still dancers and other people milling about and
none of them knew that the two people min-
gling amid them had a grimy past: one of us a
well-seasoned whore at eighteen and another
a killer ex-drug dealer. When he passed me, he
was close enough to brush against my shoulder.
He was sweaty and looked tired as he took deep
breaths. He had been out there running drills
like he was in a real game, all so the sponsors
could see what a hot commodity he was to the
team. I looked up at the man who had once pro-
tected me and, in both of our eyes, a night we
would never forget flashed.

It was easy to remember the face of the last
man I'd seen from Dame's camp on the night
his reign of terror ended. I didn't know his name
right off the bat then. Dame had so many niggas
running in and out the Trap you never knew if
you would see the same one twice unless they
were in his inner circle. The only reason this
one stood out was because he had a bull nose
piercing with a small horseshoe-type ring. He
had a patch of hair growing on his chin. The hair

on his head sat in a cut with tight, thick, silky curls; and although his square jaw line rocked a light five o'clock shadow it was his long, thick eyebrows and brown eyes that gave him a baby face look.

"Time for your set, Angel," was all he said to me.

Gina and I were the only two in the club who came with our own bodyguards, and while I missed having the security knowing Jake was protecting me, since the dude came recommended by Jake I was okay. I nodded at him and told him I'd be out in a minute. He turned to leave. The rest of the girls and I all sat talking about all the craziness that had been going on since the new girl, Ray-Ray, had been brought in. Shorty was a fighter, and until Dame had damn near beat her to death in his room, she had countered every measure he had set against her to break her in.

Most of us were still laughing when the words, "Dame's dead," echoed around the room.

Those words played over and over in my head. I'll never forget that night at the City. I wasn't even supposed to work the pole that night, but something in the air just told me to make it my business to get the hell out of that house. That, along with Jake telling a couple of the girls and me that it was imperative we head to work that night.

I had been snatched off the street on my way to church when I was fourteen. Dame was ruthless in his pursuit of me. Every time I'd seen him, he was trying to get me in his ride with him or to talk to him or something. I wasn't like those other girls entranced by his good looks or by the cars, the lifestyle he was into. I was simply a fourteen-year-old girl keeping her head in books and school like my grams told me to. I guess what they say is true: eventually most little black girls become a product of their environment.

Back then I used to live off of Garden Walk Boulevard in Riverdale. That place was the hood if you ever saw one. The street was lined with apartments and duplexes on both sides. Some gave off the façade that they were upscale, while others looked as if they were falling apart. The violence there was rampant and, just like most major cities plagued by crime, there was a no-snitching policy. Dame had the whole Clay Co in a death grip. It had gotten so bad in the area with violence that at one point someone was being raped and killed daily. The thing with Garden Walk was that you didn't know it was the hood from the outside looking in. You'd have to be living there to know the hell that lived within.

That particular night Dame had people snatch me, my grams had been sick and we were having a revival at the church that week. She couldn't drive but told me I could go ahead and walk to the church since it was only about ten minutes away walking. I was happy about it because that night was going to be the night me and the mime team did our little routine. Being on the praise team was something that I enjoyed doing so much at the time. I was a different kind of girl back then.

"Can I go to church with you?" I heard a male's voice ask me as I passed a set of duplexes. It was Dame's voice, the voice that I'd come to loath every time I heard it from that moment on. Even though his voice was even and smooth as silk, it made my flesh crawl because I'd heard stories about him. I knew the voice because every day I'd get off the bus from school Dame would be riding through the neighborhood. I knew he had dudes who slung dope for him who lived in my complex. Rumor had it that he had some girls who were prostituting for him, too, but I tried to steer clear of that side of things.

"Damn, shawty, you cutting?" Dough Boy had asked me that. Asking a girl if she was cut-

ting was just like asking her if she was fucking. I scowled at him because even when he was driving Dame around he would ask that same stupid shit to almost every girl. I guess me looking at him like he had Black Plague bruised his ego, especially when Dame laughed along with the other goons. Then, I wouldn't have fucked Dough Boy to save my own life. The sight of his whole face sickened me, mostly his lips. There were some dudes who had sexy, thick lips, but Dough Boy's lips made it look as if his breath smelled like ass.

I kept walking hoping my silence would make them leave me alone. They had to know I was just a little girl. My grams hadn't allowed me to dress beyond my age. I held my Bible clutched to my chest. The church was only a few minutes away when the hairs on the back of my neck stood up. Only then I had no idea how to read that as a warning sign. I was too afraid to turn around to see what all the shouting was about. It was only when Dough Boy snatched me around by my arm that I realized I was going to get either beat up or raped and killed.

Shoot, out of all the shit I would be through locked up in Dame's mansion the next four years, being beaten, raped, and killed would have been a godsend. But I digress.

"Please, let me go," I said as I cowered away under his gaze all the while still clutching my damn Bible like it was going to save me. Tears clouded my vision as I flinched at the pressure he had on my arm.

"You deaf or summin', li'l bitch? You don't hear a nigga talking to you?" he growled down at me.

I didn't say anything because I was afraid to. I was scared that he wouldn't let me go if I did and even more afraid of what he would do if I said what I wanted to say. So I did the only thing I could do. I pulled out my pepper spray. He took a face full and then I kicked him in the nuts before I dropped my Bible and took off running. I could still hear his homies clowning him as I ran as fast as I could in the black Mary Jane church shoes I had on. That didn't help nothing. Two more dudes chased me down. One tripped me and I went tumbling to the ground skinning my knee.

"Ahhhh," I screamed out before they snatched me up.

The saddest part about the whole thing was the fact that people were standing around. Most either ran into their houses and locked their doors or pretended as if they didn't see a scared little girl kicking and screaming as those two threw me in the back of the car.

"What's your name?" Dame had asked me after they'd gotten me into the car.

For a while all I did was back away to the other side of the car and stare him down. I knew he had to be just messing with my mental since he had called me by name a time or two before. I had learned that was Dame's game. If he could break you mentally, he had you. I'd never been so afraid a day in my life. He sat there with butterscotch-toned skin, a tapered haircut that had been shaped to perfection, and dressed like he had been featured on the cover of GQ. His light eyes studied me as he smoked on a cigar.

"My grams going to notice when I don't come home," was how I answered.

He tilted his head and furrowed his brows. "Is that supposed to deter me or something?"

The Escalade was still sitting in place so I was hopeful that he would let me out. "People saw you taking me. Someone is going to tell."

That nigga smiled quickly then it faded like it was never there. "You think so?"

I wiped the tears from my eyes with my closed fist. Even though Dame looked like he had just walked right out of heaven, I'd learned that he was the complete opposite.

"Let's go, Jake," I heard him say.

There was glass separating the back of the truck from the front so I didn't even know anyone was up front. That didn't stop fear from overtaking me. Dame just sat there and watched me as I tried to open the door and jump out the back to no avail. I was horrified so much so that I started hyperventilating the farther and farther we moved away from where me and my grandmother lived. I screamed and banged on the windows, crying for dear life, until Dame's fist connected with my jaw and put me out of my misery. That was how my life started with Dame, his world, and his rules.

My life had never been the same after that day. I tried to run away from Dame's mansion four times before I realized that once he had you there was no escaping. It was hard for me to wrap my mind around the fact that some of the older women were there because they wanted to be. After the first few weeks of beatings, starvation, and being sleep deprived, I finally started to get with the program. Dame took my virginity then introduced me to drugs and alcohol. I'd started to learn that as long as you did what he said when he said exactly how he wanted it done you could pretty much survive day to day unscathed mostly, but that was only if that nigga was in a semi decent mood. Sometimes

Dame would fuck with me just because. I could either be too quiet for his liking or not paying him the attention that he thought I should have been paying him. I also found out another secret: the better I was at dancing, the more he kept me at the club bringing in money. The more I was at the club bringing in money, the less I had to worry about a nigga in the house trying to make me fuck them.

My name was Bianca, but since day one Dame had called me Angel. It was his play on the fact that he'd taken me on my way to church. I had been called Angel so much that sometimes I forgot my own name. Being under Dame's umbrella had been hell so when the words "Dame's dead" were spoken to me, it took me a minute to wrap my mind around who was saying it and what it meant. It had been four years since he had taken me. So all I knew was Dame, his world, and his rules.

I turned away from the vanity mirror I had been sitting at applying my makeup for my last set of the night. "What?" I asked, looking up at the girl who'd told me.

Most of us in the City were shaking our asses for Dame, but it was only me and another girl, Gina, who had brought in the most dough. She wasn't there that night and the fact of the rea-

son why she wasn't there hurt me to my core. I wanted to cry thinking about her. Word was the girl had sliced her own throat after the last time Dame took her to the basement before he had died. The basement was a place in Dame's mansion no one wanted to go. So much shit happened in that place that it would make the worst of the best serial killers cringe. From beatings to sodomy, committed against males and females, it all happened in the basement.

It had been me who had helped to get Gina cleaned up after her first trip to the basement thanks to that bitch Sasha. If Dame was dead, I hoped that bitch was killed with him. Gina had been the only cool one in the house besides Coco, Trigga, and Jake. I mean, it was a few dudes in the house who were okay and normally those were the ones hanging with Jake and Trigga. Any of those other niggas I tried to steer clear of.

Coco was a few years older than me and had a kid she hid away from Dame. She was a pretty girl who kind of took me under her wing when I got in the house. It was her who taught me how to shake my ass like I had been born to do it. It was her who helped clean me up after Dame had ripped my pussy to shreds while taking my virginity. That nigga's dick was like *nothing I'd ever experienced, even after he'd made me take other dick to make him money. No man's dick had ever come close to ripping me from the front to back like Dame's had done. But it was Coco who taught me how to stay on his good side as much as I could.*

There had been plenty of times that nigga would come in on a rampage, but shit, me, Coco, and Gina had mastered the art of taking as few ass whoppings as possible. Gina mostly knew when he was coming home in a fucked-up mood because she was closest to Trigga and Big Jake. They would tell her some kind of way and she would tell us. Then the three of us would either steer clear or triple team that nigga in the bedroom to make sure he didn't pop off on us. Sometimes even that was hard to do with that bitch Sasha, Dame's supposed bottom bitch, thinking she used to run the girls in the house. Eventually Dame got tired of Coco, too, and he killed her. Coco had been doing all she could to keep her kid hidden and sometimes she went through this emotional phase were she would just dope up and zone out. That would cause her to miss work at the club or even not perform well when Dame sold her out to other people. She started costing him money and that angered him. He beat her to death in front of the whole house. I often wondered what happened to her kid, but since nobody had even seen the kid but me and Gina, that I knew of, it was a long shot to find out what happened to him.

"Yeah, girl. Look," she said, pointing the remote at the TV and turning up the volume. There was Dame's mansion, the place we used to live, up in flames. The reporter was claiming there had been no survivors.

"I don't believe that shit," Niya said behind us. She was an Asian and black chick with exotic features and a ghetto booty.

"That nigga ain't dead. Don't let this shit fool y'all," another girl said.

"Let me get my ass out here and make this money I lost last night before this nigga try to break my fucking arm again. Y'all stupid asses sit in here and believe this shit if you want to. When that nigga get here at closing time and y'all ain't made his money we'll see who's gon' be dead by the end of the night," Niya said before stomping her six-inch spiked heels out the door.

Her round, tanned ass bounced and jiggled as she walked out. Part of me was wishing that nigga was really dead, but knowing who Dame was and how he rolled wouldn't allow me to be so lucky in my thoughts. So I, too, got up and finished dressing up to work my set. Wasn't any need for me to get all happy about shit that wasn't true.

Bubbles looked at me one last time. "You think he dead?" she asked.

I shrugged and glanced from her to the TV. She was still holding the remote in one hand and the other hand was on her stomach. She was pregnant and scared shitless Dame was going to find out and do to her what he had done to Gina and countless other girls who'd made the mistake of getting knocked up. The only reason Coco had been able to get away with it was because she got good at lying and hid her sickness by pretending she had doped herself up one too many times, she used to tell me. When she had the baby, Dame had been somewhere in London handling some business with a shipment of girls.

"I hope he's dead. Jesus, let him be dead," she whispered.

I could hear the cracks in her voice because of the emotions she was feeling. We didn't have time to talk about it though.

That night after all the girls had finished the sets for the night we waited out back for the van that Dame would normally send for us, but it never showed. Surprisingly, the guard who was *supposed to be watching me had disappeared too. What if that nigga is dead? I got to thinking.*

"Y'all think he ain't gon' show up?" Niya asked.

"They said this motherfucker was dead on the news," Bubbles added. "What if he is and this is our way out?"

"Our way out?" another girl repeated. "What we gon' do if he is dead? All I got is the couple stacks I done made tonight and I ain't got anywhere else to go. What the fuck I'ma do if this nigga is dead? I ain't got nowhere to stay, nothing to eat, no clothes, nothing. Everything of mine was in that house."

I listened on as most of the girls murmured agreeing with her. There we were, six young girls with no skill sets other than shaking ass and selling pussy. There was only one thing that made me different from them. I had $10,000 cash in my bag from the take on the night and a couple more stacks from what I had made the night before. Sometimes, if we made real good money, Dame would let us keep a couple thousand or so as a bonus. I'd been making enough bonuses to have a little stash saved up. While the girls were trying to decide their next move, I quickly called a cab.

"Where you going, Angel?" Bubbles yelled out once they all realized I was trying to make a quick getaway.

"I don't know, but if this nigga Dame is dead, I can tell you I'm never going back to the Trap again."

Bubbles rushed over and hugged me tight. "If I never see you again, thank you for always being there for me."

All I did was smile and kiss her cheeks. I really didn't have time to talk. I hopped in the back of that cab and told him to take me to the Westin.

I hadn't looked back or been back to the Trap since. Yeah, at least that was the plan for me not to go back to the Trap. Life or God had a funny way of doing shit and at this point in the game, after all that I'd gone through, I wasn't too sure there was even a God anymore. See, my intentions had been to run away from the life that Dame had forced me into. I had planned to do whatever was necessary to keep my nose clean, head above water, and stay out of trouble. Shit didn't work out that way though. That $10,000 ran out quickly. Between staying in a hotel and buying food, that shit went as fast as it had come.

I was too damn scared to show my face at the City for a while for fear that Dame really wasn't dead. Then one day I was out and I swore before all that was holy I'd seen that nigga walking into a restaurant talking to other bosses. That shit scared me so badly that I stood at the window openly gawking at the man sitting there. It was as if Dame had been resurrected. I stared for so long that he calmly tapped some cat in a suit and pointed in my direction without even looking at me. When the man got up and looked at me before moving toward the door of the place, I damn near killed myself in traffic on Peachtree Street trying to get away. I'd had no idea how close I'd come to falling into the clutches of a man who made Dame look like Mother Teresa.

"You keep watching me and people are going to start to talk."

The voice startled me, bringing me back to reality as I sat on the bench next to the showers in the locker room. I went to turn around but he stopped me. I knew he was behind me but didn't know how he had gotten in there.

"You wouldn't know I was watching you if you weren't watching me," I responded.

"Put your headset on, then talk to me. That way if someone walks in it can look as if you're just singing along with the song. And, for the record, I wasn't watching you."

My heart was beating in my chest because I'd known my past would catch up with me sooner or later. I did what he suggested then asked, "What do you want?"

"To know if my secret is as safe with you as yours is with me."

"I don't know you," I told him.

"Good. I don't know you either, li'l buddy."

I responded, "Good."

I could feel he was still there watching me although he was quiet. I didn't know the method to his madness, but I assumed he wanted his secret to remain intact for the same reason I wanted mine to remain intact. He had a lot to lose, way more than I did. He'd built a solid image in the last few months, poster child for the NFL. If they had any idea that he had been a drug runner and hired killer, he'd be back in the Trap quicker than he could blink. Me, on the other hand, I just wanted a fresh life and a new start.

Chapter 3

Angel

"So, you're the new girl, right?"

"Yes, I am, if you want to call it that." I smiled and looked at the bulky football player sitting next to me. His big, beefy hand was on my thigh and, every so often, it would inch higher and higher toward my pussy. I just smiled and played it off. I looked at the man decorated in so much jewelry the lights in the room were dancing off of him creating a light show. He had a few things I wanted and needed. He was the means to an end. There was a party going on, one where the best of the best in the NFL were invited. In order for any chick to be there she had to be a part of the Bounce Girls and she had to be one of the main dancers. I mean, there were some other girls walking around, but they were all entertainment, which meant the man in charge had gone to Magic City and Diamonds of Atlanta and grabbed the cream of the crop.

Me, I was a Bounce Girl but only as an alternate, which was fine by me. All I'd wanted to do
initially was get a job so I could be sure not to fall
back into my old lifestyle.

"I'll call it that because you have a different
style about you. All these other chickens walking
around here trying to catch a nigga's pockets,
but the fact that you bought me a drink says
you're different."

"I don't buy every nigga a drink, so the fact
that I liked you enough to do so says you stand
out to me. Look at you; you're not all loud and
boisterous like these other clowns."

Reggie grinned; or at least I thought his name
was Reggie. I couldn't remember. And while he
may not have been loud and boisterous in the
sense that he wasn't shouting about fine bitches,
big booties, and liquor, his jewelry spoke loud
enough for him.

I watched the man's eyelids droop some more
then scoped out all of his jewelry. I knew he had
a bankroll in his pocket, too, since he had flexed
just minutes before buying another bottle just
to show me he could. That would be his mistake
in the long haul. When I'd purchased him that
drink, I slipped an Indigo pill into it. I didn't
know who had made that shit, but if you mixed it
with alcohol, it put the biggest of niggas on their

backs. It would be my fourth time running the scheme. The first three times had worked like a charm. Like I said, it would be a cold day in hell before I went back to shaking my ass and selling pussy.

He slid closer to me and I gave a fake moan when his fingers finally found their way up to my clit. I opened my legs a bit more so he could get a feel of what he wanted.

"Fat pussy, huh?" I asked with a smirk then leaned closer to his lips so mine could brush his as I spoke.

"Damn, girl," was all he could say.

"Why don't you meet me in the bathroom downstairs in the kitchen?"

His eyes widened. "Why not up here? Shit, we can get down right here if you want."

"No, because what I want to do to you, you're not going to want anyone to see. So meet me down there in ten minutes."

I let my hand massage the ever-growing bulge in his pants. Since he was damn near slobbering from the mouth, I hoped this fool could actually make it down the stairs to the bathroom before passing out.

He stood then snatched me up with him, grabbing a handful of my ass in the process. "Ten minutes?" he asked with a hungry look in his eyes.

The grip he had on my ass actually hurt, but I smiled and played it off. "Yeah. Now go. My pussy ain't gon' stay this wet and hot all night."

I was more than happy when that nigga turned and bumped into a few people as he made his way down the stairs. I looked at my watch and started counting down to my next victim. Everything for the night was going as planned. All I had to do was get to the bathroom downstairs in ten minutes and I could have my bounty. If you haven't figured it out by now then let me explain it to you: I drugged a football player and when the drugs finally took a toll on him, I would rob him of his jewels and his money. Then I would make my escape through the back door of the kitchen since it was the easiest escape route. At least that was the plan until shit went way left.

"This is how this shit is going to go, my man. And I'm only going to say this shit once, you're going to take this shit, and you gon' like this shit, understand?"

I watched Micah as Tino cried in front of him. What I had come to learn since joining the Atlanta Nightwings cheerleading squad was that nothing was as it seemed. From the auditions to where I was at the moment—some isolated mansion in the backwoods of Alpharetta—everything was a farce. Music bumped and blared around the place. There were hundreds of people in and out of the house at a time. The pool was live with half-naked men and women. The backyard was filled with people dancing and partaking in alcoholic poisons. Football players from all over were at the party. It was the big throw down before the next game with the Angels versus the Nightwings. Their rivalry was almost celebrated like a holiday.

"Micah, you ain't tell me this many niggas was gon' be in here like this," Tino whined.

"Nigga, I don't give a fuck how many niggas in that room. They paying so you playing, you feel me?" Micah gave a sarcastic laugh then wrapped a muscled arm around Tino's neck.

To others passing by, it looked like Micah was just hugging his boy up, giving him dap, but I'd come to know better.

Micah spoke through clenched teeth. "Let me tell you something. I own you. Do you understand? I own everything about you including that loose booty of yours. All these down low niggas done heard about the way Tino swallow big dicks and take big dicks up the ass, no lube. They want to see what all the hype is about. So you pop this pill, drink this liquor, and make my money. And don't act like I don't break you off nice at the end of the night, too."

Tino looked like he was about ready to fold into mist and disappear. He was one of the only three males on the cheerleading squads. To the outside world they were just guys there to spot when the girls were doing flips and tricks on the field, but those of us on the inside knew that all three of them were a part of the ring of prostitution and drugs: two of the dudes were candy for the down low dudes in the NFL who didn't want anybody to know their secret.

"Micah, you told me this was about fun and I ain't having fun no more. Some of these same niggas raped me last time," Tino cried, but his voice was raised just a little bit too loud.

He drew attention with his antics and that was a no-go. I wanted to feel sorry for Tino because on the day that I'd made the team, he was one of the first ones to congratulate me. But I found out he was only being nice to me so he could introduce me to Micah. But I had peeped game from a mile away.

"Oh, so I see we using threatening words like rape and shit now, huh? I don't know nothing about no rape, but I got this video that shows you sucking and fucking two niggas at once. The same niggas you screaming rape on be them same niggas on the tape. You got they cum all over your face, my nigga. So rape what?"

Micah had pulled away from Tino, and took a defensive pose. The crisp, ironed designer jeans cuffed over the fresh white Air Force Nikes, thick white designer T-shirt, and white blazer complemented the platinum and white gold sitting on Micah's arms, neck, and in his ears. He was the squad's manager. It was funny how Micah could be this smooth-talking pimp one minute, and then be a corporate executive when the time called for it.

"That was different, Micah."

"Ask me if I give a fuck. I can take you out of this shit in a heartbeat." Micah snapped his thick fingers. "Just like that."

Micah glanced around quickly then clapped a hand on the back of Tino's neck, bringing him closer so he could whisper in his ear. Whatever Micah said to him caused his spine to go so straight that one would have thought he was a statue. All the color drained from Tino's face before he walked out of the room. Micah turned his attention back to me as he rolled his shoulders then brushed the lapels of his blazer over like it had some dirt or lint there.

"Now, where were we?" he asked me. "Oh." He clapped once. "When you gon' let me introduce you to all this money?"

As soon as I had walked into the party Micah summoned me. His main priority? To get me to do what he made Tino and most of the other girls on the team do: sell pussy. He'd cornered me just as I had been trying to leave to get downstairs.

I sighed and set down the champagne glass I had been drinking from. "I done told you, my pussy ain't for sale."

"You sure? Because I heard from some people who know some people that you used to shake that pussy down at Magic for my nigga Dame."

I stood and glared at Micah. He and I had history. Being that he was one of Dame's inside men, he got the pick of the litter when it came to the girls. I responded, "I don't know what you're talking about."

"Oh, but you do. I know you do, Angel."

My whole body started to shake from the inside out. For months I'd been trying to hide all evidence of my old life. I knew that Micah was trying to force my hand. He had been talking loud enough for those standing around to slyly look on.

I licked my dry lips. "My name is Bianca," I told him.

He tilted his head to the side and licked his lips in a way that reminded you of the singer D'Angelo. "I like you, Angel," he said then chuckled. "My bad, Bianca. You're beautiful and I can see why any man would want you on his team."

He said that then got quiet, studying me like I was a test he couldn't figure out. Men didn't have to tell me I was beautiful; I knew I was. No, I wasn't mixed with anything as far as I knew, but from the pictures my grams had of my parents, they had just been good-looking black people. I had a head full of hair, but the shit was wild and straight out of Africa. I loved my hair, but the business I was in had no use for it. So, I kept it braided down and sewed in the best weave money could buy. Although money had been tight, I knew a couple of guys who broke into hair shops and stole hair then sold it on the street for the low.

I kept my body in tiptop condition because I didn't know any other way to be. I knew how to use it to get what I wanted, too. But if I was going to be selling my pussy then all the money was coming to me. Long gone were the days I lay on my back then handed over all my money to a nigga.

"I think it's time for me to go," I said then tried to walk past Micah only to be body blocked by two massive guards.

"Come on, now, Angel. Give me a chance to make this shit right. You ain't like these other bitches, I can see that. I was testing you. A nigga can see you ain't at all impressed by the lavish life I live, and I could use a down-ass bitch like you on my team. Fuck with me for a second, *mamí*."

He was blocking my money and it scared me more than annoyed me. If I didn't get my last hit for the night then I wouldn't have anywhere to sleep for the rest of the month. I really couldn't risk revealing myself too much. It was my paranoia that my old life would come back to haunt me. That was why it was easier for me to live in hotels. After checking in, I could pay for my rooms weekly or monthly in cash. The credit card and ID I had didn't tell my real identity.

I knew Micah was full of shit so I didn't know what made me turn around to face him. And I probably would have told him just how full of shit he was had the whole house not erupted with shouts of, "Enzo!"

"Oh, shit. My nigga Enzo in the building." Micah grinned and rubbed his hands together like he was Birdman from Cash Money.

Bitches started pulling their dresses up a little higher, pushing their tits up a little farther and fluffing their hair. Micah rushed out into the hall through the sea of people and yelled over the balcony, "Yo, my nigga Enzo. Ey, yo, bring my man up to the suite," he ordered then turned back around and ordered his guards to clear the room.

He selected only the baddest of chicks to stay in the spacious room that had different styles of lounge chairs and sofas scattered about. The only men left in the room were those of importance. I turned to leave the room because I really didn't want to be a part of whatever was about to go down; but, more importantly, I needed to get to the bathroom downstairs.

"Naw, naw, where you going?" Micah asked.

He didn't give me time to answer before he grabbed my hand and yanked me back in the room. Every Sunday Enzo's name was everywhere: ESPN, sports talk radio, *SportsNation,* et cetera. So I knew that by being in the same room with him it would be hard to pretend I didn't know him.

"You need to be here to see this history in the making. You know why they call this nigga Enzo? Because every time this motherfucker gets the ball in his hand, he touches the end zone. Been watching this nigga since he was in camp. Knew he was gonna fuck some shit up once he got to the NFL," Micah bragged around the room.

I could tell when the famous Enzo had finally made his way up the stairs. People parted like the Red Sea and my heart stopped. Nervousness swept through me when I saw that familiar face. My hands started to sweat and my knees got weak. I tried to pull away from Micah so I could get the hell out of there.

"Micah, I need to go to the bathroom," I whispered to him, trying to snatch away, but he wouldn't let go of my hand.

"Hey, you'll be a'ight, okay? Work them pussy muscles and hold shit tight until you meet my nigga Enzo. Keep in mind you're only a fucking alternate dancer. You ain't even supposed to be at this party. I made shit happen and I can take shit away. Just relax. You wit' me so naan nigga going to touch you unless I say so, you feel me?"

Micah was so arrogant and cocky that he thought I was afraid of some random niggas trying to fuck me. But no, I had made up in my mind that if I ever ran into anybody from Dame's old days I wouldn't make contact and would act as if I never knew them. The only reason I'd stayed on the dance team after finding Micah was the manager was because it was easy access to the players. And that meant I was closer to freeing them of their jewelry and money. Enzo was one of Dame's old henchmen. He was the one guarding me in the club the night I learned Dame had died.

Enzo walked in like he knew he owned the night. He didn't roll with an entourage, which was noticeable as he dapped niggas up and smiled for the cameras. His smile was something that I couldn't explain. He only gave a half one that looked more of a snide smirk than anything else. He was dressed like he had just stepped off the pages of *GQ,* which made him stand out among the other dudes who looked like they just came from a rap video set. Minimal jewels adorned him, a black diamond-filled watch on his left wrist and a horseshoe ring in his bull nose piercing. I couldn't front like he wasn't sexy because he was. I just didn't want to be in the same room with him.

I could tell the moment he noticed me too. His smile faded and his eyes darkened. We didn't know each other that well, but we both knew the world we'd come from. I could tell by the way he took a deep breath, stared me down, then moved to the other side of the room that neither one of us wanted our secret to ever get out. He didn't want anyone to know he was an ex–drug runner and I didn't need anyone to know I was an ex-whore. Micah could pull down our façade anytime he wanted to. That was what scared me most.

"Yo, Enzo, get over here, my nigga," Micah called out to him before he could get away.

I watched on in silent horror as they clapped hands then gave shoulder bumps.

"What's good, my nigga?" Enzo greeted him.

"You. You're what the fuck is good these days. You ready for the game on Sunday?"

"Always ready. Just get the ball in my hand and I'll do the rest."

"Ha-ha! My nigga. Yo, check it, I got some business I wanna holla at you about. Let's go back in my office and hash some shit out."

I could tell that Enzo wasn't really feeling the suggestion by the way he thumbed his chin then glanced away. "Yeah? What about?" he asked Micah.

"Not out here with the peasants, my man. Let's step in my office."

When Micah tried to pull me with him I balked. He turned to look at me with a frown. I told him, "I have to take a piss. Do you mind?"

He looked as if he was about to get belligerent. "Bitch, you can't hold that shit for a few more minutes? A nigga trying to talk business and you worried about pissing. Calm the fuck down. I know the pussy tight, you can hold it. I know you can . . . Angel."

I inhaled loudly then ran a hand through my hair. I caught Enzo glancing at me and so did Micah. I knew when he called me Angel that if

Enzo wasn't sure of who I was before, he damn sure was then. I could have sworn I saw Micah smirk.

"So, check it," Micah stated as he sat behind the big oak desk in his office. "I need to run some shit by you, my dude."

The music was drowned out as soon as we walked into the room and Micah closed the door. Two big, burly niggas stood at the door as I sat down on the chocolate leather Tudor-style sofa. Micah had offered Enzo a seat in front of his desk with one of the wingback maroon chairs.

"What's up?" Enzo asked casually.

Micah reached in his desk, pulled out a Bank of America money bag, then slid it across the desk to him.

"What's this?" Enzo asked.

"It's your take for the game last Sunday. I bet on you twenty to one that you would catch that Hail Mary and win the game for the Nightwings. You made me half a mil in one game. So, I wanted to show my thanks."

Enzo quirked a thick brow then tilted his head to the side. "On some real shit, my dude. I ain't here for this, feel me? I appreciate all the parties and shit and I appreciate the love, but this here, this all you. I ain't trying to be a part of that life."

Micah smirked. "Anymore?"

"What?"

"You mean you're not trying to be a part of that life anymore?"

While Micah smirked, Enzo quietly sat back in his chair and studied the con man before him. "I don't know what you mean," Enzo told him.

Micah laughed as he stood and walked around his desk. He propped himself on the left side of it as he looked from me back to Enzo. "You've met my girl Angel, right? Angel, meet Enzo. Enzo, Angel."

I didn't say anything as Enzo cut his eyes at me. The whole thing had me on edge.

"Oh, wait, you two should already know each other, right?" Micah then asked, feigning innocence as he rubbed his hands together. "I mean, you both used to work for the same dude so I don't see why any introductions are really needed, but you know. I'm just being polite and shit."

"Damn, nigga, you act like you the feds or something asking all these damn questions and insinuating shit," I barked out before I could catch myself, immediately regretting it.

Micah's gaze instantly turned cold as he stared me down. Enzo stood and rolled his shoulders. The two big, burly guards at the door moved toward him but stopped when Micah held up a hand.

"Look, man, I done told you, you can do what you want. I don't give a fuck how much money you making off me, you feel me? Just keep it the fuck away from me."

"Nah, see. I need your help though. So, I figured if I tell you how much I'm betting on what particular thing, then you go out on the field and make it do what it do. Like in this New Orleans game, I'm betting you score seven touchdowns as opposed to the four you scored last week. You can do that, can't chu, my nigga?"

Enzo's eyes turned to ice, but Micah only smirked.

"Nigga, just how the fuck am I supposed to make seven touchdowns one game? I'm good, but a nigga ain't got wings. You tripping."

"See, all you need to worry about is catching the ball when it's thrown to you. Me and the quarterback got an agreement just as me and some of the members on defense for the Angels have an agreement. You make sure that ball stays in your hand and get to the end zone when the time calls for it. So you can do that for me, right?"

Enzo shook his head. "There really is no honor among thieves. You undercutting your own people."

"Yeah, you can do it. I'd hate to leak to the media that the NFL's poster child used to push drugs and help a well-known kingpin sell women and young girls across the globe for a profit. I mean, come on; imagine all the criminal charges and all the bad press. What's going to happen to that sickly but oh so beautiful aunt of yours, and your little brother once you're locked away? So, I'm saying"—Micah stood and matched Enzo's pose—"we got a deal or what?"

Chapter 4

Enzo

The sound of screams rent the air in a jarring, "Ahh!" and "Yes!" as a thud and clatter of glass echoed behind it then mixed with a thumping baseline of Lil Wayne's "Gunwalk" in the background. I stood glancing down at the body of a dead man. He was hired to protect a man, aimed to make me his bitch on paper, and his packing mule on the field. I had a forced meeting earlier that had caused me to return to an old place I didn't want to go. It went a little something like this.

"We got a deal or what?" Micah had asked.

Now, in my head, this shit was going down one of two ways: one, the Glock I had secured against my spine was about to meet this nigga's mouth as his brains leaked on his wack-ass chinchilla rug; or, two, I play the game. Suffice it to say, I went with option three.

Staring down this nigga was nothing for me.
Not another motherfucker was going to put
me back into a place of servitude and fear. Yeah,
I had obligations to my fam, and this bitch just
showed me his hand too fast, but he also didn't
know who I was trained by. All I heard was, *"use
that shit to your advantage while building up
your arsenal,"* so I did.

So while I looked down my nose at a man who
was one of the biggest payers for our team, I
scratched the side of my clenched jaw and held
on to my anger.

Micah's hands rested on both of my shoulders. He gave a slight squeeze with a laugh.
"You're my moneymaker. You know you got a
gift out there on the field, but you also got a gift
in the streets, don't cha?"

My mouth made a straight line as I cut my
eyes at him. "Don't even know what you're
talking about. People like you always get us
black dudes mixed up, right? No matter if you do
look like one of us."

His hands clapped my shoulders. He stepped
back, but stayed close enough to be in my face as
he watched me. "But you're a killer, right?" he
said, putting emphasis on the word "killer" while
a wide Kool-Aid grin spread across his face. He
shaped his hand like a gun, clicking it off at my

head, then dropped his hands down to slide them into his pockets. "I have need for your . . . gifts, all of them."

My spine in that moment felt as it were made of steel. I stood erect, jaw clenched, not saying a damn thing, just watching a man who made me wonder why he was coming at me the way he was.

"Sir, I don't even know what you're talking about. I don't even want any part of what you are thinking you know about me."

Amusement flickered in his eyes and he made a slight, curt nod behind me. His two bodyguards disappeared through the double oak doors of the opulent office we all stood in. The sound of a protesting feminine voice flowed back into where were both stood, sizing each other up, and Micah's grin seemed to become more menacing as my own anger become more chilling.

Suffice it to say, shit went downhill after that. Even though Angel and I had tried to play it off, we both knew what it was. Micah knew us very well and playing dumb wasn't flying anymore. Angel still stuck to her story even though Micah wasn't hearing it. I watched him turn that finger he was using to mimic a gun and shoot it off toward the chick I was very much trying to keep my distance from.

"Naw, see, every day you leaving bodies on the field, so what I ask shouldn't be something to trip off, right? The both of you are used to getting specific jobs done." The sound of Angel shifting against the leather sofa had me checking her out in my peripheral. Dude's innuendos were killing my vibe, and by the way she dug her nails into her arm, I could tell it was the same for her.

"I'm not sure what's going on. Why do you keep assuming things about me? Like, I really don't want any part of this. I just need to go piss please and get back to the party," she said.

The tone of her voice was one of complete cluelessness, but everyone in that room knew she was a liar. We both were. She quickly stood, pulling down her tight skirt. The muffled sound of her heels on the chinchilla rug then clacking on the marble floor traveled toward the door but the nigga who held us for ransom wasn't having it.

Micah cleared his throat then snapped his finger. "Ah, ah, I think your pussy will be just fine if she just sits her pretty ass back down on the couch and you cross your legs. You should be good at that, right? Keeping your legs closed? Or nah?"

He laughed as if he had said some important joke then pointed at the couch. "Sit. If you need to piss so bad, squat over that plant then take it with you when we all are done. I mean, we all are family here, right?"

Through their discussion, I stayed where I was. Music for the party drifted occasionally in the room. The sound of laughter from different giggling chicks would float past the door and the smell of weed, laced with Indigo, had the whole mansion turned up. Angel's reluctant pause stilled the room before she sat back down. I was unsure about how all this was going to play out, but I was really hoping he'd hurry the shit up.

"So this is what I want from you both." Micah rubbed his hands together, then leaned to sit against the front of his desk. "Get with my program and we'll all have us a nice time together just like it was originally planned, much respect to our lost amigo, understood?" He crossed his chest, left, right, from the stomach to the heart before kissing his fingers and pointing to the ceiling.

A curt laugh reverberated from me in a reply to his showboating. "Do what you want. I mean, shit. I play how I play. What you think you know about me, I don't even care. Not my problem. In the end, you only hurtin' yaself, not me."

Micah shifted forward then stepped back to me, his eyes locked on mine, but his comment was directed behind me. "And what is your reply, Angel? Not down for the cause anymore? Family ties mean nothing?"

I wanted to turn just to see how she was looking, but I wasn't about to be disrespected just because one nigga was in the grave, and this fool thought he could pick up the pieces. It didn't always work that way; besides, he could just be playing us to see how we'd act.

"Ah, like I said, I really don't know what's going on, so I have no comment on anything," she reiterated.

Micah sucked his teeth, giving us both a bored glare as he smirked. "That's right. You playing dumb, good look."

Nerves had the planes of my abs clenching. I wanted to cap this dude. Wanted to just wrap my hands around his neck and twist, but that wasn't a possibility right now. In this world, there was a certain way to handle things, and today I was going to let my reputation get a little shaky.

Micah gave a laugh and reached out to squeeze my shoulder. "Ah yeah, just fucking with you both. It's not a good look if anyone thought what I was saying was even truth. Could make us lose a lot of money, so I had to test you."

White teeth flashed before me. He really was going to twist it like this was some test. I laughed with him and he held his hands up then gave me a hug, his left hand gripping my neck as he whispered in my ear, "Nigga you're my buck, know that. Just because Dame is gone doesn't mean the agreement I had with him is over. Know I'm watching you and you will be my bitch and enjoy it. Now smile and get the fuck out of my office. I have things that I need to speak about with our female friend." With that, he let me go and grinned wide. "Yeah, this season is going to be major." He chortled.

Micah let me know he remembered exactly who I was. He also let me know he had eyes on me and my family, something I immediately knew I was going to have to handle as soon as I stepped out of that party, and it also ended with me blacking the fuck out.

All I heard was, "It would be a shame to see your aunt wonder why her medicine has stopped coming in. Or why that school voucher your little brother had into Nasir Prep has fallen through. Would be a travesty, right?"

The quick left, then right jab, and a quick uppercut was my reply. I saw Micah's body tumble over his desk. That cocky fucker was raining red. Each droplet stained his shirt as he opened his mouth to pop his jaw back into place. He yelled for his guards to get me the fuck out his office. I was set to go for him again until his guards grabbed me and dragged me from the room.

I shouted, just to be an asshole, "Let me know if you need me to sign that ink on the dotted lines again, dog." I chortled while being led back to the party.

Just by the tension in the room I could tell nobody was expecting me to fuck that nigga up like I did. Self-preservation had me doing it. I had to because he needed to understand that if I lost, he lost, simple as that. Mathematics often worked that clear cut.

In my struggle I heard Micah's raspy bark travel down that empty hallway with me and the malice in his voice flowed with it: "Yeah, that contract is mine, Enzo. Make sure you handle what I said! All eyes are on you, playa."

Hissing, I only kept to the game and spit out, "Right, and watch your back, my dude, since we all talking secrets."

My mouth always got me in trouble, which was why I was snatched to the side where our meeting continued on the balcony. I wasn't about to let that nigga play me out the gate. Micah was on some dirty shit. I knew since the very first day of playing with my team that he was one of the bitches of Dame. Nigga sat in on all of my games, watching me with glassy eyes. Mouth gaped open, watering over what I had to assume he could get off me. His vibe always stank. Even when I played back on camp, he would watch all of us, and tick off the money he was going to pocket. Nigga stayed in a pimp mentality, but even pimps could end up sucking a dick or two.

There wasn't a damn thing I could do to keep him off my back in the moment, outside of feeding him a bullet. Since we were both in a public situation, that wasn't going to happen so I had to strategize something different in order to end his game. He had dirt on me, but he failed to think, failed to tap the marbles in his simple-ass dome and think on the fact that I got dirt on him. Power ain't shit when an agenda is set in motion.

I guess Micah was still sour about the way a nigga had rocked his dome. That was how I ended up on the balcony with both of his guards and him surrounding me again. Yup, let me explain a little something. When I blacked out, a brotha was no good, and at that moment, I blacked out.

Not even a heartbeat of a second had passed when I reached up to drape my arm over one of the guard's massive shoulders. Yeah, I wasn't some small dude, but I wasn't huge either. My time and practice in the streets as well as on the field helped me learn how to take down a chunky motherfucker as if they were nothing but a bag of kitty litter. Knowing this fool wasn't going to be down with me touching on him for long, I moved as fast as I could.

My jaw clenched tight. I shifted my feet quickly to pivot around the guard. I slammed my shoulder against that cat's chest, and then leaned the shocked dude against the railing of the balcony. I watched him struggle to move my forearm from his throat.

I then sent him flying with a slight grin on my face as he flipped over the edge. Standing shocked on the balcony and wide-eyed, I shrugged my shoulders with my hands out. I had purposely sent Micah's goon over the edge of the balcony we both stood on. Micah had just played a slick card, one that was a veiled threat against me and my family, one I didn't take kindly to. I needed to show him that I could be just as grimy as he could be.

Micah's eyes narrowed watching me, his chin tilted upward, and he scowled watching me before flashing a mischievous smile. "That was one of my good ones," he simply stated, still watching me.

My hand traveled up to my jaw where I scratched it, stubbed the patch of hair I had on my chin, and then thumbed my small hoop-pierced nose. "Again, my bad, since you got me contracted, I figured you needed more room and here I am."

Sharp, maniacal laugher erupted from the sharply dressed man I wanted to spit on, as he assessed me while rubbing his large hands together in thought. Micah's laugh settled in the wind, making me anxious. We both continued to watch each other before he finally spoke up. "My friend. I'll let that slide 'cause you're right. Your freedom is now tethered to me, patna, and once you accept that, then we good. I think it's clear you know what I will do, so now, nigga, we on an equal understanding. Test me again."

I walked forward to rest my hands on Micah's shoulders, patting them. My head dropped in contemplation and I gave a slight sigh, keeping my gait nonthreatening. "Not my intention," I said, letting it settle between us like a bullet ready to go off.

Already content with how things had played out, I decided to smooth that nigga's ego and hop 'n' fetch it out. "You're right, homie. You and me are good, my bad. The old me came out, but that's what you want and need right? So, I got you. Understand you. Whatever you need,

I got you. Bet on me and that money will keep dropping, a'ight?"

Flashing a mocking smile, apprehension had me worrying about my aunt and brother, but right now, I had to keep my game face on. Lines had been drawn, and an understanding that my old life was now coming into this new one of mine was finally settling in. I dropped my hands and moved by the two bodyguards in front of me, once Micah let me pass through.

I could tell he was already calculating whatever plan he had going and that shifty motherfucker had me on edge. As I walked on, my ears twitched when hearing him snarl, "That's my money. Let him do him, but Sunday, he better make my dough."

Damn, here we go again. A snide smile spread across my face as I strolled through the party making my way out only to be stopped by that asshole Micah again. "Don't forget your money, homie; now smile for the camera."

Lights flashed as everyone crowded around us. That thick envelope was back and being tucked into my hand. Irritation had me frozen staring at that nigga's back as he left me where I stood in a hallway, with him leading everyone back down to the party. Music bumped and had the hallway I stood in vibrating with its tune.

Micah's shifty shit had me digging my fingers into the palm of my left hand. I dropped the envelope of money, annoyed more now than I had been before. I wasn't some bitch you threw money at. I wasn't that nigga's whore. So, he could miss me with the bullshit. I had the numbers he needed, the commodity he was betting on, and he was going to learn that when he fucked or threatened what he thought was his mule, it would only cause more issues for him.

I heard, "You really not going to take that money?" which had me turning toward the feminine voice that said it.

"I don't need or want whatever he got. As far as that, I'm good on it. One of his goons left it as far as I'm concerned," I said.

The sound of teeth being sucked on grated my nerves. "Well, I'll take it. Fair exchange is no crime," the voice said.

While I was heading away, I saw it was Tino who stepped into view. I glanced down at the dude who was an inch or two over average height. He studied me with amusement in his face. Both of his arms snaked over his chest as he matched my gait and he gave off a masculine vibe, but it was the tone and the subtle tilt of his head, like that guy Lafayette from that vampire show on HBO, that had me knowing his true colors. Dude was all off on that quote, which had me shaking my head in laughter.

Intuition in my gut made me pause for a second to clear up what was going on. Everyone in this game was grimy and had their hands ready to snatch whatever you got. It didn't matter if you came from the purest of backgrounds or was an advocate of sainthood. If you were gullible enough to get played, be it small or major, then you were going to get played. Tino was a good-hearted weasel from what I had seen and heard.

Nigga was about that other life. Gripping what he could while uppin' the ass for players who played the pit bull but was thirsty for that Tinker Bell. No judgment on his lifestyle but I got no respect for his type of dudes. Tino was in a squatting position, reaching for the envelope. Both of my hands dropped into my pockets.

I turned to address him. "Do what you want, but show that shit to the guards. Do it."

Tino's eyebrow rose at the tone of my voice, but from the way his eyes lightened and shifted, it was clear that I wasn't in a testing sort of mood. He nervously stood then quickly made his way down the hall to do what I asked. Holding his hand in the air, he shook the stacks under the nose of one of the bodyguards, flashing a playful smile while he spoke. One of the guards opened the door to Micah's office and then told him that I hadn't taken the ducats.

Content in that, I walked away. As I tried to leave, I found myself back in the middle of the party with honeys surrounding me. This was the one time being as popular as I was hindered me. Still, to keep up the façade, I let some of the Bounce Girls dance with me. I noticed Tino parting through the crowd of females around me as if he were Moses parting that sea. He came my way with a stern look on his face.

It seemed like he was pissed because, the moment he got in my face, he shoved a white envelope at me and furrowed his brows. "Him said take this, don't argue about and don't diss him about it."

My face contorted as I looked down at the cash resting against my chest. "Told that nigga I don't want it and don't need it. Take that."

"No. I'm not fucking with him, okay, so just do it. Thanks and buh-bye." And like that, Tino blended back into the crowd, melting into the party groove, leaving me with cash.

I needed to get up out this mansion party. I needed a distraction so once I decided to leave, no one would stop me. I didn't have time to keep playing at Micah's bullshit games. Fisting the envelope, I moved through the party. People asked for autographs, some of my teammates gave me dap, and I headed to the bar where I saw Angel standing with a scowl on her face.

Signaling the bartender, I ordered up some round and kept my position straight as she sat rigid playing as if she wasn't paying me any attention.

"I saw you ride out slick like. You go piss?" I said in a low bass. "Know you ain't got shit to worry about from me. I don't know you, you don't know me, and we can keep it just like that," I said looking down at the envelope I held on the bar table.

Angel took a sip of her drink and kept her back to me. "Whatever, good to not know you then." She gave a slight humph and tapped her finger against her glass. "So that money still found you then?"

"Naw, it found you."

She turned quickly in her seat to glance at me before waving down the bartender for another glass. "So you going to share the wealth?"

"You going to stop looking like you got to shit?"

Angel rolled her eyes. She gave a slight pout then quirked her lips as she held out the palm of her hand and wiggled her claw-like nails. "Scratch my back and I'll scratch yours."

A casual smirk played across my lips and I turned, grabbing the bottles I asked for, then glancing at the guards who kept watching me. "I'll remember that."

"Right because we fam-i-ly," Angel drawled rolling her eyes and mocking Micah.

Music continued its thumping. I scanned the party, and I started shaking up the bottles, "Yeah, we are, and that nigga needs to remember how we do." I flashed a lofty smile and held the bottles in the air. "Check under your glass," I told her.

I popped them bottles spraying everyone and threw the wade of cash in the air.

"Check it! Straight from our numba one fan Micah! Show that nigga love, because he got nothing but love for y'all!"

Congestion filled the dance area. I pointed at Micah, who stood flanked by his security. He had changed his outfit and had a set of girlies near him. He also had on a pair of shades to off-set the bruises I gave him. Watching the chaos spread out, I stepped through and chucked the deuces at Angel, but saw that both the money I left and she were gone. People pushed and scraped to get at the money I threw up. I strolled through heading to the nearest exit, smacking some asses and playing the budding celebrity. My mind immediately went to battle mode.

Chapter 5

Angel

$9,000. That was how much money he had left for me when he'd told me to look under the glass. While I'd missed my hit for the night, Enzo's gift was more than enough and I wouldn't look a gift horse in the mouth. The room at the Embassy Suites was $120 a night and a far cry from the suite at the Westin, but it was what it was. I paid in advance for a month then pocketed the rest. While the money Enzo had fronted me was good, I knew nothing came without pay. No good deed went unpunished and sooner or later I felt like Enzo would ask for a favor in return.

When Micah called my phone later that night, I ignored him. I would ignore him for as long as I could. But knowing that shifty nigga, he would don a suit and call a meeting with the whole squad just to get me in closed quarters so he could run his agenda by me.

For the next two days, I laid low. I didn't have any friends or associates and didn't want any. It was better that way. If I rolled solo I'd never have to worry about a bitch trying to double-cross me. I'd only have to look out for me and watch my back. Back in the day, in order to survive Dame's world, you had to form allegiances anywhere you could find them and even then you had to make sure they didn't cross you.

"Today the egos and attitudes are real on the field. Shawn 'Enzo' Banks is on one. I don't know what they put in his water or Gatorade," the announcer said, then laughed, "but that boy has got the Angels defense's game figured out."

The other announcer laughed and nodded his head while agreeing. "He's scored four touchdowns in the first half. Ain't no telling what that boy is about to do next. I tell you what, Coach Payton better get back there and try to help his defense figure out how to handle this dude. He ain't playing out there."

I had the game on, yes. I had to wonder if Enzo would do what Micah told him to do. He was three touchdowns shy of the seven Micah had demanded. If he scored seven, I'd know he was on Micah's payroll and I would proceed with caution. As an alternate dancer, I should have been down waiting on the sideline with the rest of the girls, but there was no way I'd let Micah get that close to me again.

Halftime was over; by the time the fourth quarter rolled around, Enzo was on his sixth touchdown. I had to admit the boy was playing like his life depended on it and I had to wonder why. He could have fooled me, but on Friday night it seemed as if he would rather sell his soul to the devil than to play by Micah's rules. It was sad to see actually because, believe it or not, I was looking for someone to connect with who I could trust. Not sexually or no shit like that. I was off dick for the moment. I had seen enough in the last four years to be disgusted with it. The thought of sex with any man repulsed me, to say the least.

The alarm went off on my phone alerting me to the fact that I needed to get dressed. I had a good three or four hits lined up for the night. Between the Angels and Nightwings players, my bounty later on that night should be enough for me to start looking into leaving Atlanta. Micah made me realize that no matter how I tried to hide it, as long as I stayed in the A, someone somewhere would recognize me from my old life. It was time for me to get the hell on. That was the thing about me: I wasn't greedy, but I was looking for a come up. I was looking for just enough to get me out.

When my phone rang out, I already knew it was my contact at the jeweler. "Hiya, lassy, you got something for me this evening?" his British accent asked as soon as I said hello.

"Last night didn't turn up anything like planned, but I got something in the works as we speak. Can I have another few hours, and I promise what I bring to you will be worth it?"

He was quiet on the other end of the phone, which scared me. Every jeweler I'd gone to had turned me down until one told me about this dude who traveled between the States and overseas. It took me months to track him down, but when I did, it took me another couple of months to get him to agree to do business with me. He was very elusive and didn't like to be made to wait.

"Oi'ight then. A few hours more and then I catch a flight out of here. Make it worth it or we're done doing business."

After that he hung up the phone and I jumped up rushing to shower. I'd just gotten my feet in when a knock came to the door.

"Who?" I asked with one foot in and one foot out the bathroom door.

"Housekeeping," a female's voice rang out.

I sighed. "Can you come back in about an hour?"

"I just wanted to leave you some fresh linen since I'm leaving. Another worker won't be in until—"

I didn't let her finish. I snatched the door open. My first mistake. Micah stood leaning against the wall with one foot crossed over the other at the ankle with a smirk on his face. There was also a Hispanic maid there who took off running as soon as I snatched the door open. Gone was the thugged grilled-out ice-chained pimp street hustler. A business man in a tailored suit, wing-tipped shoes, and cuff links had replaced him. With Micah was a young boy with wide eyes and a bright smile. The young boy was dressed in khakis and a polo shirt with fresh red, white, and black Jordans on his feet. He looked familiar to me for some reason, but I couldn't place him. There was something about his eyes that I'd seen before. His eyes also looked as if they were glossed over like he'd had a hit of something in his system.

The erratic side of me made me try to close the door before he could rush inside, but I was too slow for the big, meaty guard I hadn't seen. When I tried to close the door, he shoved it and me backward. The hard push forced me back then down into an awkward split. My knees hit the floor hard and the towel flew open. Micah grabbed the young boy and made him stand over me as I fell back.

"Your first time seeing pussy I suppose?" he asked the young boy who just stood there gawking at my body.

"What do you want?" I asked Micah trying to cover myself and sit up.

He nodded at his guard then kicked the door shut behind him. I could already feel the pain in my knees from the fall and the inside of my thighs burned and ache because of the forced split.

"The question is not what I want; the question is what you want," he casually replied. "I can take you away from all of this, Angel. I can put you in a condo in midtown. Give you the life I know you want. All you gotta do is fuck wit' a nigga, ride wit' a nigga, you know?"

Micah's chocolate skin glistened under the glowing lights of my room. If you didn't know how evil the man was, the fact that he looked like he could play Lance Gross's brother would appeal to you.

"I don't want shit you have to offer me. I just want to be left alone. I don't want to work with you or for you."

"Who said I wanted you to work for me?"

I was confused, nervous, and scared. One because I had no idea how he found out where I was laying my head. "Then what do you want?" I asked, finally being able to stand.

He sat down on the bed then tilted his head to the side. "You know, you're pretty as fuck, but you don't comprehend well. I just said I wanted you to ride wit' a nigga. Be down for me and I'll look out for you."

"So, you're doing all of this because you want me to be your girlfriend, nigga?"

He chuckled then looked at the young boy. "Brah, this bitch 'bout stupid," he told him before looking back at me. "Fuck no, you can't be my girlfriend, but you can be my main bitch. Give me some pussy when I ask for it, when I want it. Give a little pussy away for a nigga when the time calls for it. Oh, and go out and find a nigga some new pussy when needed."

My head jerked back and I looked at Micah like he had fallen and bumped his head on somebody's pussy. Did he really think that I was about to become what I saw Sasha was to Dame? Did he really think that I would be a part of subjecting any young girl to a life that I had lived? "You must be out of your motherfucking mind, nigga," I snapped at him.

His smile widened. "Of course I am. That's what makes me who I am."

Micah turned his attention to the young boy when he jumped up with his arms in the air yelling, "Touchdown." I'd forgotten the TV was even on. "Yo, my brother got seven touchdowns in one game. Seven touchdowns, one game! My bro, that nigga is on one today," the little boy bragged.

Then it clicked for me where I'd seen those eyes before. I glanced at the TV to see the fans in the Dome going crazy. While everyone was celebrating, Enzo had snatched his helmet off looking around like he was trying to locate someone. It didn't take a long time for me to put two and two together. Micah had called Enzo's bluff. The fact that Micah had the little boy in his possession scared me, more so for him than me.

Micah smirked again then looked back at me. "I can be very persuasive," he chided.

The one thing that Micah hadn't counted on was the fact that I had nothing to lose. I had no family he could bribe me with, no little brother, no little sister, nothing and nobody. "You ain't got shit on me, Micah. So you can't do me like everyone else."

"Wanna bet?"

"Do you? Find someone else because I ain't her."

"Don't you ever wonder why nobody came looking for you when Dame snatched you up?" he asked out the blue.

I couldn't front like it hadn't caught me off-guard because that question had always plagued my mind. I knew Dame used to have pull in a lot of places, but I did always wonder why my grandmother didn't come looking for me.

"I made that happen," Micah spoke up. "I can make girls like you disappear as if you never existed."

The smirk that had once been there had all but disappeared. It had been replaced by a sneer that made him appear to be every bit of the menace to society he was. I made the mistake of blinking. He jumped up so fast that before I realized he had me hemmed up against the wall, I was gasping for air.

"Ask me how Coco's body disappeared. Ask me how many bitches like you who Dame wanted dead I've bodied. Ask me how I snatch girls off the street and ship them all across the world without a fucking trace. You know who you playing with right now, bitch?"

Micah was a lot stronger than he looked. The fact that my feet were dangling from the car-

peted floor attested to that. He carried me then
tossed me onto the bed. The towel had long ago
fallen to the floor. My naked breasts swayed and
jiggled as I bounced clumsily. When I tried to get
back up, Micah's closed fist caught my eye. That
slowed me down. I'd only been hit by one man
and that had been Dame. His hits had always
instilled fear in me. Micah's punch had done
the same, only because it hurt so badly that it
knocked tears, snot, and spit from me. My head
started thumping, and my eye socket felt as if it
was coming unhinged.

He hopped on the bed caging me in. Some
kind of way I was able to glance at the little boy
and he was glued to his chair. You wouldn't have
been able to tell he was afraid just by the look on
his face. It wasn't until I saw the way his hands
were clenching the armrests of the chair that I
saw his fear. He had them gripped so tightly it
looked as if he was trying to rip them off. I felt
sorry for the kid in that moment. He was probably about to witness something that he would
never be able to recover from.

Micah hollered for his guard to come in the
room. There was a hungry look in the big man's
eyes as he watched me like a predator. "What
chu need, boss?" he asked Micah eagerly. There
was no mistake that Micah had probably allowed

him to partake in any woman he chose to set his sights on.

"Give me your gun. Lock the door. Call down and tell Hemp not to let anyone up here. Tell our man at the desk to evacuate whoever else is on this floor. Then tell Hemp to bring me my little black bag up."

After giving those orders he sat back on his haunches and snatched his suit jacket off.

"What I'm about to show you, li'l dude, what you're about to witness is how to tame a bitch. Some of these hoes get out here and forget who the fuck runs this shit in the A. They forget real niggas move in silence. I may be the boss, but I like to get my hands dirty, too, you feel me?" He stared the young boy down until he nodded. "Good, now come here," he ordered.

"All taken care of boss," the guard said once he had done what Micah had ordered.

"Good, grab that bitch's legs and hold her still. We're about to give li'l man his first taste of pussy."

I closed my eyes feeling weak both mentally and physically. Even though I'd tried to kick the shit out of the big nigga who had gripped my ankles in a death lock—his lock was so tight around my ankles I could feel them starting to go numb from the shortage of blood flow—there was really nothing I could do physically to stop them. I opened my mouth to scream and as soon as I did so, Micah cocked the nine back and shoved it in my mouth.

"You really want to test me with that screaming shit today, Angel?" he asked coolly.

I'd never really been a fighter. That was why I had always tried to stay on Dame's good side. I couldn't fight Dame. I wouldn't have even attempted to defend myself against him because it only seemed to make him angrier, same with Micah. I shook my head and he removed the gun.

Tears had long ago started to form in my eyes. "Please, Micah, don't do this."

He acted as if he hadn't even heard me. He brought the gun up and brought it down over my eye, almost blacking me out. That pain was so numbing that it made me grind my teeth. I said almost blacking me out because for the brief few seconds I was out, he slapped me to bring me back. Through blurry vision I could see the young boy trembling where he stood. The door of the hotel room opened and in walked who I assumed was Hemp with a black medical bag.

"I think I should go back home now. My aunt is expecting me at a certain time," the boy said. His voice was emotionless as he spoke.

"Nah, you good. I can't let you go until your brother calls me. See your brother and me have this deal going on and in order for him to keep up his end of the bargain, I have to do some hostile negotiations, you feel me?" All the while Micah was talking he was putting on latex gloves. God only knew what that nigga was about to do.

Micah shrugged as he kept talking. "You're kind of like a causality of war, li'l dude. And besides, your aunt just might be dead once you get back home. I may or may not have unplugged this or that IV or, shit"—Micah stopped talking and laughed—"I may have just put the wrong shit in her IV all together. Who knows, you know. I never finished my last year of med school."

All three men laughed while Hemp snatched the boy up and threw him face first between my legs. Micah grabbed the back of his neck and forced him face first in my pussy. I tried to snap my legs closed to no avail. The kid struggled, but Micah held his face there for as long as he felt like it.

"Even tho' this pussy is previously used merchandise, I'm sure it's still top shelf. Dame only allowed the best pussy to work at Magic. What we're going to do is show a young nigga how to fuck good pussy properly."

Somewhere between Hemp telling Micah that he had already laced the boy's coke with Indigo and me gaining my senses back after the hit to the head with the gun, I realized my hands weren't tied down. They'd just felt that way because of the blows to my head. I smacked the guard holding my legs as hard as I could. That nigga's neck was the size of my thigh so all my slap had served to do was make his dick hard. His eyes watered as he licked his lips.

"Damn, Kruger, she slapped the shit out cho ass," Hemp teased his man.

"I'll return the favor later," he replied. "Trust me on that."

Kruger's voice sounded like he had sucked on too many lemons and had a frog in his throat. He looked like a menacing bull and his eyes were too far apart. Meanwhile, Hemp laughed and handcuffed my hands above my head. He reminded me of Shrek because of how big his nose was.

Micah finally allowed Enzo's little brother to move his head from my crotch. The young boy was fighting mad as he was held with his arms up behind his head.

"Yo, my brother is going to murder you niggas," he growled out.

"Fuck yo brother, li'l nigga," Hemp shot back.

Micah ordered, "Let me get that Indigo out the bag and that White Girl."

Hemp grabbed what was asked of him while Micah put the gun to the kid's head. "I'ma need you to strip, my nigga, and believe me when I say this is not a request. You mean nothing to me so I will leave your little ass stanking right next to this bitch quick."

"Fuck you, nigga. You don't scare me," the kid shot back.

My sweat and pussy juices was all over the boy's face and it pained me to look at him. His face was twisted in anger and he had his fist balled like he was ready to fight. I think he surprised us all when he drew back and caught Micah with a left-right combo. The kid was pretty tall for his age so he could square up with the grown man pretty solidly.

Hemp laughed. "Whew wee. Little nigga is a fighter I see."

Micah ran his tongue over his teeth as he nodded his head while his lips were turned down.

"You told my aunt you was from Nasir Prep. You's a liar, nigga."

A backhand from Micah caught the kid across the face and sent him sliding to the floor. Micah grabbed the Indigo pills and a bottle of alcohol. While Hemp grabbed the struggling kid and held

him down, Micah shoved two pills in his mouth
and then poured Rémy down the kid's throat. No
matter how the boy tried not to swallow it, the
fact that Micah held his big hands over the kid's
mouth then held his nose made it so the kid had
to swallow to breathe. If they had already laced
his drink with liquid Indigo, giving him the pills
and the alcohol was about to take him over
the edge in no time at all.

I moaned in protest because that was all I
could do. My head was heavy. It felt as if I was
about to lose consciousness again. Even when
Micah kneeled on the bed and forced me to snort
coke up my nose by having Hemp give me a blow
to the stomach—of course I would have to sniff
to try to catch my breath and cough—I took a
full hit of pure powder to the head. The high
was almost instant. I could feel the hit in every
nerve cell in my body. My nose burned as the
coke hit my cerebral. Eyes fluttered and rolled to
the back of my head, hand started to tremble as
my body involuntarily rolled. My heart slammed
into my rib cage hard. Micah and his henchman
sat back for at least another fifteen minutes and
watched the effects of the drugs take me and the
kid over.

Somewhere between me trying to hold on
to any cognizance I had left, I saw Enzo's little

brother stagger up. I knew what Indigo did to males once you mixed it with alcohol. That was why I had slipped them into the players' drinks before robbing them. It made them horny, made their dicks hard, made them want to fuck. It made them incoherent. I was sorry to say it had done the same thing to a thirteen-year-old boy. His first time having sex would be with an eighteen-year-old whore who was high off a hit of pure coke.

I heard Micah tell Hemp to hold the boy back until he set the camera up. Meanwhile Kruger was busy finger fucking me roughly, priming me for a case of statutory rape that I was an unwilling participant in. My head lolled from side to side as I moaned and groaned out, "No," over and over again. My pleas fell on deaf ears as they tossed the young boy on the bed. For a while the young'un just sat back on his haunches and stared at me. My body was very well developed. It had been that way since Dame had got a hold of me. If I hadn't been so high I probably would have flinched and kicked the little boy when his hands curiously reached put to grab a hold of my breasts. It was clear my breasts were the first he had touched. He kept pinching my nipples like he was fascinated with them.

"Li'l man," Micah egged him on, "you got a hard dick and willing pussy. What chu gone do with that?"

I tried to fight as hard as I could not to let the high overtake me, but somewhere between Micah shoving the boy on top of me and the boy fumbling clumsily to insert himself inside of me, I let Scotty take me away.

I didn't know how many hours later that I woke up, but the boy was in bed beside me, still naked and snoring with his hand on his dick. I jumped up so quickly that the world tilted and I fell back against the wall. Pain in my back shot through me. I looked around the room and saw a torch with a wire hanger and baby oil. A weird smell, like charcoal, lingered in the room and the fact that my pussy ached told me that more than a boy had fucked me while I was knocked out. I couldn't stand. My legs wouldn't work for me so I crawled to the bathroom. The toilet was my destination. The fact that I had fucked a thirteen-year-old turned my stomach. I didn't see how any grown person could violate a child and be okay with it. As I emptied my stomach then tried to grab a towel to stop the bleeding between my legs, I cried because I felt as if I had repeated a fucked-up cycle in this underworld.

But I had to get myself together. Micah was a mastermind and there was always a method to his madness. My back was still burning and that weird smell assaulted my senses. It wasn't until I stood and caught a glimpse of my back in the mirror that it finally settled in that Micah was indeed straight from hell. I'd seen Dame use what had been done to me as a method of torture in the underworld. The torch I had seen was to make the wire clothes hanger a certain degree of hot. My back was oily which meant baby oil had been poured onto my back right before the wire hanger seared my flesh. It was to ensure that my skin burned and blistered once the hot wire hanger touched it. Micah had burned angel wings onto my back and carved the name ANGEL above it.

No matter how far I ran, Angel would always follow me. I knew I had to get the hell out of that room. I quickly cleaned up as best I could. I grabbed any- and everything that would place me in that hotel room. Tears filled my eyes as I did so. I knew I had family in Florida. Maybe I could run there and be safe or maybe even to Cali. I didn't know where, but I knew I had to go. As I rushed to put my shoes on, my intent was to leave the boy in the bed, but when he started to come to, I watched the way his eyes darted

around the room and the way his body flinched.
I knew an OD case when I saw one. As I rushed
to get the child dressed as best I could a loud
banging on the door startled me.

"Police, open up!"

My eyes widened and it was in that moment
that I wished I had a gun. I would have killed
myself on the spot. I looked around the room at
the drugs that Micah had left behind, then to the
half-naked kid in my hotel room bed and knew I
was fucked.

"Fuck," I mumbled.

The phone rang just as I laid him back on the
bed. I snatched it up quickly because I didn't
want the cops to hear it.

I didn't say anything when I answered it but I
was sure the person on the other end could hear
me breathing.

"Tell me, Angel, do you want to go to prison or
do you want to stay free?"

I frowned upon hearing Micah's voice but
didn't answer as the banging got louder and
harder.

"Police, open up!"

"Press play on the remote, Angel. It's on the
table beside the bed."

Even though I didn't want to, I did anyway.
What I saw when the screen came up made the

bottom of my stomach fall out. There was Enzo's little brother sweating, clearly high, but pumping his hips like he had been born to do it. And there I lay. Because I was so high, the moans I gave off sounded as if I liked what was happening.

"Is that kiddy porn you're watching? Tsk, tsk. Another federal charge. Add that to the kilos of coke and stash of illegal pills I left in your room and I'd say you were on your way to prison for a long time, pretty girl. So, answer me, prison or free? And all you got to do is ride with me. Yes or no. That's all I want to hear and all of this will go away."

I closed my eyes and dropped my head. I didn't want to go to prison. I couldn't, but if the cops came into the room there would be no way I could fight or deny the charges that were sure to come.

"Think fast, Angel. Oh, did I tell you that the kid in your room was reported missing? Oh, man, imagine what is going to happen. You kidnapped a minor to drug him and fuck him."

I knew that nigga could hear me crying. He had pulled my card. "Yes," I yelled.

"That's my bitch. Now watch in silence as all the cops go away like they were never there. I run this shit, Angel. Don't fuck with me, ride with me. And your first order of business is to deliver little man there back to his brother Enzo. It's time he knew that I ain't fucking around."

Chapter 6

Enzo

Light flashed all around me with the chanting of my name, adding to the anxiety building within my body.

"Enzo! . . . Enzo! . . . Enzo!"

Each shout of my name became bullets that burrowed into my flesh. I had done what that nigga wanted. Played and dug my feet into the earth itself pushing myself beyond the limits of the game to score what he wanted, not for him, but for my fam. In my mind, my thoughts fought me, telling me that I should have hidden my aunt and brother before I stepped into this world. I had stupidly thought that with Dame gone, maybe they could stay with me. Even if some of the fallback from his world trickled into what I was doing, I thought me and mine would be okay, but I was wrong. I felt it in my bones, felt it in my psyche.

It had me pushing past reporters excited about how I played and asking questions that I just wasn't feeling. The sensation of pain in my fingers and palms let me know I was gripping the fuck out of my helmet all while I rushed into the locker rooms and blocked out my teammates' excitement. I didn't have time for the extra shit, not that day. My baby brother Drew was missing. But it was the picture I had received in my cell before the game of him with a hand pressed on his shoulder that sported an initial black diamond and platinum letters MT that let me know what was up. If I didn't play for my life, then he would lose his. It was payback for ending the life of one of Micah's goons and cold clocking that bitch at the party a few days back.

Both of my hands shook and pressed against my dirty, sweat-drenched face. The loud chants of my team blasted the locker room. As I sat trying to get my mind right, my leg bounced up and down. Everything going on around me was a blur. I didn't want to play this game. I wanted to do shit on my own terms but no, life had a way of playing me cruel. He had told me to call him once I did his work. In that moment, my cell looked like the enemy to me.

"Enzooo! Damn, rookie, you played that shit as if you were a pro. If you weren't so fucking good some of these veteran niggas would fuck you up for showing them up like you do. But right now you made us all look fresh, li'l dude, so why you sitting here looking down, man? We got drinks, pussy, and money to blow, brah!" one of my teammates shouted behind me. Dude's voice was slurred already and I knew he was beyond high and drunk.

I kept my back to that fool, not even feeling like being in the mood for this shit. Nigga used to come to Dame's to get his fix all the time. He was an addict and I really ain't have time for him right then.

Dropping my head, I stared at my white-covered legs, breathing in and out keeping my cool. My baby brother and I were close. Close to the point that we oftentimes could finish each other's sentences. I knew if something happened to him, life wasn't going to be good for me.

"Naw, just my ritual to cool down after a win, man. I'll hit you all up later, it's all good," I said, speaking to my legs and not to my teammate.

The way he slapped me on the back with a laugh had me fisting my hands while I listened to his drunken banter. "Cho, a'ight, man, don't sit here being lame, dog, handle you then get back at us, rookie."

The temptation to slam my fists in his face eased away as he left me alone. I abruptly stood, peeled off my shirt, throwing it in my locker then grabbed my gym bag, my cell, and headed out of the locker room.

My teammate called after me, "I'll keep Coach off ya back since you know we ain't supposed to leave and shit until he gets at us. I'll holla at cha."

I ignored him. Hitting dial on my phone, I took an alternate exit route that gave me privacy away from the reporters who were lurking around.

Several rings kicked up my temper as the phone was finally picked up on the forth ring. "There go my money. I see once motivated, a nigga can conquer the world, eh? How that shit feel, nigga? I know I feel good. Ooowee! I feel very good."

Heated, my eyes narrowed and it took every ounce of strength not to get at this dude. "Yeah. It was a'ight. Where's my brother?" I asked as I dropped my bag to the floor.

The sound of laughter in the background with music and female laughter let me know Micah was celebrating. The reception on his end rustled and I listened as he snorted and laughed hard. "No, man, I told you though, that little nigga got feet of gold! Don't I pick them niggas right? Never doubt me, man, never doubt my chaotic method, 'cause you'll be left out somewhere floppin' like a guppy," I heard him say on the other end.

I stood waiting in the hallway, pulling on my tank, and picking my bag back up from the floor. Laughter blasted from the cell. My anger rose the longer I waited.

"Yo! I did what you wanted!" I found myself barking into the cell. Silence replaced the background noise, and my nostrils flared as I breathed in and out in anger. Heat rose to my face while this motherfucker made me his bitch.

"So you understand me now?" Micah's voice questioned me in malicious enjoyment. "You get who got the power and who don't? Because I don't think you do. Check your text and you'll see the good time me and your brother had today. Go 'head, flip that cell on speaker."

Not even waiting a heartbeat, I moved him to speaker and ground my teeth as he spoke to others on his end of the cell, laughing, sniffing, and clinking glasses. "I'm telling you, Enzo is that nigga. The best of friends we are and with my sponsorship and working with his coaches, he is going to lead us to championships," Micah boasted.

As he talked up my game, I found my messages then checked the video sent from "unknown." I watched in silence as a scene that would sicken some other niggas only made my world tilt back. Blood drained from my face as I watched my baby brother be pushed into the screen. Deep male voices sounded in their malicious laughter. I saw Angel writhing on the bed as my brother was pushed onto her naked body.

My eye twitched as I watched my brother touch her in curiosity before he fell into natural law and rode her like he was pro at it. I glanced around in panicked anger. I felt moisture rim my eyes as I bit my lower lip to keep from screaming in fury. The jarring pain of my fist hitting the brick wall of the hallway I was in, leaving blood to mark my hit, didn't help the pain I was feeling watching my brother be forced to fuck some broad. Not any broad, but one I used to have to protect.

I felt sick in that moment, only because I was supposed to protect him from the streets. I had taken him from the same place that raised me and thought he would be safe, but no, I was wrong. Everything in the actions of my past was wrong, and the video I was watching was proof of that.

"Good look, ain't it, nigga. Ain't nothing like experienced pussy to make hair grow on a little nigga's dick, right?" I heard Micah's voice say to me, drawing me back to reality.

I ended the video quickly, not able to take any more of it. I couldn't say I was a weak nigga. Being brought up by my aunt but also by Dame, I had seen everything and experienced worse. But it was something about family being subjected to that violence that cut my soul out and left it at my feet.

My tongue ran over my lips and I swallowed a couple of times trying to work my throat muscles. "What do you want?"

Glasses clinked again with Micah ordering everyone out of whatever room he was in. "Now we get to that understanding, don't we? Niggas like to play King Kong in this bitch, but remember it was a motherfucking plane that took that monkey down, and, nigga, I'm that plane."

He paused then cleared his throat before making a "ssss" noise as if inhaling before speaking back at me with a croaking tone to his voice. "Eh, yeah, shit a'ight. What I want you'll continue to find out. Once we hang up here, you can expect to find your package being delivered to your private residence. On that thought, I have to say, nigga, you made that place look damn good. Dame would be impressed with how you got it; your pretty aunt must have helped you."

No words could be said to express how much red I was seeing. My hand pressed against my thumping skull, sweat ran down the curve of my shoulder blades. I knew I was about to black out and fuck some shit up. This nigga had been in my home. He knew where I lived, which meant he had to have snatched my brother from where we lived. This nigga had upped the ante on the playing field and stepped into my spot.

"Do you know how much money I could make off your sweet auntie's sick pussy? It's a world for such places, bet all the dick I could give her would make her heal up like Saint Matthew, ha! Anyway, kid, tell me, if you understand that, you have no way out. That freedom you think you got, you can have, but know I own the strings. You fuck with my jimmy and I fuck with your mammy. Understood? Your brother was just nice little piece of fat on the steak. You keep playing and I'll take the whole entrée, yeah?"

My jaw was set in a hard line. I could feel the veins popping out on my forehead. My forehead pressed against the cold wall of the hallway and I listened to a nigga just pull power on me. If it were just him and me I could simply handle this with ease, but because he had my family, I had to play this point to the tee.

"I understand," was all I stated while waiting.

The sound of a chair squeaking echoed back to me. "Good. We'll be in contact." With that, his cell went dead.

I stood in place where I was for what felt like hours before I heard several females scream and jump near me. "Oh, my God! It's Enzo! Enzo! Ahhhh!"

Their squeals were sharp like razors while I stood bowed with my forehead pressed into the wall. I stepped back and started at the two women. I couldn't see shit in the moment. Everything was a blur. But the quick silence then stunned murmurs that I was bleeding made me turn then snatch up my bag before stepping off with my dark thoughts trailing me.

As I walked off, I felt them following me. I growled, "I'll be good! Just part of the game. Back off."

Dizziness claimed me while I slammed open twin steel doors and headed to my ride leaving the groupies behind me. Getting to my place didn't take long. I drove there by rote, in a daze. The shotgun I had in my ride was in my hand the whole drive over. I walked into the place I was calling a temporary home and dropped my bag not missing a step. Tunnel vision worked me as I searched every room stopping once I got to my aunt's room. The familiar sound of her machines pumping chemicals into her system brought me back to reality while I watched her sleep. In her hand was the house phone and I could see her cheeks were damp with shed tears. I hated to wake her up but I had to. I had to know how that nigga got my brother.

Carefully moving around the bed, I checked her machines, having memorized every drug she needed. I made sure she was all good. I moved to sit on her bed. As I did, the sound of a pistol cocking alarmed me. I turned to find myself staring down the barrel of a gun. My aunt was slowly sitting up, starring me down with hatred before it melted away in pain and sadness.

She dropped the gun then reached out to hug me. "Shawn! I thought you were someone else. I'm sorry, baby."

Shifting my shotgun beside me, I wrapped my arms around her, taking comfort in her embrace as I spoke against her neck, "Who'd you think I was, *Tía?* Huh?"

Her hands gently slid up and down my broad back. A slight tremble from her had me leaning back to see if she was okay, as I stared into her eyes. Eyes that used to be hazel were now bluish gray from all the chemo.

"Drew didn't come home. Some man in a suit came in when I thought it was Drew. He came in looking around and asked questions about you, this chemo, and me. Said he was some rep for your team and that he was going to take care of us all. Yet all the time he was here, Drew never came home and that man kept watching me in a crazy way. You know I don't trust no one, so the fact that he was in here without a key, without Drew being in the house at the same time saying he had let him in, I knew something was wrong," she explained.

The fear in her voice had me holding her hand a little too tight. I could see a fire in my aunt, one I remembered as a kid myself. Before I had got hooked up with Dame and the game, I had been playing football at my middle school. Back then, I lived on the field. I did everything my coaches wanted, and made sure I learned everything I needed.

My team and I had been at a game in Alabama. During that time our assistant coach had to take us so, anyway, long story short, nigga found a way to try to fuck us kids, literally. He had walked into the showers with us after our win and tried to wash up on us kids. We were all freaked the fuck out 'cause this nigga had never done anything like this. I stepped out quick and hit up my aunt who drove hours to get to where we were. Before she got there, our assistant

coach had already warned us not to say anything. He tried to tell us it was normal and shit
for an adult like him to shower with us kids and
try to touch our shit. Yeah, I wasn't even hearing
it.

My aunt dragged me out with some of the
other kids and took us home. Some days after,
my aunt had dropped me and Drew off at Jake's
gram's home to stay with her for a week. I
remember that well. My aunt had that same look
in her eyes like she did now.

I watched her head out and didn't see her
until a week later. That was the same day I heard
on the news that our assistant coach had been
found dead in his car with a gunshot to the skull.
Back then, I wouldn't even have thought on it,
but I remembered my aunt had a Glock under
her bed. She had told us it was there for pro-
tection. Yeah, that shit was gone and replaced
with a new pistol. I had wanted to ask my aunt
about it. I got my answer when she turned off the
news and said, "Vengeance heals what evil has
broken."

That day she made me and Drew cookies and
told me to never let that nigga's evil pollute my
gifts. She assured me that she would always
watch out for my brother and me because that's
what family does. Now I stared at those same
eyes and my stomach clenched in response.

I inhaled slowly, bowing my head, doing my best not to watch her fragility flicker with energy bent on killing the threat that came into our home. I knew I had to tell her about Drew. There would be no way I couldn't.

"Drew—"

A knock at the door kept me from having to explain to her that he was missing. I stood then grabbed my shotgun. I glanced at my aunt and saw that her pistol was gone.

"Evil is at our door again, but that's okay, Shawn baby," she said. "We'll ride it out like we always do. Don't let it touch your power, remember that."

She had always dropped wisdom on me. Made me wish she wasn't sick anymore. Made me wish she was the happy aunt who used to dance around the house, belting out all the cuts, and who would spit rhymes and poetry every Saturday to bring extra money in the house.

A second knock, this time harder, made me nod. "I remember."

I made my way to the door, moved to the side where I positioned my gun behind me. I opened the door then pointed it at the source of the knock. A pitched, "Damn!" made me glance to see who it was. I moved my body fully into the door with a cold expression on my face.

"Where—"

"He's right here; put the gun down, please," Angel pleaded.

She looked as if she had been dropped into the middle of a storm, but she also looked high as fuck. I moved my gun gesturing with it to tell her to come in as I kept my eyes on her. I didn't see my brother until she turned her back to me then reached to the side to pull him in. He stumbled in, disheveled, slumped as he walked in drenched in sweat. I already knew what that look was about. I aimed my gun at Angel again as I slammed the door hard by reaching over her head and pressing my palm against the door.

"Sit him down and spill that shit!" I ordered.

She held up both of her hands then rushed my brother to the couch to lay him down. She pushed her stringy weave over her shoulder and kept watching me as she helped him. Sweat was also covering her paling caramel skin. She appeared red in the face and her eyes were bloodshot. Her arms wrapped around her stomach. Her tongue darted in and out to wet her lips and I could tell she was ready to throw up.

Pointing with my gun, I tilted my head as I glowered at her, "Do that shit in the kitchen sink so I can watch you then talk."

I didn't have to repeat myself because she ran to the gourmet kitchen and emptied her stomach into the massive stainless steel sink before her. Shaking hands cranked the water on, and she cupped them to splash water on her face. Through her fingers, I can tell she was crying but hiding it by the way her hunched-over back would shake and she would take deep breaths in between each retching puke.

Rustling behind me made me step back. Drew groaned and held his dick. His usually golden brown skin was now a sickly pale yellow with red tints. Heat generated from him, but he shook like he was cold.

"What did he fucking take?" I shouted, not even caring that Angel was still puking.

Angel wiped her mouth while watching me with uncertainty. "Micah made him take Indigo and Rémy liquid and pill form. Drugged us both."

Sourness in the form of bile in my throat had me contorting my face. I needed to hear her say what happened, needed to see the reality of the fucking shit that went down and tell me to my face. I asked sharply, "For what?"

Pain flashed across her face. Her head tilted to the side as if she wanted to hit me. "Motherfucker, what the fuck you think? Indigo mixed with alcohol makes a male, any age, a slave to his dick. So what you think it was for?" she screeched out.

Red flashed across my eyes again. I stomped across the kitchen with rage in my heart. Angel screamed then stumbled backward. My free hand found its way around her throat and I squeezed hard lifting her in the air with my gun pressing into her stomach. Heat traveled up my body in strengthening anger. The sound of running water and dishware crashing to the floor with my Nikes crunching into them echoed in the condo.

I could sense her slapping and kicking at me, but I couldn't feel it. I took a couple of steps forward and slammed her head back into a column in the kitchen and I growled low, "Bitch, you get off on fucking my kid brother? You so gone that you upped the pussy to a kid? You need goddamn money that bad? Huh!"

Gasping breath was all I got in response. Angel's eyes bucked out at me as she flapped her mouth trying to speak.

"I should shove this fucking Glock up your pussy, bitch, and end you right here."

"Shawn, put her down. She needs help and so does Drew. They both were attacked. Put her down," sounded behind me.

"Enzo, that nigga made us do it, big bro. Stop, please, bro!" Drew's scratchy voice also chimed in.

My teeth clenched and my stomach tightened in sickness, causing me to twist my face up and turn my head. He sounded different to me now. My own brother sounded like he now had more bass in his voice. It could have easily been my mind playing tricks on me. A taint spread through me causing my world to tilt again.

I knew he would forever be changed by this and it was my fault in reality for not hiding them. All of it rested on my shoulders. I squeezed harder, my eyes squinting in fury as I shifted my hand and pressed the end of my gun against her pussy. She had on loose sweatpants and, as she squirmed, her shirt rose and I could see a fresh burn on her side. Her hair spilled over my wrist as her tears spilled down her cheeks.

My aunt's tugging on me pulled me back from blacking out again. My chest rose up and down like a bull ready to attack. I knew I had to be looking crazy but I didn't give a fuck. My eyes kept darting back and forth. Angel's words that they had been drugged finally registered to me.

"Please . . . let . . . go," Angel gasped while frantically tapping my arm with her hands.

My aunt's frail arms enclosed me from behind and pulled me back. Out of my peripheral, Angel slowly slid down the wall then stared up at us from her crouching position on the kitchen floor.

She held her neck rubbing it, and her chest rose rapidly up and down in a pant trying to regain herself. I could hear my aunt telling Angel to go sit down as I hugged her instantly worrying about her being out of bed.

"*Tía,* you should be resting." I disjointedly stated.

She turned my jaw to look into her caring face, making me focus. "I have enough drugs in me to keep me going. You sit, and you let this girl talk as I bring their high down. Once that happen, we'll pack up like you said and figure out the next move, okay?" she explained walking me to the living room.

I didn't notice the gun in my aunt's hand until she had me sit in the massive black chair she had bought special for me.

All I could do in that moment was nod, chest becoming tighter with every tight breath I took. I heard her, and I agreed with her, but my mind was on one thing: killing Micah. He didn't deserve a simple kill. Naw, he deserved something special. Something I knew I needed to be able to do without it tracking back to me afterward. It was then that my mind started clearing up and I began setting up my agenda. I had friends in high places too. This nigga was not about to take me down, not before I dragged him to hell with me.

Chapter 7

Angel

"Ahhhhh! Grrrrrr!" I groaned into the pillow as the burning of alcohol singed my back.

"What kind of animal would do this to another human being?" Enzo's aunt, Shy, had pulled away the last bit of the T-shirt that had been stuck to my back. She continued to fuss. "This is lunacy. I'm sorry this happened to you, baby. This is going to hurt so bite the pillow and bear with me."

"While she works on you, I need you to tell me what he wants you do to for him. Obviously you're a henchman too now since this has happened," Enzo said to me.

He didn't care that I'd been drugged, raped, forced to have sex with a minor, then burned and carved up. All he saw was a whore who'd had sex with his thirteen-year-old brother. Forced or not, he didn't care. All he knew was his little brother had been violated and that I had been a part of it. I could tell in the way he sneered at me that there had been no love gained or lost between us.

I stopped biting on the pillow long enough to answer him. "He wants me to be his fuck mule. Fuck him and fuck anyone else he tells me to fuck, especially if it gets him in good with who-ever said person is."

His face frowned. "This nigga doing all this to you for some simple pussy? And you down for that?"

"No." I hissed when whatever his aunt put on my back started to burn again. "But he has me on tape with . . ." I cut my words off as I was too embarrassed to say it aloud. "I don't want to go to prison," was all I said.

Enzo grunted then turned his eyes away from mine. "You owe me for what you did to my little brother," he said.

"Shawn, you can't fault her for that," his aunt stopped working on my back and said to him.

"I can and I will. When my aunt finishes patching you up . . . Which you're going to owe me for yet again since my aunt is sick and needs to be resting. She's panting and shit try-ing to get you together. So when she finishes patching you up, we're taking a trip to Micah's place of business."

"No, no. I'm not going there," I protested.

"The hell you say? You're going because not only will this help me, this will help you. Don't forget the money I laid on you back at the party. You said if I scratched your back, you would scratch mine. It seems right now, I been scratching your back a whole lot more at this point."

"Shawn, baby, you know what you're doing when you do this, right?" Shy asked him. She had stopped patching up my back so she could catch her breath. I could tell she was too sick to be up doing what she was, but she had insisted on tending after me after she had ensured Drew was okay.

"*Tía*, you gotta let me do this. I know some people."

"Okay. I have faith in you, but you need to do me a favor before you leave here."

"What's that, *Tía?* Anything you need," he agreed.

"You promise me you gon' look out for this girl."

I turned my head just in time to see Enzo frown and smack his lips. "I don't need him to look out for me," I spoke up.

"Hush up, girl. Of course you do. Now, Shawn, you promise me you're going to look out for her just as you would Drew. I ain't saying you gotta

move her in, but once this is over, and if you
both walk away alive and well, you look out for
her, you hear me? Promise me that," she said
then coughed, hard, so much so that when she
moved her paper towel from her mouth it was
filled with blood.

I quickly sat up and was going to help her
until Enzo seemed to growl low in his throat
when I went to touch his aunt. He rushed over
to her. "Come on, *Tía*. Let me get you back in the
bed."

I looked at the woman and could tell that
before cancer claimed her she had been a rider
in the streets. I could tell by the way she talked
with a no-nonsense tone that before fate had
befallen her she would have been ready to ride
shotgun with her nephew to kill a nigga.

It didn't take Enzo long to get his aunt settled. I could hear her telling him that he was to
leave her there and come back for her after he
did what he had to do that day. She ordered him
to place Drew in the room with her. Anytime
Drew came into the room where I was, I looked
away. I couldn't face the kid. I couldn't look at
the lust that obviously still lingered in his ado-
lescent eyes. He couldn't be faulted for what he
was feeling, but that didn't mean I had to feed
his nature.

I got up, and grabbed the clothes his aunt had laid out for me and dashed to the bathroom. His aunt and I shared the same complexion so I found some of her makeup and fixed myself up as best I could. Her clothes had fit me perfectly. I used a brush, comb, and some scissors in the bathroom to fix my hair. I cut it into a bob and styled it. By the time I stepped out of her bathroom, I looked like a high-powered attorney or a high-end escort, depending on how you looked at it. My back hurt so much that I couldn't wear a bra. I could barely wear the thin button-down blouse.

As I was walking out of the bathroom, Enzo was coming down the hall. He damn near took my shoulder off as he passed me. "The car is this way," was all he said.

He had changed into some sweats with cargo pockets, all black everything. I looked toward his aunt's room. I wanted to tell her thank you for all she'd done, but remembered the look in Enzo's eyes from before and decided against it.

It didn't take us long to get to Micah's dance studio. While you would think Micah would be running some kind of strip club, the nigga had a legitimate dance studio where girls and boys of all ages came to train. He had legitimate dance instructors from all over the world as part of the staff. The scary part of the whole thing was that parents dropped their children right into the lion's den and didn't even know it.

I didn't know what Enzo had planned. I expected us to roll right up to the front so when we pulled around back, I had to ask why.

"I'm a superstar whether I want to be or not. I ain't trying to announce my arrival and that's what's going to happen if I pull up to the front of the building." Enzo cut the engine on his foreign ride and looked over at me. "Can you shoot?"

I shook my head. He reached in the back seat and pulled a bat to give to me. "When the time comes, swing it," he said as he stared straight ahead.

For a long while we just sat there in silence and I wondered why. He kept his eyes trained on the back door of the building as one hand gripped a Desert Eagle and the other the steering wheel.

"You haven't had to kill someone in months, huh? Not since that nigga Dame bit it, right?" He didn't respond, but I kept talking. "This shit takes you back, I know. I thought I was done with this life. And to be honest, I am. I can't go back to where I used to be. Wouldn't make sense to go backward, would it? Not when freedom is so close." I was rambling, just talking on in hopes it would calm my nerves. I didn't know what I was feeling, couldn't explain. It was something akin to fear and regret.

"The only time a man is truly free is when he's dead," Enzo said.

"No, I remember Jake saying something like a man had to be willing to die for his freedom."

"Same thing."

"Not really. If you think about it, we don't have to die to be free, we can just be willing to die to ensure our freedom."

The back door to the building opened causing Enzo to sit up in his seat. His whole body tensed up as we watched a young girl who looked no older than sixteen walk out in her ballet wrap and tights. Behind her came a guard I had seen before but wasn't sure of his name. It was time for my body to tense. While I couldn't remember him raping me, I knew he had based on the soreness of my body and the video they left behind. My body started to shiver, right eye twitched, and my hand gripped the handle of the bat.

Enzo took his eyes off the duo for a second to look at me. "So you and Jake were close?"

"Kind of. He used to always talk to me and keep me up on certain things. There are times when I wished I would have trained with him when he asked me to."

"You saying he liked you or something?"

I shrugged. "I don't know, but he was nice to me. He was more into Gina though. He used to talk to us all the time. There was a time the three of us spent the night together."

"And Dame was okay with that?"

"Dame just thought his bodyguard was dibbling into his free supply of pussy, but Jake took care of me and Gina. I mean, yeah, the three of us fucked, but that was all it was for me. The way he touched and kissed Gina, I'll probably never know what that feels like."

"You were fucking Jake?"

"I fucked Jake. Once, well, you can say I fucked him and Gina at the same time."

He didn't say anything to me after that. We just sat there. I didn't know what our next move was about to be. I thought about my grandmother. Word was she died alone a few months after I was taken. I guessed she just couldn't live with the thought of losing me the way she had.

"We should wait before we do anything. Micah has the upper hand on us because he watched us, learned our every move," I told him. "We should wait."

I'd said all of that to him because I knew he was about to get out of the car and probably catch a murder charge, which I couldn't blame him for, but . . . I just didn't feel right about him running in guns a-blazing. While he used to be a part of Dame's goon squad, he was running high off emotions and needed to get his head on straight. That was why I grabbed his arm to keep him in his car.

"What are you doing?" he growled at me. "You still working for this nigga?"

I shook my head quickly. "No, but look." I nodded my head toward the opening back door again. Hemp walked out with another young girl. I would never understand how those parents didn't see the change in their daughters and sons after the world had gotten a hold of them. Or maybe they had and just didn't care or didn't know how to handle it. While the young girl on her knees sucking the other guard off seemed to be into it, the young girl Hemp had brought out didn't seem to be enjoying it at all. In fact she had a frown on her face and looked as if she was about to be sick.

I knew I had told him that we shouldn't attack but there would be no way I could sit still and watch a kid be violated again.

"I can't sit here and watch this," he said to me.

I knew in his heart, he was feeling the same way I was. "Me either."

He reached in his back seat and pulled the black duffle bag to his lap. "You scared to get down?"

I knew what he was asking and the Lord knew I was afraid, but it was too late to turn back now. I knew if I didn't rock with him then I would be on my own from then on out.

"I'm scared, but I'm down. I ain't ever had to hurt or kill nobody before, Enzo."

There was a look that passed in his eyes. "First time for everything."

"How did you handle your first time?"

His eyes hardened then turned dark before the light returned. "I don't remember it like that. I just knew I had to kill or be killed." He pulled a big hunting knife from the bag and a black Taser. "You just pull the trigger on this just like you would a gun. This shit has enough voltage to take the biggest nigga down. All you do is pull the trigger. I think you know how to use the knife. I ain't got time to properly train and show you where to hit a nigga to take him down, but you know how to stick and move, don't you?"

I nodded. "Yeah; if not I can figure it out."

He nodded. "Let's move."

We both eased out of the car. Enzo was definitely a skilled killer. He slid against the brick wall hiding behind the other trash can. Me? I was clumsy as fuck. I ended up kicking an empty Coke can and that was when the shit hit the fan. Both Hemp and the other guard looked up from the young girls they were sexing and spotted me. I couldn't run and I couldn't hide. There was nothing left for me to do but play my hand.

"What the fuck? You gotta be kidding me," the other guard fumed and stuffed his stubby, thick dick back in his pants.

Hemp pulled his dick from the young girl and shoved her so hard she fell onto the ground. "Bitch, you better be looking for Micah and just happened to get lost or some shit," he growled.

I frantically looked behind me searching for Enzo only to find he wasn't there. I knew he hadn't run off and left me so he had to be just waiting for the right time to show his hand. It was now or never, I thought, especially since I didn't know where Enzo had disappeared to. With my hands behind my back I slinked forward.

"You two get off on raping and fucking young girls?" I asked with a frown on my face. I was nervous as fuck. Hands shaking like I was having a seizure.

The other guard grinned then walked up on me. "I don't, but we heard about how niggas got off fucking that pretty golden you got between your legs."

"Pussy was so good a nigga was thinking about not pulling out." Hemp smirked. "So you Willena Bad Ass now? Coming back for revenge or some shit? Don't be stupid, bitch," he barked out.

As they talked I slid the knife into the back of my pants. They were both dressed in all black and the gun holsters they had on were visible. The young girl Hemp had shoved down jumped up and ran back into the building. I could see that on one hand she was happy to get that man off of her and on the other hand she was scared shitless. Her light-skinned face was red and wet with tears as she ran away. It wasn't too long before the other girl ran off too. I was so busy paying attention to the horrid look on the young girl's face that when Hemp grabbed me from behind in a chokehold, I almost dropped the Taser. But I knew if I had dropped it, I was as good as dead.

It all happened in a matter of seconds. Hemp picked me up and tried to shake me as a pit bull would when it had a victim in locked jaws. I saw stars and could barely breathe, but when the other guard came in to punch me, I pulled the Taser. My finger squeezed the trigger and two probes shot forward catching him over his heart. He did a *Thriller* kind of shaking move before hitting the ground. That was when I heard a loud pop behind me that scared me to death. When my body was slung to the ground, I thought I had been shot until I looked up and saw the big gaping hole where Hemp's right eye had been. The hole was so big that I could see clear through his head to see Enzo standing there with his gun still aimed at Hemp's now falling body.

I jumped up and grabbed the Taser I had dropped. "Oh fuck! Oh shit! Nigga, you could have killed me," I said to Enzo frantically. My chest felt as if it had pressure on it, eyes were wide with fright, and I was struggling to breathe. Death had a grip on me.

Enzo said nothing as he walked over the guard who had fallen to the ground, and blew a hole in his chest. I could tell it was a kill shot because of the way the body went slack after he had been moaning and groaning on the ground before. I got up and stood behind Enzo.

"We need to get out of here," he said. "You leave anything in the car?" he asked.

I shook my head. "No." I was too afraid and shaken up to speak.

Sirens could be heard in the distance. People were starting to look down the alley and wonder what was going on. They couldn't see me or Enzo because of the way the three trash cans and porta-potties were set up. Enzo didn't give me time to think; he grabbed my hand and we took off in the opposite direction.

"Don't run. Walk. Act normal," he told me.

He pulled a cap from his back pocket and put it on, pulling the peak of the hat down to cover his eyes. I knew I probably looked a wild mess as my weave was scattered over my head. We came out on the other end of Peachtree Street. Just as we exited one end of the alley and turned the corner, Atlanta PD was coming in the other. We could also see them speeding in the same direction we were coming from. Enzo quickly pulled me in with the gathering crowd as I looked around to see if anyone had seen us while he held my hand. He had it in a death grip and I couldn't lie and say that it didn't hurt, but I knew he was feeling what I felt. Paranoia. I begin to question if we had made the right decision to commit murder out in the open like that.

We made our getaway while everyone was trying to figure out what was going on. While people rushed to ask the cops what was happening, we crossed the other side of the street and watched the front doors of Micah's dance studio. Micah rushed out with a young girl who reminded me of the singer Ciara. She was looking around like she didn't want to be seen as she slid into the passenger side of his whip.

"Yo, Micah," Enzo yelled.

It didn't take Micah long to realize where the voice was coming from. Once Enzo had his attention, he aimed his fingers at him like they were a gun and pulled the imaginary trigger. If I didn't know any better, for a second I would have thought Micah was shook, but then that smirk he always carried adorned his face just before he rushed around to get in his Porsche and speed off. As he passed me and Enzo, they stared one another down.

"What are we going to do about the car?" I asked Enzo.

"I know some people who know some people. Come on, we need to get to the Underground, then to MARTA. We take that back to the airport. I have a car there we can scoop up and get back to my condo. I don't know what this nigga is going to do next and I gotta get my aunt and brother out the line of fire."

He was pulling me forward so fast that I was tripping over my own feet. So much so that when I actually fell he snatched me back up and kept moving. I wondered his reasoning for keeping a car at the airport and decided to ask him. He told me it was something he had always done starting back when he was working for Dame. Dame had made them keep cars all around the city in case of emergencies. I wanted to ask more, but couldn't focus on that while we tried to get as far away from the cops as possible.

We didn't stop until we had made it to Upper Alabama Avenue. The Underground was alive with life. Nightwings fans were still celebrating their win from the day. Women were in competition to see who could wear the shortest shorts and tightest dresses. Kids who looked like they should have been home preparing for school the next day shouted obscenities while wearing saggy jeans. The gays were out in full effect and people milled about normally while a killer and accessory to murder walked among them. They had no idea that the man they had all cheered just a couple of hours before had left two bodies back in an alley. It was good that the Underground was located at the entrance of the Five Points MARTA station. We crossed the streets swiftly, paid the fee, and entered the station.

I wasn't all that familiar with the trains that pulled in and out of the station so I had to watch silently as Enzo stared at the neon-lit board to see when the next train was coming.

"We got ten minutes to wait on the south line to the MARTA Airport Station and we're home free," Enzo told me.

He pulled me to sit down next to him on an empty bench. My heart was still racing, palms sweaty and feet hurting as we sat in silence. "I'm sorry I didn't do more to help back there," I said to him after a while.

He quickly glanced at me. "You did enough. You ain't a fighter or a killer so I don't expect you to be. You did enough." He said that then looked back down at his hands as he flexed them. The muscles and veins in his arms were thick and reminded me of steel cables as his skin rolled over them.

"I . . . I don't have anywhere to stay. I can't go back to the hotel," I said. I was scared that he would just dump me on the side of the road somewhere when we got back to our side of town. There would be no way I could go back to that hotel. Before taking Drew back home, I'd asked for a refund and they gave me a partial one because of some bullshit policy. All the money I had stashed and saved Micah or his goons had stolen it when they left the room. I had nothing.

Enzo looked over at me and I could tell he wasn't all there. Ever since I had asked him about his first kill, he'd had that look in his eyes. "You're lucky my *tía* told me to look out for you. Otherwise I wouldn't give a fuck where you laid your head. I know you were drugged, but you helped violate my brother nonetheless," he spat out.

I folded my arms a little upset that he wasn't going to cut me any slack. "You ain't ever done some shit you were forced to do, but regretted it? You ain't ever wish you can take some shit back? You ain't ever hated yourself when you looked in the mirror because even though your hands were forced you still did some shit you ain't proud of?"

His upper lip twitched as he glared at me. I could see the muscles in his square jaw line flinch in annoyance. But he didn't answer me.

All he said was, "Come on, train's here. We gotta go."

Chapter 8

Enzo

Angel's words played on repeat in my mind. Ma was right in what she had hit me with; I had done something that to this day ate at me. I had done all in the name of a nigga who made his life goal to terrorize Atlanta. I glanced at my hands as I sat in thought. Sometimes I dreamed in blood. I saw the streets covered in it, with that nigga's face staring back at me. He put me in hell, so when he died, my life was officially good. Now with Micah acting on bullshit from my past, orders by a nigga whose voice was speaking beyond the grave bothered me deeply.

A soft cough had me glancing at Angel as she sat beside me. We were the children forced into a world we really didn't want to be in. Our environment was still shaping us and that shit was bloody. The sound of Pac and vibration in my pocket alerted me that a text had come through on my cell. Snatching it out of my pocket, I glanced down and saw it was a message from my aunt telling me that she had left the condo with Drew. Nervousness quickly etched its way up my spine and made me scratch the back of my neck. During the time back at the house, after she had cleaned up Angel and after I'd helped her back into her room, she had sat me down and handed me a bag that had more money than I originally had when squatting in Dame's condo.

Also in it was a letter written by a dude I had always admired. One who was not only my buddy on the football field but also one who had helped train me in the streets as I was initiated into Dame's world. My hands shook as I read Jake's words realizing he wasn't as dead as I had thought he was. The fact that he and the crew had made it out gave me pride. I read his words while my *tía* explained to me that he and the other misfits were watching out for us, that they had our back if we ever needed it.

Now, I was looking down at her text as the acronym E.N.G.A. stared back at me. My aunt was using the cell given to her and I knew their safety wasn't something I had to worry about. In that moment, I had to watch out for a chick I used to be hired to protect, one I had to respect was pushed into a situation against her will. Did

I like it? No, but I had to respect it because one day, my time would be coming when I had to trust in someone too.

Running a hand down my face, I glanced up to see our stop. "This is us, come on."

I held my hand out for her to grab. When she didn't take it, my head swiftly turned, giving her a curt glare. Angel sat in shock staring at her hand as if it held the answers to all the madness we had going on. I may have cared some but we had other shit to deal with, so I scooped her up and threw her over my shoulder, walking out of the train and finding my way to my ride. My grip held her tight as she bounced on my shoulder. I could hear her finally coming back to reality as she squirmed.

"You finally with the living mama?"

"Stop being an asshole and put me down," she squealed.

My face contorted in a frown and I snapped open my door, threw her in the passenger seat, and caged her in while stooping down to look at her. "Stop drawing attention first off. You already got me looking crazy with carrying you, so relax. We'll be at my spot and you can lay your head down, relax, do whatever, since you staying with me now, a'ight?"

I could see relief in her eyes in that moment, a flicker of thanks. I gave a grunt closing the door and walking to my side of the car. Chicks.

We made it to my crib, tired and hungry. I locked down my door and peeled off my cap, tossing it on the couch while snatching up the television remote. "I want to check to see we weren't spotted on some cameras or some shit, looking shifty. Every time they see a dude in a baseball cap, they know to go after them," I explained as I stood wide-legged with my arms crossed, watching the massive flat screen before me.

Angel stood watching me, not moving from where she waited near the door with her arms crossed around her. My bag of items I had was at her feet. I moved to grab it while being relieved that we weren't caught on camera or considered suspects in the shooting at Micah's.

Pointing, I wrapped my hand around my mouth as I dictated to Angel what to do with herself all while watching the TV. "Your bag is behind the couch. You can sleep and make my aunt's room yours. All her stuff is cleared out and she has her own bathroom, too. We got some food in the fridge if you're hungry. Towels and whatever are in the wall closet behind the huge Basquiat painting; just push the frame to the side and it's there."

I listened to her move around me and I quietly turned off the TV after looking through all the news broadcasts. Heading into the kitchen, I made a couple of sandwiches, set her out one, and then walked into my room closing the door. My mind was still processing everything that happened by the time I got into the shower. Scalding hot water, just how I enjoyed it, ran down my back as I pressed my hand against the Italian marble wall of my shower.

My eyes closed for a second before I turned and pulled out a gun that had been resting in a compartment in the shower. I aimed it at the person before me. "What?"

Angel stood gaping, and wide-eyed. Her usual soft brown eyes were now a hazel brown I had never noticed before. The steam of my shower made the oversized simple T-shirt she had on lightly cling to the curves of her body. I could see she was wearing what appeared to be lilac bikini underwear.

I glared hard at her as she gawked. She probably did that shit on purpose, just to see me for whatever reason. My hand reached out to turn the shower off and I snatched a towel to wrap it around me. It was then that I saw her hands fly up to her mouth and she stumbled back to the door.

"I didn't mean . . . was knocking to tell you there is someone at the door . . . didn't realize until . . . Yeah, my bad," she stammered while turning around and rushing out of the bathroom.

A sigh escaped my lips. I stepped out of the huge steam shower, grabbed another towel to dry my wet hair, and I tucked my Glock near the small of my back causing my towel to hang low. Brushing past Angel, I moved to my walk-in closet, changed into my Nightwings sweatpants, and a white beater. I headed to the front room, clutching my Glock behind my back.

Pointing toward the table, I glanced at Angel who was still gawking at me with something akin to curiosity in her eyes. Her eyes trailed up and down my body, then stopped at my dick. Normally I would have found that shit amusing, but considering everything that had gone down, I wasn't sure what feeling I had. I figured she was tripping off the fact that I had a piercing on my dick and on the lines on my pelvis. I didn't really care what she thought about it. For me, I was into what little pain I could give myself without literally harming myself. The little bit of ink I had and the piercings I sported was enough for me right now. Each piercing and ink I had represented the shit I went through in my life that I almost didn't make it out of, so I was cool with what I had for now. If that scared Angel, then it wasn't my problem.

"Hey, hit the camera button on the remote and point it at the TV, ma," I snapped.

Angel was still in a daze before she jumped and did what I said. She paid little attention to the TV as her eyes were still scaling my body. I turned and saw it was a group of people who were thought to be ghosts. I quickly opened the door and stepped back in awe, watching my old crew walk in as if they hadn't a care in the world.

The loud thud of the remote hitting the floor made me turn to look at Angel. She stood flabbergasted. Tears rimmed her eyes as she opened and closed her mouth trying to talk. "You . . . Trigga . . . Jake . . . Gina!"

Quickly closing the door, every cloaked person around us dropped his or her hoods. I saw Angel rush forward to wrap her arms around Kelly Rowland's twin, Baby G. A smile spread across my face when I saw the back of a nigga whose name had become synonymous with legend in the street, Trigga. He stood checking the crib as if looking for something. When he didn't see it, he turned his braided, loc'd head and tilted his head up in greeting. I returned the nod, and then locked eyes on that nigga who trained me, Big Jake. He stood intently watching me. The pit of my stomach quickly knotted as I studied his posture.

Licking my lips, I looked around at everyone who was here.

I almost jumped when Angel squealed, "Ray-Ray!"

Shit had become a huge yack fest as the females started talking it up. I noticed two new faces, a young girl who kind of had some of Trigga's aspects in her, and a light, bright, kinda biracial-looking cat, with tats that covered his neck and a set of interweaved braids that fell into long braids over his shoulder. Curiosity had me wondering what was going on when another knock sounded at the door.

"You're gonna want to let them in, homie," Jake suggested.

I quirked an eyebrow, reached out, and opened the door. Two hooded people walked in. It wasn't until I looked down by happenstance that I saw it was actually three, the little hoodie person was sporting a pink and purple backpack with matching shoes. I watched the shorty make a beeline toward Trigga. The little kid looked up to say something in code to him, code I learned from the both of them. Trigga muttered low then tilted his head back behind him. It was then that the kid slipped behind him and moved to plop down on my couch.

I stepped back to lock the door, glancing around at the group before shaking my head. "What up, strangers?"

Low laughter from the fellas made my shoulders relax the tension within. My eyes darted back and forth before stopping on the face of a beauty I had only been privy to seeing a couple of times since working with Dame. Before me was the African Queen. Her head was a crown of twisted braids. Her lips covered in purple gloss and her charcoal-lined almond-shaped eyes kept my attention before I realized I was staring too hard.

Reaching to rub the back of my neck, my head shook again in confusion. "The African Queen? The Misfits? Damn, to what do I owe the occasion?"

The African Queen stepped forward, her arms stretched out in welcome. Out of respect, I went to her and hugged a woman I knew could kill me without blinking. She leaned back some assessing me, as if memorizing my features, before she gave a slight nod and a disappearing, knowing smile.

"Your aunt is resting well with your brother. She's starting a new regime of medicines that I know will get her cleansed out so she can truly heal and not be poisoned by these Western medicines."

I honestly did not know what else to say other than, "Thank you."

My eyes traveled over her head toward everyone that watched me. Dumbstruck was an understatement through it all. Anika had been one of the only females in the game to run with the big dogs when Dame had been alive. She was also the only person alive who could check Dame and make him back down. To see her with the Misfits made me question all I thought I knew.

A soft brush on my cheek had my attention focusing back on the African Queen as she cupped my jaw then stepped back.

That was when Trigga crossed his arms, watching me as if he knew some secret too, and nodded. "Jake, man, it's all you."

My eyebrow quirked and I stepped forward to talk. "Jake, man, thank—"

Before I could finish the front of his fist made contact with my face. I stumbled backward, almost slipping because I was barefoot. Instinct quickly had me squaring off. No motherfucker was about to come at me without letting me know what the play was. Not even one I had the utmost respect for.

I inhaled deeply, curved my back, and sent my fist bowing upward to connect to the underside of Jake's bearded chin. His loud grunt sounded the air.

I heard Angel yell, "What the fuck is going on?"

I didn't get to focus on that because I was quickly being charged by a wooly mammoth motherfucker who sent me backward yet again, but this time crashing into the glass table that once was Dame's. My teeth ground and I started fighting back, punching each fist into his rib-cages and anger that had been put on check from earlier that day suddenly cracked up like Pandora's box and I saw nothing but red. My hits landed harder, and I moved to push that dude off me as he sent beefy pounds into my face. Playing dirty was suddenly my thing when I pressed into his old gunshot wound. I knew if I pushed hard enough I could send a spasm of pain in him that would have him pushing off me, which it did.

He barked out a yell. "So it's like that, nigga? Don't fucking act like you don't know what this shit is about. Ain't take long at all for me to learn truths after killing those niggas. Dame was a talker too, motherfucka!"

It was then that I realized what he was talking about. I held a piece of broken glass in my hand. Cuts lined up my back, chest, arms, and sides due to not having a shirt on. His words hit me on rewind and the red I saw disappeared quickly as I came through.

Dropping on my knees, I bowed my head and laid the piece of glass I had down before me, pushing it his way. "I ain't have a choice in it. Take your bounty, homie. Just know I ain't have a choice and I'm sorry, brah."

Silence hit me. The cold press of steel instead of glass was my reply and I sat and waited until the slam of a fist, then a kick in my side hit me back in reality.

"Nigga, your bounty is mine and vice versa, ya heard me? That shit was done to make us kill each other in the end. You know that nigga had a bullet out for you anyway for being good in the game. Ain't no way I'll take you out like that; you my fam and no matter how bad I want to defend my gram . . ." Jake's voice broke off.

I glanced up through the blood that ran in my eyes to see him looking over at Trigga for a moment before kneeling down to offer his hand.

"She was your gram too, and I learned awhile ago that I can't kill a nigga who was my own brother, who was thrown in the same pit of lions as I was. After everything I went through with Cain and Abel, me and you are even on this. Just tell me, did you give her respect with it?"

I knew the Cain and Abel reference meant he was talking about Dame and his demented twin, Dante. Thinking back on that day was something I had dreams of since it going down. Willingly thinking on it though was something I never wanted to do, but for Jake I had to. I slowly stood up and squeezed the hand that was locked on to me. "Yeah, man. I told Dame one thing, but yeah. I placed a pillow over her head and let her go out. Then I shot her, just to give Dame something to drool on. I'm sorry, man."

My hands began to tremble as I thought back on it. Dame knew I could get into Jake's house with ease. I broke in the back way using a key I had, and quietly walked into her room where she slept. It took me hours to work up the nerve to take her out. I sat watching her, remembering the church songs she'd sing to us on Sunday mornings when she'd fix us grits, scrambled eggs, salmon patties, and pancakes. *Tía* always called her a guardian angel and that was what she was for me too. I laid the pillow over her head, and then held her hand as she struggled. I could tell how she held me that she knew it was me. She simply patted my hand then went off into the light. I later told Dame that I sliced her throat then shot her in the head.

Jake's voice pulled me back into reality. His hand reached out and pulled me into a brotherly hug before letting me go. "We all got our demons. Me and you are good."

Glass crunching under a pair of boots made me look to see the African Queen standing between us and pointing for us to go sit. Something about her ways reminded me of my *tía,* especially with how she was looking up at me with a look of authority in her eyes. I didn't hesitate to move. I walked through the crowd of people sitting down next to the kid who had earlier been speaking to Trigga.

A kooky laugh that sounded like the Joker had me ready to grab my Glock.

There was a sinister yet playful quality to it. "Ah ha! Ya wanksta trashed that dope table, bruv, and still ya both fucked each other up! It's a draw all ya ducats are mine, pay up."

Grumbles sounded all around us as everyone dug into their pockets. The kid next to me gave a huff and bounced up unzipping his or her book bag. "You cheated and that shit ain't cool, Speedy!"

That laughter sounded and the one with the two ponytails bent down and gave a smirk. His voice was thick with a British accent. "No, doll face, the dealer always bets on both sides, especially when you dealing with dudes like those two. Don't hate me, love me. Here, keep a dolla 'cause I hate to see ya salty. Ha!"

"But I won that," Jake grumbled then sharply cursed through the stinging of his cuts that were being cleansed.

All jokes continued and I flinched at the sting of rubbing alcohol on my body as the African Queen patched Jake and me up. I watched the one they called Speedy stroll through the condo making his way into the kitchen opening up cabinets then the refrigerator as if he lived here. Something about him amused me so I let it fly as he pointed at a bottle of coconut water then bent down to grab some food.

"So what up?" I asked.

Trigga stepped up and he laughed at the kid who plopped down next to me. The kid pushed off the hoodie and I saw mounds of thick, twisted braids fall everywhere. Hoop earrings peeped from under the thick mass. I sat back in awe at the realization that the kid was a girl. She looked up at me, looked me up and down with eyes that seemed to match my own, then tucked her iPod ear bud in her ear as she dug in her backpack pulling out a notepad.

She flippantly pushed it my way and spoke to me without looking, "Since ya in the family 'n' stuff, sign ya name here."

I chuckled low and did what she said, giving her my autograph. I handed her back the notebook. She stared the signature down then gave a wide smile before putting it away. Shaking my head, I looked up toward a chuckling Trigga.

"She a rude girl for real. So check it, like it or not, beef now settled. We here to help you with that nigga who's a loose end. This is my family; let me introduce you all, and we can talk business."

Trigga walked around the room and made his introductions. I was all smiles and humor before the last hoodie came off. A young Ciara-looking chick stood before me, winking her eyes at me, and grinning hard. "You that dude Enzo on the Nightwings. Damn you fine in person."

The moment that chicken opened her mouth, I felt my Glock in my hand on the side of me as my body became ridged like steel and a scowl formed across my face. "Yeah, Trig fam. I'm good on that help, brah; don't need it, don't want it."

Chapter 9

Angel

As soon as the girl took her hoodie off I moved behind her. I was all set to knock that bitch on her ass until I felt a blade at my throat.

"You may want to rethink that thang, pretty gyal," the boy I had come to know as Speedy said to me.

Enzo jumped up and pointed his gun at Speedy. The chain reaction was immediate. Those same people we had been glad to see just moments earlier held guns pointed at both me and him.

"Bruh, you better speak your piece or you and li'l shawty 'bout to bite these bullets," Trigga said to Enzo.

"Nah, what's about to happen is you're about to be a member short and if that means I gotta die to ensure that my aunt and my brother remain safe so be it. But y'all need to make sure each member of your crew is legit and not working for the devil," Enzo growled low.

I could have been wrong, but I knew I'd seen that lanky bitch get in the car with Micah earlier.

"You better use this fucking blade you got against my throat, nigga, because if not this bitch is dead," I told Speedy. The hunting knife that Enzo had given me earlier was already drawing blood from the girl's side.

"I don't really know you like that, Angel, but I respect you because you were one of the only girls who was nice to me in the house with Dame. But I ain't that same girl I used to be and will split your fucking skull in one shot if you push that knife any deeper," Ray-Ray told me.

I could tell by the look in her eyes that she was dead serious, but it was the semi smirk on Gina's and the other young girl's face, the one they had called Chyna, that gave me a little less fear in what I was set to do.

I noticed that Trigga and Jake had their guns aimed at Enzo who had his gun aimed at Speedy. The African Queen, a woman I had always wanted to be like simply because of the woman she was, stepped in between the melee.

She held her hands out and looked between all of us. "Obviously, we have a problem here. Cooler heads need to prevail. Angel, why so hostile toward Dominique?"

"I saw this bitch get in the car with Micah today," I quickly spoke up.

"I don't even know who the fuck Micah is," Dominique finally said.

"She's lying," Enzo countered. "I know I saw a girl who looks like you ride off with that nigga."

"Looks can be deceiving, bruv," Speedy said behind me.

The low, growled threat in his voice told me that he would have no problem slicing my throat from ear to ear.

"Moseif, relax," the African Queen told him. "Why don't we all calm down and think this thing out. They say they saw someone who resembles Dominique with Micah today and considering what they have gone through they have a right to react this way. However, Dominique is a part of this crew and we protect our own. Shawn." She turned to Enzo as she spoke. "Talk to Angel because if she hurts Dominique, Speedy is going to kill her and I assume that means you're going to try to kill Speedy, which is only going to make Trigga and Jake kill you. Is that really what we want?"

Enzo's face turned into an all-out scowl. "I don't really give a fuck about Angel if you really want to know. I made a promise to my aunt to

look out for her and that's it." I saw the confused look on everyone's faces. "She fucked
my thirteen-year-old brother so her living or
dying means shit to me, but that bitch she's got
hemmed up . . . Real recognize real and this ho
looking very unfamiliar to a nigga right now."

"I swear I was nowhere near downtown
Atlanta today," Dominique frantically pleaded.
"I don't know who this man is."

I was prepared to die in that moment. I had
been prepared to die anyway, but the words
Enzo spoke made it clear to me that all I had
was me, myself, and I. I knew death was my
companion because I wasn't built to survive this
part of the game. The only reason I'd survived
with Dame for so long was because I had people
who had my back and looked out for me when I
was too weak to look out for myself. I was no fool
and I knew that once we had gotten rid of the
entity that was Micah, I was as good as on own
my own. With no more money, no education as
of yet, and no means to an end, I was beginning
to feel like I ain't have shit to lose so why fight to
live. Besides, there was a real strong possibility
that I was going to die anyway, so why not go out
on my own terms.

Either way, one thing I knew for sure was that
I'd seen Dominique get into Micah's car.

"You lying bitch," I said through clenched teeth.

I grabbed Dominique by the back of her hair, shoved the knife farther into her side. Speedy's shank caught my neck; while the pain from the slice hurt like I would have never imagined, I welcomed death like a kid at Christmas.

"That broad is crazy, yeah? She musta really thought she see that gyal Dom down at di place fi not give fucks 'bout her own life. She shank di bitch proper, too."

Was I in heaven or hell? I didn't feel like I was burning. There was a cool breeze whishing over my body. I tried to open my lids but they were heavy. My throat was sore on the outside and I could feel my hands absentmindedly rubbing the wrap around it.

"But Dom say she wasn't down there, Chyna. Speedy said she was with him. Somebody lying or this bitch is really crazy," I heard Gina mumble. "I don't like that bitch, Dom, anyway if you want the truth. She got my boy Speedy all caught up and shit."

"It's gon' right kill mi blood when he realizes—"

Shit, my mind screamed. I was alive? Still fucking alive? God had a real cruel sense of humor.

"No, it just wasn't your time to go," a smooth voice washed over me.

I opened my eyes and saw the African Queen walking into the room. I looked at her crazy thinking she was in my head then realized through my grogginess I'd spoken my thoughts aloud.

"I thought I was dead," I grumbled.

"You could have been if my aunt hadn't body snatched Speedy before he got the blade deep enough."

I cut my eyes in the direction of the door to see Ray-Ray was sitting there with an unreadable expression on her face.

"Well, did that Dominique bitch die?" I asked in disgust.

"No one died," the African Queen. "The shock of being cut probably knocked you unconscious. You only received a scratch compared to what Speedy could have done to you had I not been there. I see that you're just like most of these girls out here who have become a victim of their environment. So allow me to tell you like I've told my niece," she said nodding toward Ray-Ray.

"Wait, Ray-Ray's your family?" I asked with furrowed brows.

"Yes, she is. Will tell you the story later, but listen to me, just because life has dealt you a fucked-up hand doesn't mean you have to play like you got nothing to lose. Trying to get yourself killed may seem like the easy way out, but don't be chicken shit. Fight for your life. Give no man, woman, or child your life so freely. You're beaten, but not broken. You're down, but not out."

"I ain't got nothing anyway."

"Life, you got life. When this is all over, find me, and I'll help you get your life on track. But know I won't help you unless you want to be helped. But first, tie up your loose ends. Come on, ladies. We got to disappear. Phenom wants us back at base camp."

I watched as the three stood up and with the way Ray-Ray was watching me I knew she was feeling salty that I'd tried to off one of her friends.

"Wait," I called out behind them. "I never said where we'd seen Dominique so why would she automatically say she wasn't in downtown Atlanta today?"

I was talking to all of them, but my eyes stayed on Ray-Ray and Gina. They knew me more than any of the people in the house and Gina knew me best. There was an unspoken message that passed between the women. When the African placed a comforting hand on Ray-Ray's shoulder, I knew that something deeper was going on with that group behind the scene. I didn't care. I needed them to know I wasn't lying.

I sat up and threw my legs over the side of the bed. It took me a few minutes to get my bearings enough to stand to go in the bathroom. Once there I stood a moment watching my reflection in the mirror. Even though I'd gone through hell the last four years of my life, I still had my youth about me. Bags sat underneath my eyes and I flinched as I pulled the white covering from my neck. Stitches sat there perfectly sewn and like the Queen had said, Speedy didn't do nearly as much harm as I'd expected or wanted. His blade had only come halfway across my neck and looked to only be a serious flesh wound.

It was late at night/early morning. I walked downstairs to find Enzo sitting on the couch with his hands steepled in front of him as if he was praying. The bruises, cuts, and scars were visible on his bare shoulders as he sat with his elbows on his thighs. He seemed to be in deep thought until he looked up at me. The words he had spoken earlier echoed loudly in my head. I rolled my eyes and headed for the kitchen. I was shocked to find Jake and Trigga sitting at the table near the bay window. Glocks were laid out on the table like a Thanksgiving feast.

Jake stood and walked over to me. "You good, Angel?" he asked me after giving me a comforting hug.

I gave a brief smile. "I'm okay, I guess," I lied. "It's whatever. Y'all should watch ol' girl though. I know what I saw."

A look passed between Jake and Trigga. As always they were communicating without words. Trigga didn't say anything to me, just gave me a curt head nod and went back to watching out the window. That nigga may have been finer than the most expensive of wines, but he wasn't a talker still, I could see. Not too much had changed about him. He had longer locs and more muscles, but he was still the same silent Trigga. His hoodie was off and all he had on was his white wife beater. There was a tattoo of the word GHOST over his heart.

"And I ain't no pedophile or child molester. They drugged me and the kid and made us do it," I said again, feeling the need to defend myself against what Enzo had said.

"Angel, we know the story. He told us afterward. We can understand why he's mad, but we know you wouldn't have done it had it not been forced. We got you."

I thought about saying something else but only nodded and went to grab food and water from the fridge as I had planned to do. Enzo's fridge was stocked with all organic foods, fruits, and juices. It told as to why his body was so fit. Trigga and Jake spoke on things that I didn't understand, which meant they had been speaking in coded language. I grabbed what I needed to and walked out of the kitchen so they could get back to doing them.

"Angel."

When I heard Enzo call my name, I wanted to keep walking, but turned to look at him. "Yeah?"

"Are you trying to kill yourself? Let me know so I can just quit looking out for you now."

I tilted my head and looked at him as if he had grown two extra heads. "Looking out for me?" I repeated. "You just told everyone who was listening that you really didn't give a fuck about me or my well-being. You're full of shit, Enzo. Either you're full of shit or you're fucking bipolar. Either way, fuck you for that shit."

"I will never fuck you, so no, thanks. I'm just making sure my aunt doesn't have her heart set on saving a woman who doesn't want to be saved. She told me to look out for you but if you're just going to try to get yourself offed, I ain't wasting my time."

I stood there and just looked at the bare-chested man. Earlier when I'd seen all the piercings he had on his body, I'd been intrigued . . . more like turned on but I would never admit it out loud. The piercing he had in his dick piqued my curiosity. The piercings he had on the V cut of his pelvis made me want to touch him in ways I've never willingly wanted to touch a man. Seeing him naked, earlier, had given me all kinds of thoughts. But I knew there would never be a way that my curiosity would be satisfied. Enzo had made it quite clear that I disgusted him.

And that was fine, but he would not stand in front of me and play mind games with me. Dame had been the master of mind games. And to think about it, the more I stood there looking at Enzo, the more that nigga was starting to favor Dame in small ways. It fucking annoyed me that Dame was so engraved in me that any man who got close to me would probably start to look like or remind me of him in certain ways. The way Enzo was standing, his eyes, the way he used his words to cut me earlier all reminded me of that nigga Dame. It wasn't a good time for Enzo to be fucking with me.

"Go to hell," I told him and rushed up the stairs.

I knew he wouldn't come after me, which was fine by me. I needed to be alone anyway.

There was something that I needed to do. Dame
had brought some of us here a time or two and
because I knew he rarely used the place, after
he'd died, I climbed through a window and hid
some money. The only thing was it was in a
small wall safe in the room Enzo had as his own.
One way or another I had to get that money.

As I sat and ate my food in silence I thought
back on what happened in the alley. I'd helped
to murder someone, two people today. I really
didn't want to think about it, not because it sickened me, but because seeing Enzo kill the way
he did had turned me on. I didn't know if it had
been the way he killed them with no remorse or
if it was the look in his eyes that said he had no
problem doing it that turned me on. My feelings
behind the whole thing freaked me out. One
minute I was scared and paranoid, the next I
could feel my pussy muscles clench and release.

It made me want to fuck him the way I'd never
done willingly to another man just to show him
that what he had done was worth it. Images of
Micah's scowling face played before me. He had
been too quiet for my liking. I'd expected him to
come back guns blazing because that was just
who Micah was. I'd rather know what he was
doing than to have him this quiet.

As if the universe was reading my mind, my cell phone rang. I didn't know the number but picked up anyway. "Hello?"

"So that's the move you're making? You're rocking with Enzo," Micah's voice said on the other end of the phone.

My whole body went rigid. "What do you want, Micah? Why can't you just leave us alone?"

"Us, huh? So you and this nigga a team now?" he asked. "Been running ya mouth?"

"I guess you'll never know," I snidely replied. We both knew what he was asking, but only I knew if his secret was still safe with me.

"I see. So, it's like that?" He chuckled. "And you think this nigga gon' be easy if you've told him."

"I think you need to go fuck yourself."

"After I fuck you. Are you sure this is the move you wanna make? Your life would be much simpler if you just got with the program, Angel. Nobody gonna take care of you like I will."

I scoffed. "I think I'm fine just where I am."

"That's funny considering he told a houseful of people that you don't mean shit to him."

The hairs on the back of my neck stood up in that moment. I rushed to the window to look outside. I could see hooded and masked figures rushing up. I'd been right. Dominique was the bitch I'd seen with him at his dance studio. I knew she was the only one who would have told him what Enzo had said. I dropped the phone and rushed down the stairs when I heard Micah tell someone to "make it happen."

Enzo jumped from the couch and looked at me as I clumsily fell down the last few stairs. Before I could tell Enzo that Micah knew we were still here, the windows shattered as bullets rained through. I was trying to get back up when Enzo tackled me to the floor as shards of glass flew around us. From somewhere in the kitchen I heard return gunfire and knew Trigga and Jake were doing what they did best.

"Stay down," Enzo yelled at me.

I kept my head covered, peeking through my arms to see him crawl to the fireplace and lay his hand against a wall panel. Somewhere in between windows breaking and bodies rushing the house, I heard myself scream. I watched on as the wall parted and showcased a hidden area that was decorated in every gun you could imagine. Bullets kept coming, but it was when the front door flew off the hinges that I really knew shit got real. I expected Enzo to come out with a gun, but when he pulled what looked like a bat with nails poking out of it in one hand and something that looked like a chainsaw with a handle in the other, I didn't know what to think. As soon as a man in a ski mask stepped over the threshold of the door, Enzo rushed him, swinging the bat backward to connect with his face. The nails from the bat caused it to stick in the intruder's face before Enzo snatched it back. Before the goon could yelp out the chainsaw-looking club split his face in half when Enzo swung it upward.

Another one stuck his arm in the door with guns blazing. Enzo took his arm off. The limb fell to the floor with the finger still squeezing the trigger while Enzo used the chainsaw concoction to gut the man, shoving it into his abdomen hard making the intruder's entrails fall out when Enzo pulled the weapon back.

The look on Enzo's face was a mean one. One minute it looked as if he smelled something foul, the next it looked as if he was enjoying the violent barbaric way he was killing people.

"Angel, grab the gun under the sofa. Safety's off. Get that shit and shoot," he fussed at me.

I didn't hesitate to do what he said. I could hear bodies dropping in the kitchen and just outside the window. I grabbed the gun and shot the first person who didn't look like they belonged in the house. I'd never used a gun a day before in my life, so the recoil of the heavy object damn near took my hand off. I didn't even know if I'd actually hit my target, but I was shooting anyway, shooting and screaming. I saw bodies moving by the window on the opposite side of the room and opened fire.

A yell sounded so loud that it made my flesh crawl. I ducked a barrage of gunfire and glanced to see that Enzo had a knife stuck into the back of a female who'd made the mistake of joining Micah. He had her by her ponytail as he pushed the knife into her spine then took it in an upward motion. Her screams got louder and louder. Enzo bit down on his bottom lip as it looked like he was ripping the woman's spine from her back. When he released her and pushed her forward, he cupped his hand where the entry of the wound was and pulled. The woman's gargled scream got caught in her throat as she fell face first onto the marble flooring.

I lay there with my mouth wide open in shock. Enzo looked down at me then wiped his bloody hand across his top lip. It was official, there was a side of Enzo that scared me and turned me on at the same time. In that moment he looked more like Dame then he ever had and that made my flesh crawl all the while making me question my attraction to his madness.

Chapter 10

Enzo

Blood for blood, flesh for flesh. I stared down at my bounty of a pound of flesh, stepping over the body of the chick that thought she could take me down. Her screams and that glossy look of shock, then terror rocked me. It had me flashing a satisfied smile over the fact that I had taken down an enemy. Let's just be clear in this, I really didn't want to have to go into my dark place. My blackout mode, but since niggas decided to take me there, my killer mentality was very obliged to come out and play.

As I cocked my head back, smiling at the ceiling, enjoying the rush of the kill that ran through my body, my heart automatically felt as if I should be on the field playing for the masses as I murdered the opposing team. Shouting drew me back to my surroundings. I saw from the side of my eye Angel staring in shock. Bullets were flying all around us, niggas were busting into the crib as if it was some drug bust. It felt as if everything I had worked for was coming to an end. There was no fucking way this shit would go unnoticed. My days as a player were numbered and it put a large amount of resentment in me.

I wanted Micah. Wanted to torture that nigga like I had to do in the underworld from time to time.

Which was why I stepped forward and bared my teeth shouting, "Where is Micah!"

I stepped over bodies, planting my feet to drop to one knee then lift up and body block a nigga to the floor. My fist followed through as well as the two knives in between my fingers slid into the jugular of that fallen nigga. I quickly stood up, turning to snatch another chick who rushed me, pointing Glocks at me. I used my blades to slice at each of her wrists, and then grabbed her by the neck. I snatched her close then stuck her multiple times in the stomach, watching the light in her eyes quickly fade.

Hot blood ran over my hands, and I noticed Angel ducking and sending her fist into random attackers' faces. "Grab the Glock, mama!" I shouted.

She turned my way and stared at me in a strange way before doing what I told her.

Trigga and Jake were in the hallway of the condo blazing it up with bullets and helping keep the enemy's guns away. I used that time to go to my room, grab my bag, strapping it to my back along with Angel's. A grimace flashed across my face as I kicked the door closed to shield me from bullets that rained into the room. I hunkered behind it, pulled out my shotgun, and then yanked it open, pumping steel into anyone who wanted to get it.

"Angel! Get your shit, we outta here," I yelled.

She whipped around my way to see where I was and then ran as fast as she could. Her pink and black Nikes hopping over bodies, broken glass, and other fallen items. All of this shit had been Dame's. Only thing I came in with was the machines my aunt needed, and she took that when she left. We all were living out of luggage still, just in case of something like this. Throwing my gun down, I pushed through the madness, snatching a big wrestling-built dude. His face was covered in a mask but his throat was accessible to me. I remembered I had another blade, so I pulled it out from my pocket and let it play between my fingers with a smile.

My fist went flying, connecting to the big gorilla's throat. He reached out to snatch at me but I was too quick. Though my body was in pain from fighting Jake earlier and by getting dirty now, some dark place in me kept me going. I knew I was in blackout mode and I rode with it to leap up, wrap my arm around the goon in front of me, tightening it, letting my bicep choke any breath from him. I flexed and tightened my hold as I stretched him backward and rammed my blade up his back severing his spine. It was my favorite move. It left my prey vulnerable for me to flip the blade again and easily slice it across this throat. The sound of the jerky heavy body in my grasp dropping made me laugh.

A shout kept me following through. "Enzo! It's clear; we gotta go."

I was a soldier in the streets. Moving out was what I always did best. Jogging forward, I moved Angel behind me and we headed into the hallway. Bodies lined the floor like roaches in a forest. Some moved and wiggled and those who even dared to reach for us I had Angel stomp out with the nail bat I snatched back up for her.

Holding her back, I leaned to peek around a corner, making sure it was clear. "Jake and Trigga handled this shit. Forgot how clean they were with it. Seems like they only got better."

Angel's soft breaths traveled my way. The warmth against my back let me know she wasn't moving from where I had her, which had me reaching back to pull her with me as we headed down the hall.

Crunching of bone and Angel's grunt let me know she was one with watching my bat.

"Yeah, you all are . . . crazy as hell," she said in between each swing of the back.

My head tilted to the side. I opened the emergency door to the condo and motioned for her to come on. "Says the chick who just bashed in some niggas' heads and pumped steel into bitches' faces."

We headed down the stairs in a rush. The sound of gunplay was greeting us below in our descent.

"You told me to do it and I had to or we were gonna die," Angel huffed out while trying to keep up with me.

I chuckled low and held up my hand motioning for her to stop as we made it to the exit. "Oh, yeah? Then get ready for some murder kill, killer. If I disappear don't worry about me." Tossing her my bag, I stared into her light brown eyes. "Go to Dixie Motel. There's a card in my bag; and make sure no one is following you."

I reached forward to show her also pulling out my skullcap and fitted cap. She watched me put both on, and I glanced her over. "Change your look up too, mama."

A slight frown played at her lips as she adjusted the bag and flipped her hair up, twisted and created a messy knot. She reached up, snatched my cap, and put it on her head then gave a sigh turning when the sound of guns going off sounded around us.

"Done; let's go because I hear your song."

Angel stood behind me with white knuckles gripping her bat hard, whereas I scoped my area then frowned when I saw a waiting silver car watching the battle continue. Rushing forward, we both took out several other gunners coming head-on with us. Angel took to a corner where both Ray-Ray and Gina were positioned. I guessed they had gotten caught in the crossfire as they'd been leaving.

Out the corner of my eye, I could see Baby G digging her nails into the eyes of another chick. She gave a wicked yell as her knee connected with the attacker's face. All in one move, Gina's grip seemed to tighten and she spun in a way that allowed her to snap the broad's neck with a slam.

I wasn't sure where the hell she learned some shit like that, but I was impressed nonetheless. Ray-Ray had something that looked like claws of simple razors between her fingers. She slashed out and cut, ducked, then brought her fist in to gut another chick that came after them. Both chicks seemed to have moves that mirrored some of Trigga's style and it had me shaking my head at the organization of a group of kids who seemed like almost a year ago had no one to pull them together. Today the fight was real and everyone was on their game.

Now when I say everyone, I meant it. I stood in the middle of bodies staring at Micah who sat in the back of his silver Jaguar XJ with a smile on his face smoking a cigar. He had a struggling Angel in his arms, who kept trying to hit him with my bag. My guns were empty and all I had was a makeshift piece of metal I had found nestled in my hand like a machete.

Sinister laughter like that of the Joker sounded around me and my eyes widened when that dude Speedy dropped on top of the Jaguar, stuck his tongue out laughing then punched his fist in the sunroof of the car.

"Grab that nigga!" sounded from the opposite side of the car from Trigga.

My feet planted and before I could run forward, the sound of something rolling toward my feet made me look down. In front of me were several colored pencils with razors plated into the sides. I glanced around to see a set of Pastry kicks swinging from a fire escape near me.

Eyes that mirrored my little brother and me smiled from their hiding spot and I heard, "I ain't supposed ta fight anymore, but I can give yuh stuff ta play with."

Snatching them up, I slid each one through my fingers and I scanned back to where the little girl was. "Thanks, baby girl; keep back," I said but saw there was no one where she had just been sitting.

"Damn," was all I could say.

Shouting echoed and I ran forward. Speedy was gripping the sunroof hard, his many zig-zagged braids flying in the air. He used his hands as weapons, snatching at the many guns that pointed his way.

Micah snarled trying to slash at Speedy's fingers. He glanced my way, saw me sprinting his way then shouted to his driver, "Go, nigga, go!"

Blood ran down my face from the fight. My eyes stayed locked on my goal, that nigga Micah's throat my ideal goal. Speedy kept his hold as if he were surfing, and I ran after the Jag.

I laughed as I hyped him up. "Swaggin', surfing," I shouted.

Making my way to the Jag, I gripped the open window staring inside. The Jag wasn't able to move fast enough due to the many goons in the alley and I was able to pull myself where I could look into the window. The piece of metal I'd turned into a weapon surged into the car, its nails slamming and cutting into the leather of the Jag as well as Micah. I knew from the flashes of my face that I could see in the window's reflection that I looked like a demon. My eyes were dark as coals, my teeth were bared in a snarl, and blood covered my face.

"Why you scared, bitch? Ain't expect that I'd die so easily huh?" I snarled at Micah.

Micah's face went from malicious to displaying a flash of concern.

Angel used my bag to ram his face but he punched the shit out of her while trying to keep from being snatched.

Micah gave his own laugh then tried to use his feet to get at me, but Speedy was still snatching at him, using chicken wire to lasso whoever's neck got in the way. While we both tried to grab at him, the sound of screeching brakes sent both Speedy and me off the car. I lay on my back groaning, rolling from side to side, seeing that Jake had stepped in the way of the vehicle.

Micah shouted out, "Run that big bitch down!" The driver backed up the Jag and complied.

I pushed to get up as fast as I could, only to see Jake quirk an eyebrow with an unamused smirk and then sent a bullet into the driver's head with his silencer. I could hear the car door opening and glanced back to Micah where Trigga had snatched him up. Angel scrambled out in a daze. She turned to pull out a cigar lighter, flicked her nail against the gauge, and then torched that nigga's neck by pressing it against his jugular.

Trigga gave a haughty laugh, and then signaled with his eyes for her to step back. "Damn, dude, it's that serious for you, huh?" he asked sending his fist into Micah's contorted face.

The sound of sirens coming our way to the back of the condo complex had everyone pissed the fuck off, including me. I rushed forward, stepped to Trigga who held Micah out to me, and then took that weasel by the neck digging those pencils given to me into his back.

His shock and pissed yell gave me utter pleasure as I pushed deeper near his spine. "Tell you what, I won't kill you today, because yeah, we both got a reputation to maintain. But how 'bout we finish this at another time, this time of my choosing?"

Micah's hand came at me but I pushed harder feeling the trickle of blood cascading over my fisted hand.

"Yeah. Truce, nigga, truce!" he hissed through clenched teeth.

My face was close enough where I could feel the heat of his breathe. I had every intention of killing him where he stood but it was Trigga's hand that pulled me back.

"Get at him later. Ride out, fam," was all he said.

Jake stepped up, pulled out a syringe, and then stuck Micah in his neck. "Night, night, nigga."

The sirens got closer. Trigga shouted to Speedy to take the Jag and dump it in a safe spot with Micah and ordered the rest of the Misfits to clear out.

"So, man, we'll meet up and have a true conversation later," he said.

I ran my hand down my face then gave a nod. "Yeah. Don't trust that bitch Dominique. She's that ho who will fuck up your whole world, man. I can't get with you all a hundred percent until she's gone."

Trigga watched me without saying a word. He turned then stopped. Blood seemed to blend into his reddish brown skin. His locs were now loose but he also had his hoodie on, which cloaked his face. "Then I ain't teach ya nothing, my nigga. Know thy enemy but not yourself, then wallow in defeat every time, my man. It's always a method to the madness get in track on that and then we'll talk again."

My brain comprehended what he'd told me. He didn't say much but he said more than a State of the Union address. I trusted them enough with my aunt and brother. I knew I had to trust them enough to know that they were aware of shifty bitches in their crew and that they'd handle it when it was time. For now, my fight was still with a nigga who wanted me dead and for some reason wanted Angel badly.

"Angel," I called out to her.

She scrambled to grab my bag and hers then came my way. Her hair was everywhere. Blood speckled her tattered clothes and shoes as well. Her face was flushed red and her eyes were mad dilated. She looked like a deer caught in head-lights.

"How'd you get caught?" I asked as the Jaguar peeled off behind us, and we were left alone in a back alley full of bodies.

Cutting through a sideway, we waited until cars went by and we headed to a parking garage several buildings away from where I lived.

Angel peeked around in fear, and I could tell she was hoping no eyes were on us. "I was doing like you said. Went past Ray-Ray and Gina and was heading out when I ran into one of his guys, that's how. I tried to fight but . . ."

I pulled her to the side then opened a door to the parking garage guiding her inside as I closed the door then reached up to dig into a space above the framing. A set of keys appeared in my hand and I motioned for her to keep walking.

"Yeah, if you riding with us, we'll have to train you up."

Our feet echoed in the garage and we made our way to my covered Land Rover. I helped Angel climb in, noticing the cuts on her waist, and seeing the branding for the first time through her slashed top. My jaw clenched in anger, because she had been burned into like that and because it was also a reminder of the bullshit Micah made her do to my brother or made my brother do to her. My eyes narrowed and I slammed her door. I walked to the driver's side of the ride and hopped in. I pulled out into traffic, blending in with the normal ATL traffic.

We drove past the condo where dozens of cops flanked the area. A place that was once where I could lay my head without thought of being bothered was gone. We were on our way back to the Trap where I knew we could hide without being directly tracked. The drive took some time because I made sure we weren't being followed. No one knew this ride I had but still caution was always necessary. I received several texts from the Misfits telling me that Micah was handled and that my aunt and brother were worried about me.

I knew I couldn't go to wherever they were hidden and I knew I couldn't completely go missing because I had a job to handle. So I let them know that I was okay and eventually made it to Dixie Motel. Once pulled in, I bowed my head, resting it against the steering wheel. Angel sat asleep, bloody and dirty beside me.

My eyes took her in, watching her for a few moments before I slapped her thigh hard waking her up. "We're here; get out."

Getting into the motel room didn't take long. I ordered her to go shower while I went out to get some ice and smoke a blunt. I knew I'd have to get food but I had to shower and clean up. A Chinese takeout deliverer came into view and I memorized the number on the side of their car as I let tendrils of smoke roll through my slightly parted lips. Chinese sounded good right now and we could lay low as they delivered us food. It wasn't something I'd normally eat, but I could make an exception to the rule since I was hungry and on the run. Snuffing out my blunt, saving it for later, I walked back into the room and kept my eyes away from the bathroom.

"I'm hungry," Angel whispered behind me.

I hadn't heard her come out of the bathroom while I stashed the ice bucket in our mini fridge. "It's a Chinese food spot, here's the number," I said writing the digits down, dropping a roll of money near it then moving toward the bathroom.

She stood in a towel with wet, crinkled hair. It had me frowning because her hair wasn't as long as it was just a few minutes ago and it was that sandy-brown red again, curling around her head in a fro.

"Order two large fried rice, shrimp, and beef. Get whatever sides, too, with that hot sauce and add whatever you want with it plus drinks," I said stepping into the bathroom.

I got ready to close the door then almost tripped over myself. It looked like World War III in that fucker. Towels were everywhere and hair lay over a toilet, over the floor, over the sink and at my feet.

"The fuck is this?" I yelled.

Angel rushed behind me and pushed me to the side scrambling around the bathroom. "I was about to clean it up but you headed in there before I could."

My hands ran down my face and I stared down at a chick who had turned into Mystique. "Fucking chicks straight shifting like chameleons. Damn," I griped.

She bent over in her towel cleaning up everything, snatching things with an attitude, and my eyes found their way on her ass. The towel was so short that I could see that separation between her thighs. "Look, it's cool, I'll deal with it."

"Nah, niggas act like they never seen weave before. I got it," she spat out, moving quickly then walking past me.

My hand reached out to grip her arm and I saw a slight spark of fear hit her. "I'm tired, my bad okay? Sorry. Just order our food and think on why the fuck Micah wants you so bad, because that shit just wasn't about me, but about you too. Don't answer your cell anymore either. We're ghosts for right now."

Angel gave a slight nod, and then pulled her arm out of my touch. I kept my eyes locked on her and she pulled her real hair to the side as her almond-shaped eyes kept displaying her exotic looks. "I really don't know but I will. Wash your ass, nigga. Bye."

Then like that, I was pissed the fuck off at her again and slamming the door to the bathroom behind me. I glanced around the bathroom, peeled off my clothes, and then hopped in the shower.

Drills were coming up and I knew she would have to be with the Bounce Girls too, training for the next big game coming up in two weeks. For now though, we'd have to keep clear of Micah and any shit he was coming with.

As water made my wounds sting and ache in pain, a wad of clumped hair appeared at my feet and I roared out loud, "This that shit that I don't like! Fuck! You don't even need the fucking horse hair; get your shit right, mama! Fucking Chewbacca!"

Chapter 11

Angel

I looked around the drab hotel room and gave a long, deep breath. The double beds were nothing fancy. Just regular old beds with country-like bedspreads on them. While Enzo had showered, I went to the front desk and bought some of the off-brand Febreze-like spray to take the dingy, mildewed odor out of the air. I paid the lady an extra fifty for her to give us fresh sheets. The old bitty had been so thankful for the extra cash she went into the storage room and gave me two brand new packs of sheets. They were only 180 thread count, but at least I knew no one had pissed, shitted, died, or fucked on them.

"The extensions in my hair were Brazilian, not horse hair," I said.

Enzo looked up from his food then frowned while looking at me as if I was crazy. He shrugged. "And that is relevant why?"

"Was just saying is all since you called me ugly and was fussing about the hair in the bathroom."

He wiped his mouth with the napkin while still watching me. "I didn't call you ugly."

"You did. You called me Chewbacca."

He gave a visible smirk then went back to eating. "I called you that because your ass was shedding hair and shit all over the bathroom and shower, mama. A nigga like me don't too much care for a bitch and her weave being all over the place. The fuck you got weave in your head for anyway with that African bush you got on ya head?"

I cut my eyes at him and subconsciously ran a finger through my puffing-up hair. "So now you have a problem with my real hair, too? You're an asshole, Enzo."

He gave a lopsided grin. "So I've been told. But, nah, mama. I gives no fucks about your hair one way or the other. Just keep the shit out my way."

I really had a mind to toss my whole plate of food at him as he sat there and stuffed his face. But because he was my safety net and a way to keep a roof over my head and food in my mouth, I didn't want to get too flip at the mouth. So, I stayed silent as we both watched the news. Enzo's condo was up in flames as cops milled about. Really it was Dame's condo. We listened intently as the news anchor spoke about a drug and gang war that was still taking place months after Damien Orlando's death.

The woman went into detail about his twin brother being found burned to death in a warehouse in Morrow after he had been shot, mutilated, and had his head severed from his body.

"Damn," was all I could murmur. *Twin?* My mind came to life. That had to have been the man I'd seen that day when I was passing the restaurant. *Oh my God,* I thought. Thank God I ran my ass away from that nigga he'd obviously sent after me. I paid close attention to it all. I didn't want to miss a thing. It wasn't until the reporter was talking to the plainclothes detective that I tried to turn the TV off.

"The fuck you doing? Turn it back on," Enzo demanded as he snatched the remote from my hand.

I watched as he stood; the gym shorts he had on did very little to hide the bulge between his legs. Maybe I was crazy, but I would have paid to see the piercing in his dick again. I'd never seen anything like it and it fascinated me. Still, with all that had happened and all that was going on, it was safe to say that I would never get that eye treat again.

"As you just heard, police are saying that Micah Tems, a major sponsor of the Atlanta Nightwings Football Camp for Kids, was found passed out in his car. It looked as if he had been beaten, assaulted with some kind of sharp knife-like weapon, and left for dead in the back of an abandoned building. As of now, we do not know where Shawn 'Enzo' Banks is or if his disappearance and Mr. Tems's assault are connected in anyway," the news anchor reported.

Enzo grunted, "Humph. Damn, all a nigga wanted to do was play football as a kid, make the NFL, and take my aunt and brother up out the Trap." I didn't know if he was talking to himself or me. I remained silent. It seemed as if he was zoned out, in another world.

"Micah is after me because Dame sold me to him. Only Micah had to work off a debt to get me. No matter how much money he gave Dame, you know that nigga always had a bargain going. Dame had been plotting to have some people killed and of course Micah was to see to it being done. Micah works for the FBI, Enzo."

He tossed the remote and walked to stand over me. "Keep talking," he growled. The look on his face told me that things could or would go way left in the blink of an eye.

"When Dame sold me to him, Micah was to get me twice a week and one weekend after I finished working at the City. Drugs, alcohol, and pussy will make a man careless no matter who he is. He messed around and said too much one day. Said something about needing to call his captain. At first I thought he was talking about Dame, but when he almost freaked out because he'd left his phone in Dame's limo I knew something else was going on. Then he left me in his hotel room alone for too long one day. I found his badge."

"So, he's an FBI agent?" He must have been thinking Micah was an informant.

I nodded. "Yeah."

"And you've known this the whole time and ain't said shit?"

I watched as Enzo's fist balled by his side then slid back a ways from him. The dark clouds rolling in his eyes put the fear of God in me. His jaw was twitching and his breathing deepened.

"Because I was hoping he wouldn't find me after all of the shit that had gone down with Dame. He always tried to say little shit to get me to say the wrong thing."

He asked, "What chu mean?"

"Like, he never quite knew if I'd seen his badge or had picked up on what he'd said that day. I played a dumb, stupid bitch. I played the dumb ho I was supposed to play until that day he had us in his office and I asked him if he was a detective or something with the way he was questioning us about our old lives. He knew in that moment. I know he knew. And he played his hand again when he called the cops off after he left me in the hotel room with your little brother. I know a lot, Enzo. A lot. When I was snooping around and found his badge, I found out a lot more stuff, too. I know he has files on Dame's old faction, DOA,

and he has something on some street legend
named Phantom or Phenom or some shit. He
has a file on the African Queen and I'm sure by
now he is after you and anybody associated with
Dame's empire. And he can't kill me until he finds
out how much I know and if I've told anyone."

"Doesn't mean I can't kill you though. You
snitching, bitch?" Enzo asked through clenched
teeth.

"What? No, no. Why would I be snitching? If I
was working for him would the nigga be trying to
kill me too?" I explained hurriedly, hoping that
he wouldn't flip out on me.

I expected Enzo to ask more questions, but all
he did was stare at me for a few more moments
before walking away. I looked back at him as
he lay down on the other bed in the room with
one hand propped behind his head as he mean
mugged the wall straight ahead. I stood and
threw away the food containers and empty soda
cans.

"So you're not going to say anything?" I finally
asked after Enzo had been quiet for over twenty
minutes.

He turned his head and slowly watched me.
"Trying to figure out if I believe you. I'm two seconds away from taking this gun and blowing your
fucking brains out in this hotel room. How do I
know that you ain't working with this nigga and
this shit is all a ploy? I can tell you right now that

before I go to prison I'll kill you and every mother-fucker in this hotel before I use the police to commit suicide."

"If I was working with Micah, would I have brought your little brother back to you? Would he have done this shit to me?" I snatched my shirt off and turned, then pointed to my still sore back.

"How the fuck do I know how far a nigga will go to further his agenda? Niggas could know we're in this hotel right now."

"You picked this damn hotel, boy. You're really fucked up in the head, Enzo. You know that? Paranoid as fuck. You've been treating me like shit this whole time and all I've tried to do is show you that I meant what I said when I told you I'd scratch your back if you scratched mine."

"Mama, ain't no more room left on your back for me to scratch," he quipped.

That hurt. What he'd said had hurt. His words had been cutting me all day and I was beyond tired of it. "You know what? Fuck it. I'm done. I'm out. I'll survive the best way I can," I snapped as I snatched up my bag.

I packed as best I could. I threw on the only pair of pants I had with me, pulled the mess on my head back into a ponytail, and stormed out of the room. I didn't know why I found myself depending on another man anyway. I'd said I would never go back to allowing a man to run

my life. By rote, I'd gone and let Enzo do that.
He had the power because he knew I didn't have
anyone or anything. Shit, that nigga didn't really
want to be bothered with me anyway. So I was
doing us both a favor by getting the hell on.

Rain poured down on me as soon as I walked
out onto the balcony of the seedy motel. The
place looked like cheap whores frequented
it hourly. I could tell by the cars and sneaky,
shameful look of the men who walked in and out
of the hotel rooms.

"Hey do you have a bus schedule?" I asked the
woman at the front desk after walking down
the rickety iron stairs.

"I got one, but ain't no bus coming back
through here 'til the morning." "Morning"
sounded more like "moaning" when she said it.
Her voice sounded as if there was a voice box in
her throat.

I sighed and looked at how heavy the rain was
falling. "How much is a single bed room?"

"Thirty-five plus tax."

I reached into my pockets and cursed
myself when I realized I'd taken the money
Enzo had given me and placed it back on the
table. I put the money there so he could see I
wasn't on some shiesty shit. Now I was wishing I would have pocketed that shit because
I didn't even have thirty-five cents, let alone
thirty-five dollars.

"Fuck," I spat out, inwardly kicking myself.

"You's a pretty gyal. You look like you can make a good five hunnid if you talk to summa the men out there. 'Specially at the truck stop cross the street over yonder," the old bitty told me.

In her mind, I knew she was only trying to help me and had probably assumed I was a whore anyway since I was in the room with Enzo. I gave her a wry smile and retreated out into the rain. For a while, I just stood there under the awning trying to figure out what my next move would be. Once the wind started blowing and the rain started to drench me, I moved around to the underpass of the hotel. Drunk women and lustful men passed by me as I sat with the cap's peak pulled down over my face. Once it stopped raining I would start to make my journey to somewhere.

I'd sat there for a good hour before I remembered the card the African Queen had given me. I stood and snatched the card out, grinning like a fool because I remembered her saying she would help me if I wanted it. I left my bag and rushed around the front desk only to find the door locked.

"You need summin, shawty?"

I turned quickly to find an elderly looking gentleman behind me. While I could tell he was too old to have such a young vernacular,

he was dressed like he was eighteen with his
pants hanging off his ass. I wanted to tell him
no, I didn't need anything, but I could see a pay
phone just inches away from where I had been
sitting.

"Is it possible I can get enough change to use
the pay phone? I need to call someone to pick me
up," I told him.

He looked at me for a while. I couldn't tell
what he was thinking, but was grateful when
he reached into his pocket and grabbed some
change. He counted off a dollar in quarters and
dimes. "What's ya name, shawty?"

I didn't want to be having a conversation with
him, especially not one where I had to tell my
name. "People call me Tino," I lied to him.

He frowned, then smiled. "Mena done gone
for the night. I'm taking over this shift. You gotta
nigga name like my li'l niece had. Yo' daddy
musta been a hood urchin too. My brother had a
girl and she looked so much like him we started
calling her his name."

I gave a fake faint smile just to appear as if I
was interested. "Yeah," I lied, "they named me
after my daddy too."

"I always wondered what happened to my
niece after my brother and his wife got killed.
You probably heard about it. They found they
bodies back in Clay Co in Jonesboro behind
the Woods."

He was looking at me as if he was hoping I'd heard something. To be honest, I had no idea what he was talking about. All I wanted to do was get the change so I could make the phone call. If I had been putting two and two together I would have realized he was talking about a girl closer to me than I knew.

"I'm sorry about that. I hope they found the people who did it," I told him.

"That nigga got his," was all he said as his eyes dimmed over.

"Hey look, I don't mean to seem rude or anything, but I really need to make this phone call."

He nodded and handed the change to me. "No problem. You young like my niece. I wish I could find her. You don't need to be out here at no place like this. Shit ain't safe for no young pretty thang like you."

He moved closer to the light and I could see he had a mouthful of gold. The wavy fade on his head was lined to perfection. His eyes held a familiarity about them. The dark complexion of his was rich like the darkest of chocolate. I could tell that in his younger days, he'd been hell on women just judging by the way he carried himself.

"Thank you," I told him as I rushed off toward the pay phone.

"You welcome, shawty. Hope you find who you looking for. Be careful though," he warned again.

His warning went in one ear and out the other as I passed a group of about three women who looked like they'd gone to Party City to buy their wigs and outfits. The rain beat down on me as I raced to the pay phone. I quickly put two quarters into the slot and dialed the number. I was so excited that when the phone rang seven times without anyone picking up, my face fell. I tried one more time and got the same thing. I slammed the phone down, pissed. I'd gotten soaking wet for nothing.

I huffed and walked back to the underpass to grab my bag only to find that it was gone.

"Looking for this?" a feminine voice asked me.

I turned to find a woman, or man, who stood at least six feet tall. Her makeup was flawless, but her wig was a different story.

"May I please have my bag back?" I asked as calmly as I could.

"Or what?" I turned behind me to see the other two women had walked up on me.

"You new hoes is disrespectful. You can't come to another ho's block and think you can just take money," the other, who looked like she could pass for the Sandman from the old Apollo, said to me.

All three of them had bad weaves and even worse bodies. The tall, masculine-looking one looked like Patrick Ewing in a red wig. The white one who had called me disrespectful was made like a meatball with feet. The light-skinned one looked as if she had been a dime in her day, but now she just looked like two rough pennies with bad acne scars and herpes on the top of her lips.

"Look, I ain't selling no pussy," I told them. "I'm just waiting on somebody to pick me up."

"You been out here for a while, ho, so we know you lying," the masculine one said to me.

"Mary, don't be talking to this ho. Let's just fuck her up," the white one egged her on.

"Yeah, like Bambi said. Just do this ho. She gon' learn na'day."

I knew what was about to happen. Dame had forced us to kick many bitches' asses when they had overstepped their boundaries and sold pussy without upping him his cut. I pulled the knife from my back pocket and took a defensive stance. I knew I stood no chance, but I'd be damned if I was going to let these wack bitches fuck me up without a fight. Since Bambi looked to be the weakest, I went for that fat, no-neck bitch first. I pulled a move I'd seen Gina use many times in fights. I kicked that bitch in her rancid pussy. She went down with a hard thud.

The light-skinned chick ran up on me and caught me with a blade across my shoulders.

"Grrrrr," I yelled out.

I moved her off of me, then swung out with the knife, catching her across the face. Mary ran up on me and caught me in the jaw with a left hook that damn near put me on my ass. My hand broke my fall. Broken pieces of gravel and whatever else was on the ground cut into my skin before I jumped back up. Mary was grinning. She knew there was no way I could go head up with her one on one. I tried anyway. Each time I tried to kick or punch, she dodged, bobbed and weaved, then caught me with a counter punch that bloodied me.

This bitch bounced on the balls of her feet and slap boxed me like she was a trained fighter. By this time the light-skinned chick had joined the fight again and caught me with a slash across my back. The pain that was already there because of what Micah had done to me topped with the fresh blade cut made me scream out. I could hear the pay phone ringing. I knew that was someone from the Queen's camp calling me back if not the Queen herself. Bambi had jumped up and when Mary kicked me backward, she added insult to injury by spitting on me then back-handing me to the ground.

I hit the ground rolling. I did a tumble over my head and landed on my back. Blood ran from my neck and I knew that the stitches in the wound Speedy had given had opened back up. The light-skinned chick was over me in a flash. Murder, animalistic rage was in that bitch's yellowish eyes as she brought the blade down, aiming for my face, but catching the arm I threw up.

"Fucking bitch. We gon' kill you tonight, ho," Mary said as she reached in her bra and pulled out a sling blade.

"If I were you, I'd leave her alone," a voice sounded behind them.

All three women turned around. When they did, I started crying, thanking God that Enzo was there.

"Oh, here go a Captain Save a Ho kinda nigga," Bambi quipped. "Nigga, you can get it too."

Enzo's head tilted. "Bitch, did your big pasty ass just call me a nigga?" he asked her sarcastically.

Bambi stepped forward with her blade in hand. Before she could muster another word, Enzo snatched her, spun her back around to him, grabbed the hand she had the blade in and made her slash her own throat. The rain made the blood pour down the front of Bambi's short dress. Her doughy thighs trembled and quaked before she dropped like a sack of flour to the pavement. The light-skinned chick never stood a chance when she decided to try to trade punches with a man like Enzo. I'd known from the fight earlier that he gave no fucks about the enemy being a woman. If she came for him, she was as good as fucked and not in a good way. He took his fist to her face like she was a man. He held no punches. When he uppercut her, her head jerked back, giving him enough time to pick up the knife I'd dropped. He stuck the knife in her stomach over and over; it looked as if he was giving her gut punches.

When she fell to the ground with blood pouring out of her mouth, he kneed her in the face. Her body fell backward beside mine. As soon as Enzo's feet came down on her throat, I knew she was dead. Enzo gazed down at me with a frown on his face. My eyes widened when I saw Mary rush up behind him with an iron pipe. I tried to warn him. He could see the look in my eyes and ducked just in time. Gunshots rang out just as Mary tried to bring the pipe down. She jerked violently four times before her body slammed to the ground. The man who had given me the change to make the phone calls stepped forward.

"Thanks," Enzo told him as he lifted me from the ground.

"I told shawty to be careful out here. These hoes got no regard for life 'round here," he said. "Y'all gon' need to break up outta here though. Five-O just 'round the bend. Somebody done already called 'bout the noise out here."

Enzo nodded. "'Preciate that," he said, holding his hand out to shake the man's hand. It was the first time I'd ever seen him be cordial to a stranger.

The man shook Enzo's hand and gave a quick nod. "Name's Leon Jenkins. Was watching her 'til I had to take a shit. She reminds me of my niece in a sense, you know, young and pretty. Streets treat them kinda gals rough. I lost my niece. Ain't wanna see the streets take another young gal on my watch, feel me. And I know you. They's looking for you says on the news. Best you get on outta here," he finally finished.

I could tell that, like me, Enzo didn't really care to hear about man's niece, but we both appreciated his helping hand.

"Thanks, man. We out," Enzo told him.

"Best thang to do is to hit 75 the back way down yonder by the BP," the man said and pointed in the direction he was talking about. "Five-O gon' come up this side road right here. They won't see ya."

As Enzo carried me in his arms and jogged to the car, all I could think about was being grateful that the asshole who cradled me in his arms wasn't asshole enough to let me be killed. I moaned out when he slid me into the back seat of the Rover. Lying on my back was going to kill me. I guessed he figured that out and turned me onto my stomach. We were both soaked as the rain drenched the area. Enzo tossed both of our bags in the front seat before cranking the truck and pulling off into the direction Leon had told us to go.

Chapter 12

Shy

"As of now, there is no indication that rising star, Shawn 'Enzo' Banks has been involved in the incident."

I lay watching the madness that reflected to me from the flat-screen television ahead of me. Every news station had Shawn's face flashing on it next to the sports sponsor of his team. Worry had me sitting up, and moving to slide out of the bed. Whatever war that man who was gunning for my son wanted, he was about to get more than he chewed off. This was recklessness. Shawn's career was in the balance. The Lord had already blessed him with a do-over and now some crap that none of us had foreseen, crap that was barreling back our way because of his past, was working to erode everything that had gone on. It was not acceptable. I was not about to let this happen. I had to safeguard his reputation before it was tainted. It was the least I could do for keeping secrets.

Walking toward my new walk-in closet, there was nothing hanging up, just my small bag of luggage. Because of all of this change, I wasn't comfortable yet with settling in to this new place. Regardless of all the paperwork that was shown to me, displaying my name, making me the owner, there was no way I was going to kick up my feet and start relaxing. That almost happened at the condo but now that was gone. Shawn's face was on all the major Atlanta news channels, and my baby boy Drew was walking around the house still in a daze, not focusing on his schoolwork, not playing his video games, not being the kid he once was.

My heart was broken in a million pieces because of it all. After changing into my white maxi dress, and wrapping my hair in a white gele-style head-dress with my white large hooped earrings, I stepped into the main entertainment room. I noticed Drew sitting with his arms outstretched on the huge black curved couch, watching TV. His eyes seemed lost in a daze. His typically Mohawk shaved head was growing out with soft curls and his clothes weren't the typical playful meme-designed shirts he always wore. No, my baby boy sat in sagging dark jeans, a white oversized tee, and white socks.

I quietly moved to where he was sitting and I lightly placed my hand against the top of his arm. "Sweetie, I'm leaving the house. Go on upstairs and put on a nice outfit. We're going to be on TV."

Drew sat quietly as if not hearing me. I moved to tap the back of his neck and he glanced at me with dark eyes as if he had blacked out, reminding me all too well of his big brother's episodes. He was changed. Their father's blood was rising against mine and there wasn't a thing I could do but keep raising Drew as best as I could.

"What did you say, *Tía* Shy?" he asked with uncertainty. His voice had changed over the past days and the low tremble was only a reminder of that.

"Baby, I said go upstairs to your room and grab something nice to wear please. We're going to be on TV." I reached out to gently rub his shoulders. "I know you saw your brother on TV. We need to come to his side and make sure his job doesn't get hurt in the process like that nigga wants."

Drew's eyes went back to their light shade as he leaned back, gawking. "*Tía* Shy, you need to rest. You can't go and, dudeeee, did you just say 'nigga'?"

I laughed softly. In that moment, I saw the beautiful spark of my old son and I prayed it hadn't died all the way. "Yes, I did. Don't get it twisted, baby. I may be sick, but I'm still a lion. Why don't you go upstairs and I'll tell you a little something about my past, something you didn't even expect."

Drew quickly stood to come around the couch and sit me down. "Yes, ma'am, but you sit, and rest."

I smiled and playfully brushed his hands off. "Don't you grab another white tee and pants. I know you dress better than that okay?"

"*Tía!*" Drew griped and I gave him a light laugh.

"You know I love you and am only on this earth to guide you, and I'm here to tell you, that shit ain't hot; go change." Drew gawked at me some more, his hand came out to rest over my forehead, and I pushed it away, pointing. "Go so we can talk and get our family together."

I watched him rush upstairs to change. He came back later in dark jeans, a set of Jordans Enzo had gotten him, and a button-down designer embroidered top that had the word M!SFITZ on the back.

A smile spread across my face and I patted my side. "Listen when I tell you this because I need you to be strong if I don't make it through this sickness."

Drew's gorgeous eyes widened. He had my lashes and twin dimples, marking him mine. My hand cupped his face and I began telling him a little of my background. How I was singled out when I was eighteen by one of the craziest killers in the A. I explained to him that I needed him to know that even in darkness, there is always some form of hope that can pull you out from a situation you never thought you'd survive.

I watched his head bow as he listened. I patted the top of his hand and held it within mine. "Baby, I tell you. I used that pain for my poetry. Every loss I had, my pen became my Glock. My words, my bullets. Listen."

I licked my lips, started humming one of my spoken-word pieces and let my lyrics wrap him in a healing balm. Drew opened his mouth to speak but I held up a hand reaching up to cup the back of his neck. "I know you're on the fence, sweetie. I've been there many times. You don't know how to feel, even though a part of you is falling for a girl who just took you to manhood against both your wishes. Don't let it change you. Don't let the darkness that nigga intentionally tried to seed in you grow anymore. You take that and you focus on your studies."

I could tell that Drew wanted to fight me, but I pressed on as I glanced into his eyes. "You use it to get your game up. You grow up to protect girls like her, girls like me, kids like you and your brother. Don't let that nigga's agenda become yours. You have your own. You are a future king, and you will rule in dignity, righteousness, and intelligence."

Taking a moment to catch my breath, I licked my lips and sat back. "Just take my lessons, take Enzo's lessons, and reach beyond the streets but don't forget the streets, okay? Both of us will teach you what you need if you ever run into niggas like that pussy bitch again, or even if you purposely run into them. But you promise me, this new power you got, you use it for good."

I continued, hoping he'd understand, if only a little. "That doesn't mean you are going to be perfect. I had to do a lot to survive. A lot of things I regret, but nowhere in my journey did I let another nigga's dark deeds or agenda turn me foul."

Drew watched me closely. I could see some of the old him peeking through the muddled darkness in his eyes. He leaned forward and kissed my cheek. "Yes, ma'am."

Tears fell down my face. "Be your own man, but be a good one. I love you, Drew baby."

"I love you too, *Tía,* and I always will. I got you and big bro. I ain't thinking about that nigga 'cause I got you here always," he passionately replied.

I leaned to kiss his cheek and used him as a brace to stand up. "We need to tell them media hounds that Enzo was with me at a treatment center."

"If he show up hurt, *Tía*, we need to plan for that too," Drew suggested, helping me to the door.

As we opened the door, my eyes widened at an old familiar face from my past, one who looked slightly off. A smooth British and Caribbean accent washed over me, making me warm in places I hadn't thought about in a long time. There were small differences that let me know he wasn't who I thought he was, but nonetheless something about the man still had me feeling good and feeling confused at the doppelgänger in front of me. Mirror stood in front of me. Not many people paid attention to him because of his quiet demeanor. Most people only saw him as guard to one of the most elusive street legends in the game, Phenom. But if they had been paying close enough attention, they would have noticed the striking resemblance between the two. They'd be able to see the familial bloodline.

"So you're another dude who's gonna help? A'ight, thanks, man," I heard Drew say as I came back to reality.

I nervously bit my bottom lip and stepped forward. "Yes, thank you. We need to get to a place where we know the press will be. Somewhere they will notice me and start asking questions."

He held out his arm for me. "I'll set up whateva yuh need, love, as long as yuh be good and dun overexert yuh self. Cha?"

My hand pressed into his large bicep. I could tell with how my body fit against his, he wasn't the man who had caused drama in my college years, before I was hunted by a demon. A warm smile spread across my face. I watched Drew climb into the car to help me in, as our new bodyguard also helped me in the back of the car.

"I promise," I said as he winked at me then closed the door. I settled back against my seat and began my plans with Drew. We were going to place a knife into Micah's back before he could ruin my son's empire. You don't mess with a king and not expect his mother to not cut back.

Yes, I was the gatekeeper but I was also a killer. Play on, or get got.

Chapter 13

Enzo

Darkness masked us as I quietly pulled up to a secret spot from my past. A large, unassuming building sat in front of my ride. The beams of my lights flashing on the chained door let me know everyone was gone for the night. Checking out a sleeping Angel in the back of my ride, I quietly got out and headed to the abandoned firehouse that had been converted to an auto shop. Unlocking the doors, I scanned the area seeing fresh new whips and cars on lifts ready to be worked on. I had only been there once back in the day. Last time I'd heard Trigga had said it was a private auto shop, but they had been working with someone to make it open to the public. I was always too busy to lay my head here but it was cool that I was one of the few to know about it, and use it as a safe spot to stash cars, money, or just rest up.

Heading back to my ride, I pulled in, got back out, and then locked up. Angel still lay asleep, so I picked her up, grabbed our bags at the same time, and walked through to take the spiral staircase up to the secret apartments above. I walked past a massive pool table, a big-screen TV with games, and I saw that set of color pencils lay on a table next to a drawing pad and an empty Happy Meal box. I paused on my way to the rooms.

"That Ciara-looking bitch bet' not have ever come here," I grumbled to myself. I knew Trigga and Jake were too smart for that, so I moved on, and I laid out some fresh sheets from the motel for Angel to lay on so not to stain the sheets with our blood.

I was standing in the bathroom, seeing how badly bruised up I was and if I could get away with returning to the game. My aunt's face covered all the news outlets. She stood like a queen, hiding her sickness and letting the world know that I was busy speaking with treatment specialists on her behalf and that we all were at a center during the attack at the condo.

"Ms. Banks, there are reports that drugs were involved. If that is the case, is star rookie Shawn 'Enzo' Banks involved in drug trafficking?" a reporter asked.

A spark of annoyance flickered in my aunt's eyes and her tongue was lethal in her response. "That is an assumption that we will not even play at entertaining. Like any young kid who has come from where we all have come from, he has had experiences that motivated him to be the star you all know him to be. He would not and is not tarnishing his dreams by partaking in your assumptions and stereotyping generalizations."

My aunt's eyes cut the reporter down, who looked away red-faced while other questions were thrown at her. "No, we did not know that the condo Enzo sublet had once been owned by a notorious kingpin. Had we, ladies and gentlemen, we would not be in this situation of not having a home, now, would we?"

I knew my aunt was lying and she knew she was lying, but she would say whatever she needed to protect me. I was basically squatting in Dame's old crib.

Tía Shy flashed a beautiful smile as she stared at the cameras. I could see my baby brother standing beside her, keeping her steady as she eloquently spoke. "Keep those people who were harmed in the nefarious acts that occurred late last night/early this morning in your hearts. This family is a praying one and we believe that karma will be a shield and dagger against people who conspire to do harm. Justice will come for those innocent people who were harmed today."

Cameras flashed and reporters tried to ask more but my aunt waved them all off. "Outside of that, please respect our privacy. My nephew is already dealing with a lot right now and losing our home has only complicated things. We are bystanders in a senseless maniac's or maniacs' tantrum. We should not tolerate it and we will not. Their due time is coming and the law will stand by us all. Thank you for your concern, Atlanta. We appreciate your love and support. We have set up a foundation for those families who may have been harmed in the senseless acts."

I chuckled as I turned the television off and threw my bloody bandages away. My aunt had come for Micah in a smooth way, and also fixed my reputation by giving me a way out of going to drills for a while until this was cleared up. I was deeply grateful for everything she had done.

Light shuffling of feet made me turn and point my Glock toward the noise only to see Angel staring at me with tired eyes. Her thick hair was chaos over her head and her clothes were disheveled.

"I like how your aunt speaks," she said.

Turning away from her, I washed my hands and turned my face from side to side, deciding whether I was going to shave. "I do too."

I could feel Angel's eyes on me and I knew she had some words that I wasn't even feeling like listening to, but I kept to myself and let her do whatever she wanted.

"So, I know you're pissed. I didn't ask you to save me but . . ." She held her hands up the moment my head whipped around to glare at her. "Let me say what the fuck I'm trying to say, damn nigga. I'm saying . . . thank you though. I'm not trying to be under your skin but I'm also not trying to be made to feel like shit because of crap out of my control. I'm already cutting myself because of it."

My lips tightened into a scowl and I turned away to pull out the shaving kit. "Yeah, whatever. I need you to stop being pussy and running and shit. I can't be in every place you are to have your back."

She chuckled and it made me grit my teeth but I ignored it as she spoke, "That same back you don't have room to scratch on? And if you didn't notice, I wasn't being a pussy; I was fighting back."

"Oh. That's what you call fighting? Looks like you were getting your ass handed to you. Looks like three whores, sisters after your own heart, were about to get the drop on you."

Her nostrils flared, eyes watered. "If those 'whores' were sisters after my own heart, then Micah has to know that the old Enzo isn't dead and gone. No matter what your aunt says, you are and were involved in drug and human trafficking. You did torture motherfuckers in a basement for your boss. And, no matter how far you fucking run, you and Micah are cut from the same fucking cloth," she spat out. "So fuck you."

Anger flared in my eyes. Her words tapped at something innate in me that I didn't want to face. I turned then moved to stand in the middle of the bathroom doorframe with my hands resting in a splayed position. "You know what, mama, fuck you, ho. That's all the fuck you are, a ho-ass bitch who don't know how to handle her fucking shit so as not to be used like the whore bitch you are."

The minute her fist found my face, I knew I had hit a chord in her. I welcomed the pain that she added to the additional searing discomfort that was traveling through me. See, a long time ago, I developed a way to turn into pleasure any pain given to me on the field and when dealing with Dame. So as this chick spit and clawed at me, I did nothing, only smiled, and then snatched her up by her wrists damn near dangling her in the air.

"When you stop acting like a kid then you can probably do better in defending yourself," I explained.

Her chest heaved up and down as I held her hands over her head. I'd never seen so much hate in her eyes as I saw in that moment.

"How you calling me a kid when every chance you get, you think calling me a whore is your job?"

"I calls it like I see it."

"Then, so do I. Maybe I'm a mirror that shows your reflection and you can't handle it."

"You fucking wish. If you were my mirror, you wouldn't have been about to dance with death. You would know how to hold your own, Angel."

Angel tilted her head to the side then tried to head butt me as she screamed, "Then you know what? Do me a fucking favor and please teach a *whore* to fight since you have a problem with the way I defend myself."

Her words made me scrunch my face up then drop her on her feet. She was causing a reaction in me that I didn't want. I turned back to the sink and prepped my face to shave before turning back to look at her. "A'ight, mama."

"Good then." She huffed then kicked me in my shin. "Fuck you, too, ho-ass nigga." My eyes narrowed and she stepped back then quickly walked away. "Water, let me go get some."

"Yeah, you go do that. You hit me again, and I'll show you how a ho gets done." I growled low and went back to shaving.

No lie, my dick was hard. The piercing on my tip giving me friction that had my jaw ticking. She really was affecting me and it was pissing me off. I needed a ho party to dip up into then all would be good in my world.

The sound of gunshots was my version of breakfast.

"You're wobbling the gun. Is your point to shoot every nigga in the ass? Straighten up and hold the damn Glock right, mama," I barked out.

Angel stood with beads of sweat sprinkling her temple with an annoyed frown. "I am!"

We had been practicing in the typical Atlanta heat that blazed down and cooked us both. She was in some short blue shorts and a lilac tank. I stood in red and black basketball shorts and a simple white wife beater. Behind the auto shop where no one could see us, we stood in the tall grass while Angel took aim at the makeshift dummies. Trees billowed in the wind, but the air was hot and muggy. I swatted at a mosquito that had taken an interest in the blood from my legs then frowned at her.

"Nah, man, you've hit everything but the critical zones. You need to rest?" I asked then stood behind her with my arms over my chest.

She sucked her teeth then squeezed the trigger again, hitting everything but the target before her. "It's hot. Why can't we use the shooting range inside?"

"Because with how you shooting, you need to be in the open area. Shit, you need to learn how to focus your gun outdoors, too, and not just inside the building."

"Yeah, but it's hot," she whined.

"And? The hell you gonna do if Micah rolled up on us now?" I asked.

"She'd shoot that bitch right between his eyes. Wouldn't you, honey?" sounded behind me.

We both turned quickly to see the African Queen walking our way. We hadn't even heard her walk up. Something about that annoyed me. To not know my surroundings or to not know when someone was walking up on me could be a fatal mistake. Anika's arm was wrapped around a tall, dark-skinned dude, a dude who had me tilting my head in confusion. It was the guy I had seen when I was doing my drills. He was one of my sponsors. I undid the safety on the gun that was resting against my leg and kept my eyes on that cat as I stepped close to Angel. I figured anybody who had been doing business with Micah was a cause for suspicion.

"Your coach is pissed that you aren't there, Enzo. You may want to pop back up from your trip at the treatment centers and go handle your job. You know my money is firmly invested in you and the team," the guy said. He flashed a smile toward Angel, giving her a nod before walking past us and into the garage.

Angel and I stared at each other then followed them. I watched the African Queen close the doors then walk into the kitchen to bring out several glasses, and water.

"You two should sit and rest. I got your call, love; I'm assuming that was you on the pay phone?" she asked Angel.

"Yes. Did I do something wrong?" Angel asked sitting and staring at a woman who moved around the place as if it were a castle and not a simple garage.

She set the glasses before us, poured us all some water, then offered the guy I knew as my sponsor a glass. She watched him take a sip then offer her the glass before she sat on the arm of the chair.

"No, you did not, but we have a code with it. I'll explain it later. Enzo and Angel, we wanted to sit with you privately so that we could finish a conversation that was unfortunately interrupted previously."

Angel had a look on her face that said she wasn't too thrilled with that explanation. "You do know I almost died out there, right? If there had been a code or something else that I should have done, why not give it to me first time around?"

Anika sat forward. "That was my error. A bad judgment call. I have no problem admitting when I'm wrong. That's a part of being a leader."

Angel gazed around the room then back to Anika. She looked as if she wanted to say something else, but she let it go.

My eyes darted back and forth as I tried to wrap my mind around the two sitting in front of me. "Yeah, Micah was on some bullshit, you know, retaliating."

The African Queen gave a soft laugh. The guy next to her, who sat with his finger pressed against his temple, dressed in all black from his leather shoes to his slacks and pinstriped button-down shirt, spoke up. "He's a problem. One of many that I have made note of since before the Orlando twins were killed," his ebbing British accented voice explained.

I opened my mouth to respond, but he held a hand up stopping me. Something about him had me on edge, as if not to fuck with him. He casually dropped his hand to bring them together in a steeple as he watched us. "Allow me to introduce myself correctly. My name is Mr. Ekejindu. I am the jewelry supplier A.E. Jewelry. You've worked with me, Bianca. I am also the owner of Nasir Prep, and Gentleman Elite: Tailor and Suit Specialty International House. I am also the one and only true Phenom, whose alliance to the African Queens, specifically this African Queen Anika, is not well known, except for a few special individuals. I am a man of many faces because I have to be. What I am a part of requires me to be."

Angel and I were quiet for about two minutes before we both started asking questions. Anika and Phenom waved a hand to calm us down. I listened to the two before me, both legendary street royalty, out of respect and partially to figure what was really being said behind all the intel. I had to assess the situation. I had to figure out how best to secure my spot in all of this for my aunt's and brother's sakes. I wasn't following no man but myself now that I was free and I needed to make sure all alliances were solid.

"Here is the thing. I understand you do not trust easily and that is a smart thing. I also understand that you only trust Jake and Trigga in this game because you three have a history. I assure you that I never discuss cheese around a rat, or bread around a bird. To many crumb snatchers are after the jewels of your kingdom and it's better to keep them at arm's length as you poison them by their own hands," he explained.

Anika gave a knowing smile, standing up then kissing the top of Phenom's head. "He learned that phrase from a dear friend of ours, my own spiritual sister."

"My love, I did, but that lesson was embedded in me, long before her," he countered.

Anika just smiled again and sat back down after putting our glasses away. "Of course. I know that as well. They need to understand the foundation before truly understanding the source of the lesson. Shawn and Bianca, everything we do has meaning. You are very safe in trusting your friends. We just wanted you to see that you have backing not only with your misfits, but also by us seasoned street royals. If you ever need true hiding, or find places that you need cleared out in your journey as an athlete, your journey as a dancer, Bianca, we will give you all

you need. You have a catalogue at your service.
Any friends of the Misfits are friends of ours."

I got what they were saying and felt they were
genuine in their words, but there was something
about the way they would look at each other then
back at me that had me wondering if there were
things not being said.

Phenom shifted in his chair watching me. It
was if we were speaking in codes and I gave him
a nod of respect, setting my gun down.

"Take that understanding. Both Jake and
Trigga speak highly of you and from watching
you this whole time, it didn't take long to see
that you are worth trusting. The Orlandos built
an empire that even in death still affects much of
Atlanta and beyond."

He rested both of his arms on his thighs and
continued talking. "My network is set up to deal
with those who still uplift that regime, which
is why I'm a sponsor of your team. It's a game
within it just like the streets that can get you
caught up and fucked up. Trafficking of all types,
murder, and mayhem. The game has it all. Snuff
out those lines associated with the Orlandos and
any other threats that come your way, and be
smart about how you play those cards, a'ight?
I'm not sitting here recruiting. This is all your
choices, but know we have you for protecting

my blood even when you had choices you both didn't want to make."

I sat taking in all he said. He knew about me trying to take out Jake. If he could accept that, then I knew I could accept what he was saying, even if I didn't know what those glances between him and Anika meant. I held out my hand and he took it, shaking it.

"I got E.N.G.A. tatted on me for a reason. It's in me so I'm down," I said.

Phenom gave a smile and sat back with his leg crossed on his knee. "Good. You are your own man in this part. You and Bianca, how you both build it, is all on you because you have to shape who you have around to reflect your world in the game. Keep handling Micah, but have more finesse with it; after all, you're dealing with a businessman whose hands are in many places. Isn't that right, Bianca?"

Angel blinked a moment then nodded. "Yes, he is."

"Good, then use all you have against him. You have more power over him than you even think. Use it. I'll teach you, as my husband teaches Enzo and the rest of his future leaders," Anika stated.

She stood next to Phenom's chair and he rose up to rest his hand on the small of her back. "This place is safe, but you two also need your own. On the table is a Realtor, one of my people. If you find a place that Micah tracks you to, don't move out. We'll clean the area and secure it down. For now, you have one guaranteed spot where your aunt and brother are at that he can't find. Keep that secret, because everything is for show and, in this world, you gotta be a chameleon."

A slight New York accent bled through his British one and he glanced at us, as if studying us. "You both have a good day and we all will talk. Oh, the man who resembles me is my cousin Mirror. He's my right. You can trust him to guard them."

"Thank you. I mean, I wasn't sure exactly what to do," I explained talking to their backs.

"But you did something. Keep it up. Protect your family no matter what and look out for that jewel by you. She's resourceful," Phenom said.

He stood to the side letting Anika pass him first. They walked with a swagger that said they knew the streets belonged to them.

Angel and I glanced at each other, realizing we were standing close to each other and we quickly moved apart. I sat back down, and she sat opposite of me, watching me. "So, wow."

"Yeah," was all I could say.

"So, you going to finish teaching me how to shoot then?" she asked.

I curled my lip then let out a sigh. "Are you going to stop shooting holes in ass cheeks and pussy lips?"

Angel snatched a book off the table and hurled it at me before stepping off. I followed and we began our training that lasted us a couple of days while we hid from Micah. Eventually we headed back to our game in the sports, as she helped me get a new spot. I answered all media questions accordingly. Angel and I still pretended like we weren't affiliated with each other, so I got her laced up in a condo a few floors below mine in midtown. I did that only because of my promise to my aunt; otherwise, she'd have to find her own shit.

I also began to make plans on getting my own safe house close by where my enemies couldn't find me, and one that could let me handle the underworld business now back in my life. Never lay your head in the same place twice when on the run. I learned long ago and a nigga wasn't trying to compromise the Misfits' spot.

"So you like your spot?" I asked Angel, while she stared at the midtown skyline.

A smile spread across her face as she gave a nod of satisfaction.

"A'ight, check it. We got to think of some shit to keep Micah off our backs since I plan to step back into the limelight," I explained.

She turned to me and crossed her arms around herself. "Okay, tell me what you want me to do."

I rubbed my jaw and watched her from under the hood of my lashes. There was still that one thing about her that made it hard for me not to flip stupid on her from time to time, but as Phenom had told me, she was resourceful, especially after telling me that Micah was FBI. I kept that little secret to myself for the time being. That complicated things, but the fact was that nigga was so dirty that if he even tried to wash his hands, there was no way the shit would wash off.

So, I moved to walk around Angel, as I looked her over. "I want you to think about what you are going to do when he comes for you, because he is. I think you might want to try to move from being just an alternate. What you think, mama?"

Her smile gave me her answer as we began to plan our next phase on taking down a nigga who was making our lives nothing but pain.

"Hey, you need to be patched up. Now that you got your own digs where you can bleed over everything, and throw your wolf pelt everywhere, we can get to working on you," I teased, flashing a smile.

"Fuck your life," Angel sneered, storming to the bathroom.

I followed with more jokes just to see if I could get a reaction out of her.

Chapter 14

Angel

"Tell me why you chose to work for Dame." I'd never had a chance to ask anyone that. I never understood who would willingly work for that man and why. We were sitting on the balcony of the condo he had gotten for me. For as much shit as he talked about me, Enzo had eaten the food I'd cooked like I hadn't spit in it. I appreciated the new place, but he'd made it pretty clear that I was a part of him seeing his agenda through. I'd always dreamed of living in a place like the one he'd gotten me, so there was no way in hell that I would have turned him down when he offered it to me, no matter what it had cost me. I'd rather know the devil I was dealing with than to go into a scheme with one I didn't. For now, I knew that Enzo wouldn't do anything to me as long as he had to keep his word to his aunt. And for as long as we had Micah in our sight, I had a place to lay my head.

"Why did you choose to work for him?" He answered my question with a question as he smoked a blunt.

I was already semi high just from the contact alone. I'd smoked a lot of weed in my day, but the weed Enzo had was some shit I hadn't ever had a hit of. He told me he only bought the best for his aunt because it helped her with pain when he could get her to smoke it. The little hairs on the weed was like gold he'd told me. He said since it was a lot of them there then that meant it was good weed. He had a mixture and had told me to take a pick, but I had declined just needing to keep my head clear. There were a lot of crystals on his weed, too. Maybe that was why maybe after five or so pulls he looked like Scotty was calling him. The shit was so green and potent I could smell it through the bag he pulled out. It would be safe to say that if the cops walked into the place, they'd know without asking what was going on.

"I didn't choose it. I was kidnapped."

"That nigga, Dame, had this sports camp thing. He knew all the big people in the leagues: NBA, NFL, even the MLB, and NHL. All my life, all I ever wanted to do was play ball. I can play my ass off in basketball, but it was football that called to me. To make a long story short,

Dame had what I wanted and I had something he wanted; if I moved product for him, he would ensure I got my ticket to the NFL. Of course, shit didn't go as plan until that nigga was dead."

I nodded. To be honest, I was surprised he told me that much. I was expecting him to tell me to mind my business or say some snide shit to me.

"So, why were you and Jake fighting?" I asked, pushing my luck further.

For some reason, I wanted to know about that man who was in front of me. I wanted to know what each tattoo he had meant, wanted to know why he chose to get a bull nose piercing, wanted to know why he had those piercings on each side of his V cut. And I for sure wanted to know more about the piercings in his dick.

He took a pull of his blunt then squinted his eyes as he looked at me. "You a nosy mother-fucker, you know that?"

"I was only asking because you two seemed close. So I don't understand why he would come at you like that without cause I mean."

"Some shit you just shouldn't ask people. That's one of them."

"You must have done some—"

"Shut up, Angel. Leave the shit alone."

I didn't want to push any further so I shrugged his aggressive tone off and got up to walk to the

kitchen. The hardwood floor was cool underneath my feet. Light reflected off of the golden
chandelier that hung above the dining room
table. Since the place came furnished, I made no
query about changing anything. The décor was
simple, but I could live with simple since my life
had been anything but. The plush white sofa and
love seat set boasted a cosmopolitan feel. Red,
silver, and baby blue throw pillows were thrown
about to bring out the same color accent wall.
The three colors were asymmetrical against one
another as a big black-and-white photo of the
Atlanta skyline adorned the wall. There was no
TV as of yet. Dishes were already in the kitchen,
which boasted stainless steel appliances and was
as big as the last hotel suite I'd stayed in if not
bigger. Yeah, it was a far cry above what I had
become used to since living in Dame's mansion.

I could hear Enzo moving around behind me.
I didn't really know what he had been doing
before I'd called him and asked him if he wanted
anything to eat. I didn't have any food so I told
him what I wanted to cook and he went to the
market to get it for me.

"I need you to tell me what else you know
about Micah being FBI," he said.

I turned expecting to still find him on the
other side of the room, but damn near jumped

out of my skin to find he had almost walked right up on me. I moved back a little. "I told you all I know."

"Tell me more about those files you saw," he demanded, the droopiness of his eyes making him sexier than he already was. He was in one of his moods again and it bothered me.

"I told you already."

"Tell me again, Angel."

The way he spoke my name with a low drawl made the hairs stand up on the back of my neck. I swallowed then turned to place the plate I'd eaten out of in the sink. "There were different files. Some on DOA, some on African Queens. And a file on Phenom. I didn't get to see any fully because Micah was coming back in the room. There were a lot more files I didn't see."

"Did you actually see anything on DOA?"

I shrugged as I watched him fold his muscled arms across his chest. "Not really. I mean, I saw the names of Dame and someone named Lu Orlando. There was a Dante, too, but I just thought it was an alias for Dame. I know better now. I didn't read the profiles because I was going so fast. There were cities outlined like Harlem, Brooklyn, L.A., Oakland, and Tampa. I saw something about Havana, Cuba, and Brazil, too. I do know that one piece of paper had a

timeline dating back to thirty or more years ago
showing when the FBI first infiltrated DOA.
Said something about a Battle and Phenom, but
Battle's picture was X'd out. That's all I remember."

"You're going to die, Angel," he said to me. My
brows furrowed and I backed away from him.
"Micah is not going to let you live once he finds
out you know all this stuff."

"How will he know unless you tell him?"

"You're the one who said you thought he put
two and two together when you sarcastically
asked the nigga if he was a detective. You gave
yourself away. If shit is as deep as you say was in
those files, that nigga will kill you before he lets
you blow his cover."

"So, how am I going to get to close to him and
act normal?"

"You can act like you've always acted."

"Yeah, but now I'm scared he's going to outright kill me."

"Nobody got time for that shit, Angel. If we
wanna live the life we want to, that nigga has to
go. You gone have to suck it up, mama. Of course
this nigga wants to kill you. Why wouldn't he?
One word from you and all comes crumbling
down. Truth be told I think his plan has always
been to kill you. He just used you to get to me

through Drew. Every nigga got a agenda. Act like you know."

I hadn't even thought about things that far. I had been living for the moment, trying to survive for the now. I never once thought about the fact that maybe Micah would come for me because I knew too much about him. I knew by the information I'd seen in that folder that more than one agent was undercover in the underworld of the A. For damn near a year I'd lived a semi peaceful life after Dame and just that fast, my life was no longer my own again.

I moved away from him and walked back onto the balcony. I needed the cool night air to clear my head. The scent of the dank was still in the air. He had left his blunt there. I picked it up and relit it. I took a hard, long pull. I tried to hold the smoke in and damn near choked from the burning in my throat and chest.

"Damn," I croaked out, almost slobbering out the mouth.

As soon as he walked back out I handed the blunt back to him. He handed me the bottle of Patrón in trade. I heard "Gunwalk" playing on the small radio he'd brought over.

"So can you help me not to get killed?" I asked him through watery eyes. "I don't really wanna die, Enzo."

"You sure?" he asked me. "Could have fooled me with the way you went after that treacherous bitch. Trigga said that nigga Speedy could have killed you."

"I don't wanna die by that nigga Micah's hands I mean. Anika says she'll help me get my shit together. If she gon' help me, I wanna try."

He didn't answer me right away. Just handed me the blunt back and took the Patrón. He took the liquor to the head while I choke on the blunt again. He was quiet for a good ten minutes while we passed vices back and forth. I could admit I was scared, but that weed and alcohol had me floating. "Gunwalk" was on repeat and it was putting me in a zone. Days of being in the strip club had me whipping my hair, then minimally moving my ass from side to side in a slow bounce. I was in a zone until I saw Enzo leaning back on the rail watching me.

"You gon' help me or what?" I asked him again out the blue. My speech was slurred a bit but he understood me.

"You asking a lot of a nigga, like you got money or some shit to pay for my services. Fuck I look like, Captain Save a Ho for real to you or summin'?" He snatched his blunt from my hand. I went to grab the bottle of Patrón and he snatched that back too.

"Why you playing?" I yelled. Somewhere between being high, drunk, and scared out of my mind, I was annoyed, too. I'd gone and gotten myself into a world of shit. Part of me wished I would have just said yes to Micah's little scheme. I mean after all, all he wanted me to do was fuck for money. I'd been doing that for the last four years of my life anyway. I could have just gone along with the program and not be marked for death. Then again, Enzo was probably right; that nigga was planning on killing me anyway.

"Who's playing? You been looking for hand-outs from me the whole time. A nigga done laid money in your lap and everything. Done saved your fucking life, gave you a place to stay and you still want more? Fuck is wrong with you?" he asked with a frown.

"Well, sounds like to me you are Captain Save a Ho," I snapped walking up to him. "You make me sick always talking shit; why? I didn't do anything to you." I snatched the Patrón and the blunt. I took a puff of what was left and then a swallow of the liquor.

"You ruined my little brother."

I got in his face. "Blah, blah, blah. You keep saying that lame shit like I did it on purpose or some shit! Okay, your kid brother fucked me. You mad because it wasn't you? Mad because the thirteen-year-old got to fuck before you did?"

When his eyes turned dark, I knew I'd let liquid courage make me say the wrong thing. Before I could back away he had his hand around my neck backing me up. He shoved me back so hard that I knew when I hit the floor it would hurt. The sliding door wasn't closed so I hit the floor hard. The hardwood floor felt like it split my skull, not to mention the pain from my back.

"Watch your fucking mouth, bitch," he snarled at me as he glared down at me.

I pushed up on my elbows to back away from him. I was about sick and tired of being pushed around, or it could have simply been that I was high and drunk enough to think I was. I jumped up from the floor and just stared at the man in front of me. I may have been drunk enough to say what I wanted, but wasn't high enough to try to fight him while he was in this mood.

"Asshole," I mumbled, my chest heaving up and down.

"Child molesting whore. Do you really want to start the name calling? Watch what the fuck you say when it comes to Drew."

"Then watch what you say to me," I yelled.

"You walking on thin ice, Angel. I could put you back on the streets in no time."

And there it was. "Screw you. I'm not going to take this kind of shit just because you got me a place to stay. I don't need you holding it over my head. I'll make my own way," I said slapping the water away that was rolling down my cheeks.

"How? You ain't got shit and nobody," he countered.

"I been doing it by myself this far," I snapped. "And I'll find a way to keep doing it."

"How? That little money you get from being an alternate will get you a roach motel at best and you'll be dead within a week tops."

"I got other shit, skills I can use."

"And each one will put you closer to death."

His red eyes burned holes through my head. Yeah, I had been wrong for saying that about his little brother considering the circumstances, but he didn't have to keep throwing up in my face all the stuff that he was doing for me. Shit, and he damn sure didn't have to keep reminding of what happened in that hotel room. I turned away from him and stormed to the master bedroom where I had put all my stuff. I hadn't taken anything from the bag really. Only minimal things since he had told me to lay low for the two days we had been training. I was emotional as fuck, all in my feelings. So much so that I grabbed my bag to leave, completely forgetting about what happened just days before when I'd tried to leave on my own.

Thankfully, Enzo hadn't forgotten and was at the bedroom door when I turned to walk out. I tried to get past him three times. The third time he pushed me back on the bed then caged me between his arms as he scowled down at me.

"Don't be stupid. Where the fuck you gon' go? You lucky as fuck that keeping my word to my *tía* means a lot to me. Otherwise I'd let you walk the fuck up out of here and just do you. Now you can rock with me and be good or you can go out there and get killed. All I fucking asked you to do was watch what the fuck you say about my brother. That's it. He's still a kid and what happened to him I won't get over no time soon so respect the way I feel and I'll leave you the fuck alone about it . . . maybe. Either way, you're not going anywhere so get comfortable."

"You can't hold me here against my will," I murmured, head swimming.

He backed away and pulled the belt from his jeans and turned his mouth in a lopsided grin. "You wanna bet?"

"Oh you gon' pull a Dame and beat my ass with a belt now?" I asked belligerently.

He chuckled. "Nope, I'ma tie your ass to the fucking bedpost. How you piss and shit will be your guess."

I could tell he was serious, but the way his jeans slid down on his waist distracted me. I stood back up still watching him. One of those piercings he owned on his V cut peeked out. I licked my lips as I gawked shamelessly. I let my eyes travel up the plane of his abs to his chest, his neck—a thick vein pulsated on the right side or maybe my eyes were playing tricks on me— then up to his thick lips. He was close enough that I could smell the alcohol on his breath and the weed as well, but it was wanting to know what his lips would feel like against mine that held my curiosity. My eyes caught his and I could see that dare in them. I pushed my luck, moved in, clasped a hand behind his neck, and then kissed him. Eyes closed, my mind told me that he was seconds away from tossing me across the room, but by the time my tongue parted his lips, I was too far gone. And when his tongue touched mine, the bag I was holding on my shoulder hit the floor. I stood on my toes and placed my other hand on the side of his face and took the dance of our tongues as far as he would let me. I could feel when his breathing changed. Thought that was a good thing, especially since he seemed to be as into the kiss as I was.

But when he pulled away and pushed me back, the blank look on his face told me I was probably the only one who was enjoying the kiss. The grip on his belt tightened in his fist and I was half afraid he was about to snap.

"What the hell is wrong with you?" he fussed. "You crazy or some shit?"

I got my balance then shook my head. "No. Just a whore who wants a killer to give her a chance." He frowned and tilted his head. "Or at least some dick," I continued then shrugged.

I grabbed the end of his belt and pulled him closer to me, or I tried to. He snatched me to him and then placed a finger underneath my chin to force me to look up at him. "I can't do this with you, Angel."

I looked down at the huge bulge in his pants.

He waved his hand. "I'm a man so it's natural law, but with what happened between you and my little brother, nah."

I dropped my head and the hold on the belt. He had me there and I could see where he was coming from. Just that quick, that part had completely slipped my mind. I didn't think about how it would feel for him to be in that kind of situation.

"I'm sorry. You're right," was all I said as I walked out of the room and headed to the bathroom.

My embarrassment led the way. I couldn't even look at myself so I bypassed the mirror, got rid of my clothes, and headed right for the shower. Like many times in the last four years of my life, the shower was where I washed away all my demons, hurt, pain, and shame. Even with the shower full blast, I heard when Enzo walked out of the condo and slammed the door behind him. I stayed in the shower for at least an hour. My high was wearing down and I found myself hoping Enzo had left his stash of weed behind. The weed and the liquor would be my companions.

I turned the water off and stepped onto the cold Italian marble flooring. Once I got to the mirror, I wiped the steam away and looked at myself. I still looked as if I was under the influence of something. Eyes were glazed and droopy. I was about to pick up the brush to untangle my hair when the bathroom door came open and scared the life out of me.

I tossed the brush at the man standing there. He slapped it out of the air as he studied me.

"You scared the shit out of me," I fussed at him. "You don't do stuff like that. Are you crazy?" I carried on.

He wasn't wearing a shirt. Just basketball shorts and bare feet. He must have gone to change at his place. I think it was still my shame that had me carrying on. I still couldn't look at him full on.

"Nah, not crazy. Just a killer who likes the whore that has stained his little brother's life."

I was all set to protest until he pushed his basketball shorts to the ground and closed the gap between us. He snatched my towel away then sat me on the counter. My body was shaking. I was nervous. The smell of lemon soap wafted through the steaming spot. The look in Enzo's eyes was primal, one that got my juices flowing instantly. I would have liked to talk to him to ask him why he'd come back, but he didn't let me talk. Enzo obviously knew that I could open my mouth and kill the mood so he kissed me. A quick peck on the lips at first and then a long, lingering kiss that left me reeling from its effect.

His big hands caressed my waist as I gazed up at him when he pulled back. That bull nose ring piercing he had was even sexier up close. His tongue moved across his lips and moistened them enough to make me want to taste them again. I finally realized that I could touch him. I brought my hands to his waist then his abs, traced the Adonis line and his piercings. Then my fingers traveled up to his chest. His hands caressed my breasts, massaged them, and gripped them with enough force to make it hurt but feel damn good in the process. A moan escaped my lips when the pads of his thumbs brushed across my nipples.

I was in a zone, head thrown back as his groans traveled through me and settled in the pit of my stomach. I could feel my nipples tighten while my breasts swelled. My legs started to tremble as my Kegel-exercised muscles worked on their own. His dick hadn't touched me yet and I found myself so anxious that I reached down in between us to stroke him. The weight of his dick was heavy in my hand. The fact that the more I stroked, the more he grew turned me on more. His lips found my nipples and the heat from his mouth made my legs tremble.

One of his hands came down to cover mine as he helped me to stroke his dick the way he wanted me to. Then he moved to let his fingers graze my soaked pussy. There was no hair there so I could feel everything times ten. It had been almost a year since I had been touched by a man and it had been never that I'd been touched by one the way Enzo was doing. As soon as two of his fingers slipped inside of me he caught the gasp that escaped my lips in his mouth. My hips squirmed on the granite counter. I couldn't help myself. The penetration with the way he was kissing me had me gone. His fingers were thick and he was tapping against a spot that had me seeing stars.

"Oh, shit," was all I could get out when Enzo let my mouth go.

He didn't talk, just looked me in the eyes as he rubbed the head of his dick up and down my slick slit. The friction from the ring in his dick against my clit was amazing. But it wasn't until he slowly guided himself inside of my walls that I finally knew what had made Gina throw her head back in oblivion when I'd had the three-some with her and Jake.

Head back, mouth in the shape of an O, breath caught in the swell of my chest. Enzo's slow, long strokes killed me; short steady strokes brought me back to life. My nails dug into his biceps while his hands gripped my thighs. He pushed my thighs farther apart, held them back, dipping his hips to hit that spot over and over again. If I never got another chance to have sex like the way he was giving it to me in the bathroom of the condo he'd bought me, I'd be a very pissed-off woman.

The loud buzzing of my phone jerked me awake. It took me a minute to realize I was slob-bering out the mouth and even longer to realize that Enzo was lying beside me. Our thighs were tangled. The light scent of our sex wafted through the air. The pineapple and alcohol-like remnants of his semen still coated my tongue and the back of my throat. Flashbacks of his face between my thighs, us being as nasty as we could in sixty-nine ways, added to my delirium. I sat up and looked at him to see his eyes were wide as he gazed at me.

"Answer your phone," he demanded.

I nodded, coughed, and then picked up. "Hello?"

"So Micah needs all of the dancers down at the Dome by ten this morning," Tino's voice came through.

I looked at the digital clock. Red block numbers blared at me: 3:33 a.m.

"Okay and?" I was a lot of annoyed and the satisfying ache between my thighs begged to be answered again.

"And, I did what you asked. That broad Tasha has officially contracted the stomach virus or at least, a really bad liquid laxative was put into her Sprite; so she won't be working the field or her pussy."

"You tell Micah what we talked about?"

"Of course, boo. I made sure to dress it all up nicely. All you have to do is work your magic."

Enzo stirred behind me; my pussy clenched involuntarily. I turned behind me to see his frame silhouetted in the moonlight coming through the blinds. The muscles in his back coiled and rolled as he pulled on his shorts.

Everything about him looked good, even the muscles in his ass. But it was something in his eyes when he turned to look at me that, for a brief moment, made images of our worst nightmare flash before my eyes. I had to blink to shake the image away.

"Thanks, Tino."

"Ah, naw, bitch. Thank me by giving me my pills and my money," he sang like the queen he was.

"I got you covered, Tino. You know that."

"I don't know no'ting until you pay me. See you at ten," he said then ended the call on his end.

Enzo stood off to the right of me with his shirt thrown over his left shoulder. "What he say?" his deep voice asked me.

"He did what I asked," I answered. Although just hours before we'd heated up the bathroom and bedroom, there was a sudden chill in the room that had me looking at Enzo sideways. I didn't know what he was planning to do. "What you gonna do, Shawn?"

I called him by his birth name hoping that intimacy would do something, trigger something in him that would make him open up to me. He snapped his head around to look at me after sliding his feet into his shoes. "Don't ever call me

Shawn again, Angel. And don't ask me anything about nothing."

"I was only asking because I'm worried."

"Don't ask and don't be worried. I don't need you in my business and I don't need you to worry," he said coolly as he walked out the room.

Forgetting that I was ass naked, I rushed out after him. I wasn't understanding how he could be so cold now when he'd been so into me hours before. I mean that shit literally and figuratively.

"You said when we was planning this shit that we wouldn't keep secrets," I yelled at his back. I grabbed his arm to make him stop walking.

He just turned and cut his eyes down at me. "Go take a shower, put on some clothes, and get some sleep. You need to be the first motherfucker at the Dome in the morning. Do your part, Angel, and I'll do mine. The less you know, the better, just in case shit goes left."

"I don't understand."

"If you don't know shit, you can't say shit."

That was all he said before he walked out the door.

Chapter 15

Enzo

"Pick up the phone."
"Pick up the fucking phone damn!"
Sweat pressed against my brow. I pushed up from my bed and walked into the living room, where nothing sat before me but a couch, a cordless phone on a table, and the back of a man with similar tats on his back like mine, two large diamonds on his ears, and the same haircut as mine. I blinked a couple of times, apprehension filling my chest, and I walked forward. The ringing continued. The closer I got, it seemed that the couch got farther. What fucked me more was that as I looked ahead, I saw a flat-screen TV with images flashing on it. I saw my games, then I saw Drew's basketball games, then I saw my aunt spitting rhymes that spoke about the realness in the streets. I glanced back and then I saw blood washing over his shoulders as the phone rang and rang.

"Answer the phone, man; you hear that shit, answer it!" I yelled. The shit was pissing me off, making me angrier by the second.

When I finally made it to the couch, the sensation of wetness with that of something soggy and fleshy against my bare feet and squishing between my toes made me look down. All around me was blood, blood mixed with flesh. Hands, arms, torsos, heads, all appeared from the sea of blood. I looked up in shock and saw the body was me on the couch. In my hands was Micah's dead body. His spine ripped from his back, lying on my hard thighs. In my hand was his bludgeoned face. Nigga's face was so bad it seemed that it was sunken into a muddle of bloody pumpkin guts. I stared long and hard memorizing everything. I was covered in blood. My E.N.G.A. tattoo on the side of my ribs seemed to glow, and the phone continued to ring.

I finally grabbed the phone to answer it. I opened my mouth to say hello and the voice of my aunt echoed, "The streets aren't for you but it's who you are."

I frowned and it had me looking at the image of myself in the dream again. It was then that I saw the words DOA tatted on the side of my neck.

My aunt's voice sounded again. "Make it yours. Make it what you want it to be. I love you, son."

Her words pissed me off. I reached out to claw at my mirror's neck only to see myself laugh as the letters disappeared and flowed into E.N.G.A. My baby brother Drew appeared at my side on the couch, sitting down next to me. On his neck were the same letters, DOA, but they then turned into the shape of an Angel with the letters E.N.G.A. in the middle.

"Nigga, this world is yours. Now answer the phone," was all my mirror said before he took the cord of the telephone, wrapped it around Micah's neck, tugging until whatever life that was still in that fucker jerked out. I watched him grin deviously; his eyes turned soot black then he pulled off Micah's lifeless head then tossed it to Drew, who sent it flying with a swish behind him. The sea of blood undulated on the floor, growing until it washed over me. The pieces of bodies I saw were my enemies and those pieces of bodies swallowed me whole until I woke up in a sweat at the sound of my alarm going off.

"Shit!"

The sheets of my bed wrapped around my waist in disarray. I kicked off what I could, moved to the side of my bed and slammed my alarm off, noticing it was still early in the morning. My shoulders slumped as I tried to shake off my dream, but also tried to make sense of it. I didn't want shit to do with DOA and E.N.G.A. ain't did nothing but help a nigga out. It had to be something though, but I wasn't going to trip on that shit. Fuck, for all I knew, it could be the aftereffects of boning Angel. Shit. I got my dick wet, was good, too, but my mind was conflicted on that shit because she fucked my brother, even though a part of me was liking her. I told her that anyway, damn.

I let out a loud sigh. I wasn't about to let Angel be a problem for me. We had shit to do, and to handle. Sometimes people fucked and that was that. After kicking it with Angel yesterday, I had a lot on my plate to get our plan in motion. She had done what I asked, and now it was my next move, but now it seemed as if I had some shit on the brain, shit that didn't make any sense to me whatsoever. I pushed off the bed, running both hands over my face then fixing my low-hanging pants. After heading in the bathroom to piss, then wash my hands, my cell started ringing, putting me back in the dream just that fast.

I picked it up with constrained apprehension and barked out, "Who the fuck is this?"

"Nigga, you late! Wake the hell up, new blood, and let's get to training; or did all the pussy you pulling finally catch up with you?"

I had to chuckle at Dragon's teasing. He'd been the one player on the team I fucked with on a personal level. My fingers pinched the bridge between my nose and I sighed low. "Fuck you calling me for to tell me that, homie? I know it is. I'm on my way; what you really want?"

Shuffling on the other end of my cell started grating my nerves. "Yeah, man, our mutual friend is pissing me the fuck off. Shit."

A low laugh came from me, and I glanced at my cell before responding, "I got you. We'll talk." I hung up without letting that fool continue and I grabbed my shit then saddled up to head to practice.

Working with a team of niggas who came from all walks of life was interesting to me, because it gave me the means to blend in without anyone knowing my past. The bad thing though was there were some niggas from the same streets of the A as me, and then there were others who weren't from here, but were thugs, too, who sought out the hood for whatever reasons.

Some of the faces I was very familiar with, and they knew to stay quiet because like me, they didn't want their reputation fucked up. Besides,

if they tried to ruin mine, there was no way I
could be currently linked to criminal activity
and I liked it that way. It also meant that some
of those niggas were already hitting me up with
wanting to know if I had ties to get them product. I used to ignore them and do me, but now
with Micah pressing me, the game was about to
change.

I made it without problem to the training
base. The time on my watch said I was actually
ten minutes early, which was good for me. I
was still tripping off my crazy-ass dream and
just wanted to put all that shit in the field. As I
headed to the locker, I was sideswiped. I used
the momentum of the touch to twist, and then
slam my hand and bag up into the neck of the
nigga who grabbed me. I pushed him back into
the wall, getting a good look at who it was with
a sneer.

Pissed all the way off, I brushed him off and
stepped back. "The hell do you want?"

"My bad. Look, I . . . ah, shit, you got my shirt,
homie? Give that shit back and then we're good,"
he muttered to me.

My eyes roamed over the medium-build full-
back. His hands slightly shook and his eyes
darted back and forth. He was a junky and
sooner or later it would start to be seen by every-

one else. He sported black Nike football shorts and a red Nike compression shirt. I wore Nike as well but my ensemble was all black.

He scratched at his jaw. I could tell he was nervous and the sloppiness in the way he approached me bothered me. I had given this nigga a name of one of my associates before, but he was spazzed out so deep on whatever the fuck he used that he rubbed that cat the wrong way. It seemed that this donkey was going to need a dealer who would keep him in line. I had just the right person in mind, but it all was on condition of if he had some intel for me that was reliable. I was about to see.

"Ah huh. Check your locker, you fucking tripping. I'm out." My eyes narrowed and then I walked away but not before slipping him the card of the new guy, Dragon. In return, he gave me a slip of paper with an address. What we just discussed was code for where to look for his product. His locker was his designated drop spot, and his shirt was his bags of Indigo, weed, and some Molly.

I casually headed into the locker, dropping my bag in front of my locker then reading the note. Everything on it would have to be verified later, but from a quick glance, it was solid. Micah was out of the hospital and actually somewhere in the stadium overseeing his money. With what was given to me, it had me wondering how he had time to oversee this large-ass team, its players, the girls, and countless staffers, and still have time to roll in the streets and be a Fed. I knew he had many hands then and wondered who was watching Micah's private interests and who wasn't.

Putting my gloves on, I made way to the training field. I jogged to the middle, rolled my shoulders inhaling the fresh air, then locked eyes on the man who was making my life hell. He stood in the bleachers, looking down on us as if we were nothing but his puppets. He tilted his head my way with a smirk and a wink and I glanced around then returned the nod.

I grinned, screwed my face up, curled my upper lip, and then bit my lower lip, flashing my teeth. I then pointed my fingers out like a gun and shot it off his way, letting him know that I wasn't done gunning for him. The images in my dream came back to me and it had me unsettled only because, I felt a quiet need, almost as if my dick was getting hard, at the idea of playing with that nigga's guts and hanging him out to dry. Dropping my hand and getting in step once the coaches came out; I shook off my vision, and made a note to make sure to visit my aunt and Drew later today or tomorrow.

Breathing in slowly and exhaling slowly, I crouched low to prep to run for my drills. My eyes narrowed, the muscles in my thighs and calves tightened, and I dug my feet in the ground waiting for the whistle. Each rhythmic beating of my heart had me thinking about my plan. Had me thinking about my aunt, Drew, the dream I had, then Angel. I bit down hard on my mouth guard then the sound of a whistle had me shooting forward.

Tweeeeet!

"Damn! Enzo, shit! You fucked it up hard out there on the field, homie," was shouted near my ear by one of my teammates.

I grinned as lights flashed; fans crawled around us asking for autographs. People chanted our team name and the energy around me had me buzzed up as I stepped into Club Rize. Everything in the huge two-level decked-out club was washed in black and blue lights. We strolled through the place and I felt like we were in the movie *Belly*. Sealed contact lens cases were handed up for those of us who wanted to do the glow in the dark vibe.

In the club, I saw several Bounce Girls. I saw several of the assistant coaches knee deep in pussy and titties, as dancers slid down poles. I tilted my chin up to nod at my teammate and blocker, Dragon. My boy Dragon was a huge motherfucker, I mean, nigga literally was built, and shaped like one of the predators from the movie *Predator*. It didn't help that he also sported locs that fell directly on his beefy shoulders.

Nigga's fist was so huge that he could punch a hole through concrete leaving a massive crater. It was his size and speed that got him on the team. It was his personality and size that kept pussy coming his way as well. I heard some of the Bounce Girls say it was his smile, deep voice, and dark, almost black, eyes that was pure panty wetters, even though his looks were average.

He was no pretty boy, but he had qualities, qualities that worked in my favor since he was the nigga I had sent Ross to earlier today. Dragon, from what he told me, got his name because no matter what drink he had, he always was drinking that shit flamed up. He also was known for lighting niggas on fire back on the streets before he came into the game. He chucked his hand up in the air, directing me to come his way as I noticed him passing our other teammate, Ross, a small bag.

"Sup, man, what it do?" I said clasping his forearm and knocking shoulders with him. "I thought that nigga had his full. Shit, man, nigga is a hardcore junkie ain't he?"

Dragon gave a heavy laugh, and grabbed a glass full of whatever the fuck he typically drank that required flames to be on it. I watched him down that shit in one gulp. He slammed the empty glass down all before I could order my drink. The bartender nodded my way and I watched her bring me an untouched bottle of Conjure with glasses.

"Ey yo. That's how the cookie crumble with that time fa'sho. As long as that nigga don't die, keep the paper droppin' and he follow my guide-lines and yours, shit, we coo fah real though," Dragon drawled.

My boy had a unique way he spoke. Everything always had a "fa'sho" on it, which fucked with my mental in a comical way. When we first met, I wasn't keen on letting the nigga step two feet in my world, but after Micah, and after talking with Angel about him, I let him in, learning he had beef with Micah too, because of his past deal-ings with Dame. It only made sense to do some dealings with this dude and learn him to see if I could trust him all the way with the plan.

I handed a pretty, fat-booty chick my bottle of Conjure and glasses, whispering in her ear to send it to some pretty pussy who kept looking my way while Dragon and me headed to the VIP.

"That nigga here?" I asked while we walked and lights bumped to the music.

"On the tri-level looking down on us all, my nigga, like a lame," he explained.

A cold silence entered my spirit and it had me fisting my hands. "Tino on it?"

"Yup."

"Angel?"

"You know it. 'Bout ta be some bussin' goin' down, mayne." Dragon laughed.

A smile spread across my face and I lit up a cigar that Dragon slid my way. We stood on the entry stairway of our section, nodding to the beat. Though I didn't have any contacts in, my eyes still lit up with the lighting. Dragon's eyes were red neon and he sported a set of grills that only gave him silver vampire teeth on the top and bottom of his mouth. He rubbed his chin, then fisted his hand and lifted in the air, slamming it to the beat.

"A'ight I'm out. Angel is supposed to holla at cha 'bout that product," I said as I moved to blend in with the crowd.

Dragon's steel-iron grip grabbed my arm, making me turn and eye him in exchange. If that nigga had a problem or some shit, I had no issue with going upside his steel drum head. We both stood eye to eye, and just because he was built like a freight truck really didn't put one once of fear in me.

"What up, homie?" I asked in question but with a light tone of "don't fuck with me."

Dragon stepped closer but moved to the side, he held both his hands up then rested against the wall that was near us. "We're good, man, but I wanted to talk to you about that Angel broad."

My arms crossed over my chest, and I thumbed my pierced nose then stroked my chin beard in thought. If she fucked Dragon, I wouldn't be shocked and that was no insult to her, just the nature of the world we both came from. "What about her?"

"Nigga, that bitch janked me fa' my shit last time we met and I want it back, on some real talk," Dragon growled. His eyes narrowed and I could see his nostrils flaring as they normally did when he was in a zone and ready to fuck up our opponents on the field.

I raised an eyebrow, definitely curious about how that shit happened. "How'd she do that?"

"We were kickin' it awhile back. Tossin' drinks back. I saw shawty looking sweet and tasty an' shit, shaking her ass. I went up to her, did what I do. We talked and shit, then we got to fucking around. Next thing I know, a nigga was passed out in the back of the club. My watch, my chains, my rings, and shit was all gone. Bitch even lined up my wallet with nothing but dust, homie! If you want this nigga right here to work with that thieving bitch, I need my shit back."

Laughter burned in my lungs and had me narrowing my eyes, as I tried to hold it in. I played back everything he had said and held up a hand. "Hold up. Next thing you woke up with no shit? Where they do that at?"

Dragon's face twisted up as he watched me laugh. He stepped closer with a pleading look in his eyes. "I'm serious, man. Bitch be playing niggas for they shit. Don't trust anything that broad got to give. She uses her pussy as game, and then drugs you, and then she got you."

"Oh, yeah?" I glanced around the club spotting Angel as she danced with several other Bounce Girls, working her way to get close to Micah. I thought back to when we fucked, and I wondered about if her motives would stay in line. No matter what anyone says, once your life is in jeopardy, it takes a special sort of person to not give in to their attacker and work on that side.

"Check this out though: we all got the same agenda right now, so focus on that. I'll holla at shawty and get you your gwap, and then we squash it, and let her use her gifts to better our cause a'ight?"

Dragon gave a sigh as if uncertain in my word. "A'ight, man, just saying. Was some serious shit she took from a nigga. Lot of money in it."

"Look, I gotta bounce to handle my part of this game, but now you know not to flash your house payment on your body like that, man. 2 Chainz!" I joked.

Dragon gave a laugh. "Man, fuck you."

"Nah, nigga, she fucked you.Why don't you buy some new gwap?" I quickly asked as he turned away.

"Because my shit had symbolism. I got it when Dame fell, and I want to remember how that nigga's death claimed him," he said with all seriousness.

I could respect exactly what he was saying. I got inked the very next day celebrating that nigga's fall. Dragon and me gave each other dap in understanding, and I headed out disappearing in the crowd, making sure that I saw Micah surrounded by sponsors and women. I had shit I needed to handle quickly, without him noticing; one of those things was to change into all black.

After driving away, doing a run through to ditch anyone who may be following me, I headed to the Trap, where I swapped out my ride at an old garage I shared with the Misfits. I sped out then made it to my third new piece of property hidden in Decatur. I grabbed what I needed, put on my black gloves, a black skullcap, with a jacket that had a mask attached to it. I padded up my shoulders to change the shape of my body, and then headed out in a different ride that I planned to dispose of later. Driving through ATL, I found my way back at the club.

I took the back way just in case it was still busy, but considering how late it was, I knew it wasn't. A lot of us players had moved on to after parties and I knew where this club was located, wasn't shit going to be going on outside of the club. My all-black 1972 Camaro backed up slowly as I worked the shift and kept my foot on the clutch, into a shielded blacked-out alley across from the club but close to the club's parking zone. I quieted the engine, pulled my skull cap low, adjusted my mask, and pulled the large hood of my jacket over my head while my gloved hands gripped the steel silver chain design of my steering wheel.

My attention stayed on the side and the front door of the club. My hand went to my cell then I hit send on my cell, alerting Angel to kick it to phase two. If everything was going to go right, Angel had to hold up on her end. I had scoped out his place for a while now. Monitoring every camera there was, and anyone who would be in the area, I watched my watch and saw the lights outside flicker. It was a signal that one of the team sponsors had handled business and taken out the security cameras.

It was close to game time. My eyes glanced to the back of my leather black seats, settling on my bag of goodies. I sat, and waited for a nigga I had plans to have a long conversation with for however long that I wanted. Flashes of my dream played in my mind and a slow, sinister smile played across my lips as my eyes turned ink black, and the weapon I had pressed against the lower part of my back waited in anticipation to be used in battle.

Chapter 16

Angel

"Yo, my niggas, this joint live as fuck, right?" Dragon yelled over the music.

"It's a'ight, but the party at my crib is about to better. This rat trap 'bout to close in about an hour. Bring that shit to the crib and let's keep it turned up," I heard Micah yell outside of the VIP doors.

I'd know his voice anywhere. It was something that a woman would love to hear greet her in the morning and would be even better to hear in your ear when he was fucking you. I heard most of the players yell their excitement over the music.

"You bring the bitches. I got everything else," Dragon called out.

"No doubt. Round the baddest ones up in here and let's get it cracking. Niggas thinking 'cause they caught a ma'fucker slipping that I still ain't 'bout that life, you feel me? Nothing stops me, my nigga. Feel me?"

Everybody knew he was talking about the fact that he been found drugged in his car. They didn't know the details of what had happened so Micah and his PRs started placing stories on all of the entertainment blogs saying he had been drugged, beaten, and robbed. He had been embarrassed. Everyone knew Micah was well connected in the A and even more so since Dame had bitten the dust. He was supposed to be an untouchable so the fact that he had been touched had grated his pride. This party, the fact that he was out of the hospital and showboating around the place attested to that. He had to show the A that the underworld conglomerate still couldn't be stopped.

"Damn, bitch, why you always in some shit?" Tino fussed as I kicked the man in the nuts who lay at our feet. One of the men that Micah used as his personal guard lay out cold at our feet. I knew there would be no way I could get close to Micah at this point. The look in his eyes when I'd seen him earlier said that he wanted to kill me and I knew if he got me alone, he would. So me and Tino changed up the plans after I got Enzo's text.

"I spilled most of the damn drink so that's why the pill didn't take effect like it was supposed to," I told Tino. I kicked Kruger in his nuts again just because. I would never forget that he raped me along with Micah and Hemp and I would never forget what they did to Drew.

Tino stood back with his hands on his slim hips. Sweat beads on his forehead. We both had to fight like hell to get Kruger down. Both of us sported the bruises to prove it. But it was the Taser in Tino's clutch that had taken the big man down finally.

"Bitch, you owe me a day at the spa and two days' pay for this shit, ho. Whew, chile," he said through bated breaths.

"I got you. You remember where my crib is right?"

He nodded and repeated the address off to me.

"Good. Meet me there to get the rest of your pay."

"Oh, don't worry, bitch. I'll probably be there before you do."

I only nodded, too winded to say much else. We both stood in the dark corridors behind the black double doors that led to the exit. We could still hear the club in full effect and it sounded like Micah was about ready to leave.

"We gotta get him out this hall," I said after a while.

"How we gon' move this big nigga?" Tino asked with a frown and a tilt of his head.

"I don't know, but we gotta do something and we gotta do it quick."

The double doors came open. Both Tino and I stood upright, ready to take another nigga down if need be.

"I'll meet you at the crib, my nigga," the man shouted back behind him.

The male figure that came through the door made us relax a bit; well, not me because the man who turned to look at us was a man I had robbed. Dragon locked eyes on me and the bottom of my stomach fell out. I had been avoiding him like the plague since I'd taken him for his loot.

"The fuck is you doing?" he barked out at me.

"What I'm supposed to be doing. Help us move him," I ordered.

Dragon looked at me as if I had lost my mind. He was one of the guys that I actually felt bad about robbing. He'd been a cool dude, had opened up to me about some things. But he had to understand that it was a dog-eat-dog world and a bitch was hungry.

"You know if it wasn't for my nigga Enzo, I'd put your ass to sleep back here," he spat at me. "I want my fucking chain back."

I shrugged. "I'm sorry, it's gone," I said with no remorse. I couldn't let him see that I was rattled or that I had felt bad about what I had done. He wouldn't respect my hustle then. Wouldn't respect the fact that I had to do what I had to do.

"You better be fucking playing, fa'sho, Angel, or else you on your fucking own. I'll dead this whole shit and deal with Enzo later."

His face held a malicious frown. I'd known the necklace had meant a lot to him because he'd told me the story behind it. But none of that mattered; there was no way we could not see this plan through. For some reason I felt the need to show Enzo he could trust me.

"Okay, look, maybe I can speak to my contact guy and see about getting it back, but I ain't making no promises," I finally said.

For a while Dragon just stood there glaring at me.

"Okay, are you two just gonna stand here and eye fuck or are we gonna go ahead and get down with the get on? Y'all got a bitch like me working way too hard," Tino chimed in.

Dragon shook his head then grabbed Kruger by the lapels of his jacket. He dragged the big man down the hall and then into a room before closing the door behind him.

"A'ight, Angel, this all you," Tino said as he pulled a ski mask from his pocket and pulled it over his head.

I watched as Dragon did the same. I nodded, was ready to do my part. Tino pulled football pads on his shoulder then pulled on a sweater. The pads totally changed the shape and outline of his body build. No more words were passed between us as they headed out the exit door. Micah had wronged a lot of people so it had been nothing for us to convince a couple of players to get in on the plan. Dressed in all black, I had on black skinny jeans that hugged my ass so tight they looked as if they had been painted on, a black leotard with a cut showcasing a hint of breasts, and a pair of black thigh high boots that came with six-inch heels.

I made sure no one saw me as I walked back into the party. I made my way to the bar amid getting hit on and ass grabbed a few times. I laughed and played it off like everything was everything. Did a quick scan of the room to see if I could spot Micah again. I didn't see him. But I knew he was around probably watching me from a hidden spot. I grabbed four shots back to back. Took those shits to the head then made myself the life of the party.

"Look me in my face, I ain't got no worries."

The bounce of my ass moved in tune with the loud deep bass of the music. Lil Wayne's annoying, alien-like voice floated around the club as lights flashed and vibrated because of the reverberation of the speakers. I was in my zone. All eyes were on me. I closed my eyes and just imagined it was me and Enzo back at my condo as I hopped on the small stage in the VIP, bent over, and made the Twerk Team, made famous by ass clapping and shaking on YouTube, look like amateurs. At that moment, I didn't have no worries. Money was flowing, raining down on me. Several of the other Bounce Girls stood looking like they had run afoul out some rank pussy.

I had a job to do. That was what I kept telling myself. I had probably taken one shot too many, but it was the only way I could keep my game face on. I lifted my head and made eye contact with Micah. He hadn't been in the VIP moments before. But that was okay. Just like I had thought, he had been watching me from somewhere. That was the thing that made him most dangerous: you never knew when his eyes were on you. Niggas screamed and yelled wildly at me. Some just stood gazing curiously. I'd heard one ask Micah why he hadn't showcased me before now. Then asked him how much it would cost for me for the night.

"She's priceless, my nigga," Micah told him. "But give me a few minutes and I might change my mind."

Kruger stood behind Micah watching me too. That worried me. Micah must have found him in the back room. He had an ice pack on his eye as he and Micah whispered back and forth. I made eye contact with both men then smirked. I was bold knowing that in a few short hours, maybe minutes, both of them would meet their Maker. Club Rize's VIP section had stripper poles and a small stage that was perfect for me. I stood up straight, slung my Brazilian Remy over my shoulders as I did the stripper bounce from side to side.

Micah moved to sit right in front of me, arms folded across his broad chest. There was a plush black and red leather sofa, riddled with ones that he sat on. In his eyes was a coldness. I was almost turned on by it, almost; but he was missing something. He was missing that demonic look, that predatory glare that said in this jungle called the Trap you would always be his food before he would be yours. Enzo had that look. Enzo had perfected that look. I imagined he was Enzo as I sauntered over to him. I balanced myself over his face. The softness of the couch almost made the stance in my heels awkward, but I had perfected the art of dancing thanks to my girl Coco. I could shake my ass standing barefoot on burning coal if need be.

I squatted over Micah's face and popped my pussy so hard that every nigga in the place got closer to see. It looked as if I was getting off by damn near having Micah eat my snatch in public, but it was flashbacks of the night before that had me gone. Micah had always had a weakness for my sex. This time was no different. Although I knew in his head he'd planned to kill me, that cold look in his eyes turned into another look I was very familiar with. He was turned on, ready to fuck or be fucked.

"You see pussy right there, red bone mangoes right there."

Micah licked his lips then leaned back. His eyes never left mine. Jaw twitched, eyes glossed over, he was high.

"Mad at me?" I asked him sarcastically.

He didn't respond. Back when he was paying Dame for me, he used to like when I played the seductive kiddy games with him. It used to get him off when I would pretend as if I cared whether he was upset with me and his dick would get harder and harder at the thought of me making it up to him. I smiled then dropped down to straddle his lap. Moved my ass and hips in a way that would make him remember what it was like to fuck me or to have me fuck him. I leaned in, placed my lips close to his. I knew he was mad, knew he wasn't in the mood to play or talk to me, but he couldn't deny his infatuation and attraction to me.

It must have annoyed him to know I was getting a rise out of him. He jumped up quickly, almost causing me to fall on the floor. Micah's hand caught the back of my hair. He grabbed my arm and forced me to walk toward the black double doors with the glaring exit sign above them. Kicking the doors open, he shoved me into the dark hallway I'd just been in moments before. I fell into the wall as I caught my balance.

Micah tsked. "Bianca, my Angel, there was always an innocence about you that I liked. I liked you a hell of a lot. I would have made you a *made* woman, a kept woman. I don't get how you choose to align yourself with a nigga who's the same as the nigga you worked for in the beginning."

I tilted my head and frowned at him, but didn't speak. I was clearly confused.

"You don't get it now, but one day you will and by then, it will all be too late," he continued.

I couldn't front like Micah wasn't a fine man because he was. Under normal circumstances

I may have been attracted to him, but I knew too much about him, knew all his dirt. I didn't want to be a made or kept woman under him. It required me to do his dirty work and I wasn't down for that. I'd rather take my chances with Enzo because at least I knew he would keep his word if I kept mine. A girl like me needed at least that security.

"It's going to hurt me to kill you, Angel. Truly, it is."

His dark eyes gave me a once-over as he reached behind him to remove a gun from his waistband. I hadn't counted on that, I thought as my eyes widened.

"All you had to do was treat me like a person and not a piece of meat. I wasn't going back to that lifestyle, Micah. I wasn't. You came at me the same way Dame used to. I couldn't do that shit again," I told him. It was a half lie. I wouldn't have worked for him either way, but he didn't need to know that.

He chuckled low. "The funny thing is, you're so busy running from Dame's ghost that you're closer to him than you think you are. My sweet Angel, you told him about me, didn't you?"

He moved closer to me, almost like he was stalking me as I backed away. I just needed to get to the door that was only a few feet away. But

I knew if I ran, I was as good as shot in the back and left for dead.

"Told who, what?" I asked feigning ignorance.

"You know what the fuck I'm talking about, bitch. Don't fucking play stupid with me," he snapped.

Another reason I would never be under his lock and key. The nigga was bipolar as fuck. At least when it came to Enzo, I knew he wasn't evil just because. I knew in order to get him to go stone-cold crazy, you had to push him to the limit. With Micah, all you had to do was breathe the wrong way and he was trying to kill you.

"I ain't tell nobody shit because I don't know what you're talking about. What the fuck would I tell him?"

"Cut the shit, Bianca," he yelled.

He went to grab me and I kicked him in his nuts. The guttural groan he gave as he bent forward and grabbed his dick almost distracted me from running away. I quickly ran for the exit.

"Ahhhh, fuck! Angel! Why you gotta make a nigga act all crazy and shit? Huh, baby?"

I looked behind me to see he was advancing on me. A shot rang out behind me that made me duck and screech out. I almost fell when my ankle went one way while I was trying to run another. I kicked myself for choosing to wear six-inch heels. My ankles were burning as I righted myself once against and kept running. The door was within the distance, but Micah was closer. He caught up to me and grabbed the back of my hair, throwing me head first into the wall. I screamed out, but no one could hear me over the music. So if Micah decided to shoot me dead in that moment, no one would have known. I fell backward, thankfully, and used my boots as weapons. I kicked at him like a madwoman, knowing that if I didn't get outside that door, Micah was sure to finish me off. The heels of my boots caught his arms and chest. The more I kicked the harder he came at me. I tried to kick for his face but he grabbed the foot I was aiming with. With the gun in his other hand he tried yanking me to him. He swung the gun at my head, but I fell back, using my other foot to kick him in the neck.

It backed him up off me enough for me to get up and run to the door. The cool night air assaulted me as I clumsily rushed forward. I almost fell again, but knew that was a no-go. I knew Enzo was there but had no idea where he was. The back parking lot was almost empty, except for a few foreign whips that belonged to some of the high-profile players. The wind whipped around me as the trees swayed in the

night. I turned in a circle, kind of delirious.
Something wet trickled down my forehead causing me to touch it with my hand. When I came
away with blood, my heart rate sped up faster.

Micah came bursting through the back door.
He, too, had blood dripping from his chocolate
face from the assault with my boots. "Bitch, you
must be out cho motherfucking mind tonight,"
he roared.

He charged at me so quick that my scream got
caught in my throat. I swung out as he grabbed
for me. I surprised myself with the fight I had
in me, so imagine his astonishment at the heart
I was showing. Even still, the fight in Micah
was bigger than and stronger than I was. In the
end the butt of his gun took me to the ground. I
didn't know where the rest of those niggas had
come from. But I was sure as hell glad when they
got there.

"What it is, boss man?" I heard a male's voice.

As I lay on my back, head splitting with the
pain from the hit Micah had given me, I could
see the feet of about six men. I backed away,
scrambling to my feet.

"Grab that ho," Micah ordered the man.

I smiled as I shook my head. "The only ho getting got tonight is you, nigga."

Micah looked around as the men, all clad in ski masks, all black clothing, and black boots surrounded him. "What the fuck is this?" he yelled out. "You niggas—"

"We niggas got a bone to pick," Dragon's voice called out.

"And seems that bone is coming outta ya ass, my nigga," another player's voice came through.

I wanted to stay and see them beat the cold piss out of Micah, but the text to my phone from Enzo was etched in stone. All I was supposed to do was get him to the parking lot. My heart continued to race at the possibility that I almost got killed before I got him outside. I wasn't to know what happened in that parking lot after I got Micah out there. He didn't want me to know shit so I couldn't say shit. So like the damsel in distress I usually was, I took off running like a madwoman.

Chapter 17

Angel

I made it in no time to the rental car Enzo had gotten for me. People were so busy doing what they were doing that no one even noticed me. For a couple of minutes, I sat there to get my thoughts together. I was supposed to pull right out and head back to my condo but my hands were shaking so badly that I could barely get the key into the ignition. Once I was calm, I pulled out into the Atlanta nightlife traffic.

The phone Enzo had given me started to ring and since no one knew I had the phone but Enzo, I thought it was him. "Hello?"

There was a cough on the other end of the phone. "Angel, is that you?" the almost frail voice asked.

It was his aunt. To hear her voice so sickly and to remember the way she looked last time I saw her saddened me. I could tell she was a strong woman and to know something as evil as cancer had taken a street warrior down was a sobering moment.

"Yes, ma'am, it's Angel," I answered.

"Where's Shawn? Is he okay? Are you okay?"

"I . . . I, ah, really don't know where he is," I lied. "And yes, I'm okay."

She was quiet a moment. She probably knew I was lying because of the hesitation and shakiness in my voice.

"Well, since you don't know where he is, I suppose you can't tell him that his brother has gotten away from the security here and is out there God knows where. Drew said he wanted to see his brother so I'm assuming he went to his place."

Oh, God. The last thing Enzo needed was to know Drew was out in the streets of Atlanta running around somewhere. I was sure it would ruin Enzo's plans to get Micah if he knew Drew was missing. "I'm sure he'll be back soon. I can tell him then."

"Angel, do you know where Shawn is?" she asked me in a tone that let me know she still had some fight in her.

"I can't say that I do."

"Is he in trouble?"

"No."

"Is he doing something that may cause him trouble?"

"I can't say."

"Where is Micah?"

"I honestly don't know the answer to that question."

She went into a coughing fit again. I heard a voice in the background I knew was Anika's telling her she needed to rest and let them worry about finding Andrew.

"Angel, if Shawn was in trouble, you would tell me, right?" Shy asked me.

"Yes, I would."

"If he was doing something that would get him in trouble, would you tell me?"

"Not if he asked me not to," I answered honestly.

"On one hand I'm happy to know that he can trust you. On the other, if anything happens to him and you could have prevented it from happening, I'm going to be one pissed-off woman. No one likes me when I'm pissed, Angel. Do you understand?"

"Yes, ma'am."

"Good. If Drew happens to come his brother's way you call me, understand? And if Shawn can't get to his brother, you keep Drew."

"No, I can't do that," I protested. I didn't want that kid anywhere near me, not with all that had happened. I could barely look myself in the face after what he had been made to do. There was no way I would be able to look him in his eyes.

"You can. I would consider it a personal favor if you did. Just keep him with you until his brother can get to him and bring him back to me," she ordered.

I knew there was really no way she would take no for an answer. So I agreed to her terms. After the call ended I tossed the phone on the seat next to me and it flopped down between the seat and the door. *I'll get it once I get in,* I thought.

I made it to the condo's parking deck without issue. I parked the car where Enzo had dictated and made my way to the elevator. I was still nervous, wondering if Micah was any closer to death and if Enzo was okay. I'd done my part so all I had to do was wait. My place was two floors down from Enzo's but since Shy had said Drew left under the guise of getting to Enzo, I took the elevator up to his place.

I felt the bottom fall out of my stomach as I walked off the elevator and turned the corner. There was a miniature Enzo sitting by the door. He had his knees pulled up with his arms resting over them. He was dressed in khakis, Jordans, and a black polo-style shirt. I took a deep breath because I didn't want to be anywhere near the kid, but swallowed that lump in my throat. He must have heard me coming because he looked up the moment I started walking toward him. He hopped up quickly and walked toward me, meeting me halfway. The kid was tall for his age and while he had a baby face, I could see trouble brewing behind his eyes.

"Wassup, Angel? You seen Enzo?" he asked me.

The bass in his voice unnerved me. Or it could have been that I was just so uncomfortable around him that anything he said or did would make any interaction between us seem awkward.

"Why aren't you back home with your aunt?" I counter asked him.

He sucked his teeth and made a screw face. "Here you go. Anyway, I wanted to talk to my brother 'cause I ain't seen him in a few days. Y'all acting like a nigga ain't got the right to see his fam."

I scratched my head in annoyance and switched my weight from one foot to the other. My feet hurt, back ached, and head was throbbing from the blow to it earlier. "Well, Enzo ain't around right now so you need to go back home," I said.

He shook his head. "Nah, I'ma wait on him.
Where you going? I can chill with you until he
gets back."

"Like hell you will. Enzo already on my ass
about what happened. I ain't about to have him
come home and find me anywhere near you. You
need to go back home, Andrew."

"Shawty, why you tripping?"

"I'm not tripping."

"I'm cool. I'll chill right here until he—"

"Andrew, you really cannot be here right
now. What part of that don't you understand?" I
yelled at him.

His brows furrowed. "Don't be yelling at me,
Angel. You can't keep me from chilling by his
door until he gets home."

"Your brother is not here because he fucking
out handling business. You sitting by his door
and not being home with your aunt is just making shit worse. Go home!"

One of Enzo's neighbors stuck her head out
the door. I really didn't need anybody calling the
cops or the security guards up. I dug around in
my bag for my phone only to remember I had
left it in the car.

"You stay right here, you understand me?
Stay here until I get back, Drew. Don't move,"
I ordered.

He smirked looking too much like Enzo for my liking. The way he gave me the once-over had me shaking my head and hoping that Enzo would make Micah beg for death before he actually killed him. There was nothing worse than a child ruined by the acts of an adult. I jogged back down the carpeted hall to the elevator and hopped on. The whole ride back to the parking deck all I could think about was getting the kid back to his aunt. I rushed through the automatic doors and searched out the car. I was so focused on one thing that when Kruger stepped out the shadows, I never saw him.

I opened the passenger door and bent down to grab the phone. It was then that he reached into the car and pulled me out by the back of my hair. I shrieked out not knowing what was going on. The phone dropped to the ground and shattered and I was tossed roughly to the ground. I didn't waste any time getting up to run though.

"Stupid bitch. You thought I was out when that faggot hit me, huh? Had him say your address all loud and shit like a dumb ass. Micah should have let me kill you in that hotel room," he called out as he ran behind me.

I bent the corner running like I had on Jays instead of heels. My feet and ankles would hate me later, but I had to get Kruger far away from me as possible. I prayed Drew would stay where he was or would even realize I was gone too long and head back home. By the time I looked over my shoulders I was on the second-level deck hiding between a Hummer and a Navigator. My heart drummed in my ears. Breaths came out heavier and heavier each inhale and exhale. Any chance I had of finding a weapon was dropped when my purse fell to ground as I ran. I covered my mouth to keep my heavy breathing from giving me away. I could see Kruger's shadow as he came to an abrupt stop.

"Come on, sexy lady. Don't be like that. Hey, look, maybe before I kill you, we can fuck again. And then I can toss you off top of this fucking building to see how pussy looks when it's flying," he taunted me.

I looked around knowing there was no way out for me. Tears clouded my vision as I tried to duck walk between cars. When that didn't work, I got on my knees and crawled. I knew he could hear me at that point and I didn't care. I just needed to get out of the parking deck. The faster I crawled, the faster he ran until he cornered me between the last car on the row and the wall.

"Fuck," I yelled as he yanked me to him by my legs.

I just knew I was as good as fucked up with the complete look of murderous intent in Kruger's eyes. I clawed at his face trying to get at his eyes, tussled with him trying to keep his hand from around my throat. Just as quick as he had come at me, he suddenly stopped. His eyes widened and blood dribbled from his lips. I couldn't see what was going on because I was flat of my back. It wasn't until I sat up that I saw Drew behind him. Kruger dropped to his knees, grabbing behind him at whatever Drew had shanked him with. Drew's teeth bit down into his bottom lip as he pulled the knife from Kruger's back then stuck him, mercilessly, over and over. Every time he shoved the knife into Kruger's back it was harder than the first time.

"Bitch-ass nigga," Drew growled.

There had been only one time I'd seen the look in a man's eyes that I saw in Drew's. The air around us seemed to get colder when Drew let out a low, throaty laugh that showed he was enjoying what he was doing. When Kruger's body fell face first into the pavement, Drew stuck the knife into the back of his neck, then stood and started to kick him over and over. I knew this was bad. I knew the whole thing was bad and some kind of way, I knew Enzo would blame me for it. I jumped up, ripped my shirt over my head, and grabbed the knife from Kruger's neck.

"Put your hoodie over your head, Drew. Now," I yelled.

Thankfully he didn't question me and did what I asked. I grabbed his hand and hightailed it to the upper deck back to the main elevator. I stopped and grabbed my bag along with the broken phone along the way. I didn't stop until we made it to Enzo's. I shoved Drew inside and frantically paced in front of the door.

"Shit, shit, shit! Drew, what the fuck? Why did you do that?" I asked, walking up to him to shake him.

"I did it because he was trying to hurt you," he said as if it was a normal thing he had just done.

It was because of me he was no longer a virgin and because of me he had a body on his hand. There was nothing else I could say or do. I told him to sit down while I went and locked myself in Enzo's room. For a long while I just sat on his bed with my head in my hands before heading to the shower. Afterward I walked back to the front room, thought about trying to get Drew to go home again but didn't want to release him back on the street until everything was clear. I tried to finagle the phone back together best I could, but it was gone. I had no phone to call Shy to let her know Drew was okay since Enzo didn't have a landline. I asked Drew if he had his cell and he told me he'd left it at home so Shy wouldn't keep calling him. I helped him to clean up and get the blood off him. I tried my best to get rid of the evidence.

One hour turned into two and two into four. As the night went on, my heart got heavier, wondering if Enzo was okay and what he would do to me once he found out what happened.

I already knew that I would have to deal with the fallout behind this. And I wondered how long it would be before someone found Kruger's body. My question was answered when I heard sirens in the distance. Flashing lights lit up the area down below as I looked out Enzo's bedroom window.

I walked out his bedroom in yoga pants and a tank top to find Drew peeping out the blinds. "Get out of the window," I told him.

"Think they here for that nigga?" he asked me nonchalantly.

"Drew, you killed a man. This is not funny."

"Never said it was, but I don't feel no kind of way 'bout it." He shrugged and walked to throw the empty water bottle he had in his hand in the trash.

"This isn't a fucking joke," I stressed to him.

"Who taking it lightly? You tripping though. I was always taught to fight for those who can't fight for themselves, especially chicks and kids.

You ain't a kid, but you was about to be dog food."

I just shook my head as he moved around the kitchen looking for something else to eat. How could I express to a kid who really seemed to have no moral compass of right and wrong that he was in deep shit? I watched as he found what he was looking for: a Little Debbie Star Crunch. He ate it, and then discarded the package. Anytime I found him gazing at me, I tried to make myself busy doing something else. He walked into the bathroom and I plopped down on the sofa in defeat.

"Hey, why your shit here? This yours?"

I looked up to see Drew had walked out of the bathroom and was standing there with a pair of my thongs in his hands. After Enzo had left that morning, he'd texted me telling me he had taken a pair of my thongs just to be funny. I'd seen them hanging in the hall bathroom as I passed and thought nothing else of it. Judging by the look in Drew's eyes though, I knew what was going on in his head. The kid had taking a liking to me, and we all knew that but tiptoed around it because of the circumstances.

"I just left them there after I showered," I lied.

He didn't believe me, I could tell by the way he smacked his teeth then squared his shoulders.

"But you was in Enzo's room in the shower. How they get in the hall bathroom so fast?" he questioned.

"Drew . . ."

He shook his head tossing the undergarment at me. "I knew it. He said you was a ho but he ain't say he like hoes. So you let my bro cut too?"

Frustration riddled me. There were things that a thirteen-year-old just wouldn't understand and I didn't want to explain it to him. I told him as much.

"Nah, it's cool," he said. He chucked up his deuces. "I'm out."

I moved from the sofa to block his exit. "No, I can't let you go out there. Not with all those cops out there. You staying here until we hear from Enzo."

Drew's face twisted in anger as he tried to shove his way past me. "Fuck you. You can't make me stay." The boy had way more strength than his age gave him credit for, but I wouldn't be moved.

"No, Andrew. I'm not"—we struggled as I talked through clenched teeth trying to hold my footing—"not letting you leave."

He pushed me and I pushed back. We both stumbled and ended up falling over the back of the sofa. I landed on his legs still trying my best to keep him pinned down. It was one thing to have him commit a crime in my defense; it would be another altogether to have him get arrested for it. Out of all the things that could have made the night ten times worse, nothing could have prepared me for when Enzo turned the lock and walked in to see me straddled and trying to force Drew back down on the couch.

In an instant I saw the look of utter disgust in his eyes and knew shit was about to go left.

I got up quick as lightning. "Wait, Enzo, this isn't what it looks like," I tried to explain.

But there was nothing in his eyes that said he believed me. Just death stared back at me. He dropped the black bag he was holding on the floor and charged at me. I moved backward still trying to explain because I knew in a matter of moments what was about to happen. I'd seen that look plenty of times before. I knew when a man was about to lay hands on me. I felt the same pangs of pain in my chest plenty of times when Dame snapped before taking it out on me and the rest of the girls back then. I mean Enzo had gotten physical with me plenty of times before, but he'd never outright hit me like he was doing in that moment. I was back in that mansion, back in a time when I would try to run away from the devil himself. I could hear Andrew yelling at his brother that I was just trying to keep him from running, but he was too far gone. To him I would always be a whore with no morals and no regard for anything or anyone but myself. Maybe having been wherever he was, doing whatever he had done to Micah, had taken him to a place of no return.

I didn't know. All I knew was when his hand connected to my face I hadn't felt that kind of open-palmed pain since before the Misfits burned Dame's mansion to the ground. I hadn't been slung around and called so many bitches since then either. By the time Enzo heard his brother, he and I had torn the front room up because I fought back. The straps of my tank had been ripped and my breasts were threatening to fall out of my shirt. I was breathing so hard it felt as if my chest was about to cave in.

Enzo's fist stopped mid-strike when Drew jumped in front of me. Enzo shoved his brother back, demanding he got out of his face so he could finish his assault on me.

"I was trying to keep him in here until you got back," I yelled at Enzo wiping the blood away from my nose and face. "Your aunt called, said he was gone. I came home to find him sitting by your door. If you would just listen to me . . ." I didn't even know I had been crying. "Damn, why

you always, always thinking the fucking worst of
me? Even after all the shit I do and put myself
through just to fucking show you differently?" I
continued to yell.

He didn't even answer me. He just grabbed
his brother and pushed him toward the door.
I could have gone after him. I could have tried
to make him listen to me so I could tell him his
brother had found himself in a murder, but I just
sat there and let it be what it was until I heard
him and Drew in the hall arguing. I got up and
rushed out. I tried to explain to him again that it
wasn't what it looked like between me and Drew.

"Back up off us. I ain't got shit to do with you
no more," he growled out.

Chapter 18

Enzo

Time ticked by as I watched some of my team-mates have fun with Micah. He stood circled by six niggas. Nigga's eyes got so wide that I could see the white of them where I sat. The enjoyment of this moment was sublime. It also gave me time to pop my trunk, leave the keys in the ignition, and step out of my ride. I took my time strolling to the huge fight. Niggas had pipes, bricks, Glocks, and whatever else weapon they all wanted to bring. Me, I kept it simple for right now, because I had more shit I wanted to do to him.

I laughed low and clapped my hands in a rhythm every nigga around me would under-stand. See, this was a multifaceted type of get-together. I had people who all had beef with Micah, including a few who he thought would have his back, who swore down that they could handle their business, and business they did handle.

I walked through the small crowd and shouted out, "'Rule one of Fight Club is . . .'"

"'You do not talk about Fight Club!'" echoed around me in mocking laughter.

My own melded with theirs and I nodded in amusement while walking circles around a fucked-up Micah. He sat on his knees with his fists clenched, breathing hard, and his shirt ripped with blood dropping to the dark asphalt. He had held his own, but it wasn't enough, he still got his ass kicked and it had only just begun.

"See, Micah, my nigga, you started some-thing that you shouldn't even have continued or begun. I told you, I ain't know shit, didn't want shit to do with shit, and that I was just minding my own shit, feel me? But you just had to keep playing top boss and wake up something that should have been dead," I cajoled.

The tip of my Nike nudged his at his bent knees, before I kicked, landing my foot right under his chin, snapping his neck back. "'Rule two of Fight Club is . . .'"

"None of this shit exists! 'You do not talk about Fight Club!'" everyone echoed.

"Don't you get it, Micah? You may have power, but you piss off enough people, my nigga, those ghosts you helped create turn into terrors," I explained while feeding from the energy of the group. I nodded to some of the teammates in front of me, and they disappeared, coming back with a gift.

My hand went up to my mask just to thumb it and I crouched down to pull Micah up by his shoulders and brush them off, before turning his head toward the men I nodded to.

Micah groggily grumbled. He spit out blood and his head lolled back. "Man, fuck you. I know each and every one of you. Say good-bye to life. Fuck your careers."

Everyone around me let out a laugh, and my grip on his head tightened. "Clearly you really don't understand the madness of what you created, my nigga. We don't give a fuck. Obviously, we got something set up where you can't touch not a fucking thing with our contracts. You can't touch what you don't control, my nigga," I explained.

Micah violently jerked and swung to get my face, but I pulled back and pointed. "Damn, you not tripping off your gifts."

Several bodies of his boys lay at his feet, the only one missing was Kruger. Each of the men's heads were chopped cleanly off, and each one branded on the shoulder with Micah's initials.

"Shit, man, fuck, what did you do, homie?" I joked.

I held tight to Micah's fighting form as he cursed and spit out, "Fuck you! Set me up all you want but I got each and every one of you, know that shit."

I started to hum a song, a tone so sweet that it had Micah looking at me sideways. See, my *tía* said I had a singing voice that could get me a record deal, but I wasn't about the shit. Yet something had me singing in amusement and had me slamming Micah's head against the pavement before him. "'Got killers with me right now, U.O.E.N.O it.'"

"Each missing head will be presented to each and every one of your associates who have dealings with you and dealings with us. That will be their warning, that if they come looking for you, it's game time. Understood?" I clarified.

Micah sputtered and spit. Sweat ran down his dark face and snot mixed with his blood. Both of his bruised eyes were bloodshot, and I smiled at the flicker of hope that he was about to get away that shone in his eyes.

"Oh shit, is that hope I see, my nigga? Hol' up, hol' up, hol' up, let me set something straight: you, my friend, are officially mine to fuck with. Ain't no freedom for you."

Dragon came to my side, whispering that it was close to being time for us all to ride out. I turned my back to speak with the homie, and that was when Micah shot up and moved to come after me. I let him grab me around my waist and slam me to the ground. It was hard for him to get a hold on me because of my padding, and I twisted to elbow him in his ribcage. This allowed me to fall forward and get out of his touch.

"Nigga you dead. No matter what the fuck you do, I'm ending you. All I see is your Maker in you and I was right to come at you like I did," he spat.

His words, had me giving him a screw face but I wasn't about to be bothered with whatever insanity was going on in that nigga's thick skull. I was operating on blackout mode, that mode that had my demons spilling out of me. I shifted on my feet, and the crowd around us used whatever they had to throw at Micah making him duck and try to break through the crowd.

I stood up straight and ran my tongue over my teeth. I tasted blood and saw he had punched me good. It had me walking toward where he was, as he punched, kicked, and pounded his way toward escape. Too bad for him, it was just too many of us, not that I really gave a shit since

I had plans to fuck him up like he already was. So, I reached out, tapped Micah's shoulder, and watched him turn to swing on me.

Ducking, I gave a bright smile, then swung up and snatched that nigga by the throat. Strength fueled me. He tried to buck at me, but I only gripped tighter.

"Final rule to Fight Club!" I shouted.

"Fair exchange is no robbery in Fight Club, once an enemy has entered Fight Club, it is no turning back," everyone said in unison. I continued the rest with them as Micah's eyes bucked out of his skull. "If your enemy dies here or elsewhere, it is on your hands. So it's best to make sure that nigga is DOA."

"Let's have a talk, Micah," I said as I reached behind me, slid out my tanto sword then hit him in the skull with it knocking him out. I watched Micah shake then slump before I turned to look at everyone around me.

"A'ight. You all know the other phase; handle it and I got this," I ordered.

Dragon made a call sound and the parking lot emptied. A few short minutes later, Micah lay gagged, tied up, and passed out in the back of my plastic-lined trunk.

The fight was a nice buzz for me. Dragon and I finalized some understandings and I drove off with Micah in my trunk. I wasn't sure what I was officially going to do with him. To kill him or not to kill him was on my mind heavy. Sometimes a situation presented itself where it seemed as if you could get a clear solution, then things changed. The battle with Micah was building, and killing him outright didn't seem like the smartest thing to do. Especially not after finding out he was FBI. Besides, I wanted to play with him like he played with me. If I killed him, questions would arise I was sure. I had faith in my skills to hide the body, but I didn't know how much he had in those files Angel told me about. I didn't know if he had a file on me. With the way Micah had been coming at me to do his dirty, shit, anything was possible. My moves from here on out had to be well thought out and planned accordingly. Which was why hours later, I sat in front of him in the basement of an abandoned house. He hung like a roasting pig. His arms behind his back, and his ankles tied to his wrists.

A fat blunt rested between my teeth as I sat wide-legged in front of him. I crossed my arms and tugged on the rope that had had him hoisted up. I could see he was awake but playing like he wasn't.

"Sup, homie. Took you awhile to wake the hell up; you enjoying yourself?" I casually asked with a bored expression on my face. I let the comforting release of smoke from my lips flush his face and I swore that nigga turned ten shades of blacker from it.

"Fuck you! Let me down! You just fucked up your whole life do you understand that?" he shouted at me.

It really was interesting to me that he kept saying that. Especially when I was at a point of not giving two shits. "Naw, see, football players go to prison all of the time. The industry loves its mules and as long as I'm still usable, the game will always have need of me. Unlike you. See, my PR can flip it and call me a bad boy and I'll still get money, love, and breeches, as my nana used to say. You? You get nothing but to swing here for however long I want you to."

Micah's eyes narrowed and he tried to struggle again and buck at me, but it just had me sighing, and tugging on the rope then making him drop into a slant on his head.

"I told you leave me and mine alone."

"Fuck that. I knew you'd do exactly what I wanted. I knew you couldn't let the streets not get to you, do you even know who the fuck you are? Damn, nigga, you so much like him it's fucking comical," Micah grunted, and laughed before coughing.

"Once I get out, your aunt Iya—ain't that her name, pretty name—and your brother Andrew are going to taste me in a way you ain't even ready for!" he choked out. I could see his throat muscles working to hold bile back.

"As if you could find them, but check it. Damn you drunk so much you ready to vomit? I wouldn't if I were you. How I got you set up, one of two things will happen: you'll choke on that vomit, and the blood already rushing and pooling to your skull will knock you out, and you'll still choke on your vomit. Damn kinda fucked up huh?"

My feet kicked out in front of me and I stood grabbing my bag and pulling out my toys. Micah's coughs stopped and he went back to struggling. "Let me out. Look, we can call this shit even right? I'll leave you to yours and you leave me to mine. Keep making money on all sides and we can be coo wit' it yeah?"

"Ah huh?" I said while strolling to him. I moved near him and showed him a wire hanger. "These your initials right? Let me give to you like you gave to others."

Micah struggled again and I sighed turning the wire in my gloved hands. "Nigga, ain't shit you could do to me that will put the fear of . . . Ahhhhh!"

See, he thought I was going to brand him,
naw. That wire had a loose part, small enough
to enter right into where he pissed. The smell of
charcoal filled the room and I pushed that metal
probe deeper into his dick before pulling out.

"Might want to see a doctor about that shit,
my man. Now what were you saying?" I asked,
putting the hanger down. I grabbed my tanto
sword and walked back to him, resting my hand
on his ribcage. "Because I really don't give a
fuck; everything I'm doing it's for your understanding, not mine. I told you what I want and
need you to do. All you gotta do is hold up on
your end with my needs, my wants. Yeah?"

Micah's sweat dripped down his contorted
face. I could see he was trying to stay conscious
so I tugged on the chain that held him up and
positioned him so his blood could settle in his
body again. Unfortunately, for Micah, I also
slipped my sword right into his ribcage and
turned it as I pulled out.

"Ahhhhhh!" his scream continued. I patted
his jaw and went back to his bag, pulling out a
needle full of indigo and heroin.

"Can't let you pass out just yet, nigga. So yeah,
by now I'm thinking you thinking, what the fuck
is wrong with this nigga? And it's like this: you
fucked with my brother and thought that shit

would ignite an ounce of fear in me? Yeah, it did, but, see, I got a fucked-up, twisted way in how fear operates in me. This right here is the results of my fear. I never was a nigga who understood why my old boss felt to have an underworld. But right now, between me and you, I get it and I'm enjoying having this time with you so that you can understand what you need to do," I purred out in a menacing tone.

"I . . . I understand. I got you. Just let . . . me—"

"Naw, man," I interrupted. "You just relax, because *mi casa es su casa.*"

I walked up to him, and continued my torture on him. Injecting him with poison and doing to him exactly what he did to my brother and to Angel, except in pain. I took the time to use a scalpel and tweezers to peel the flesh back from his face on one side. From his bottom eyelid all the way down his face, I peeled. By the time I was done, Micah was back upside down hanging. His flesh lay hanging off him and I finishing cleaning off his blood from my gloves.

"Money . . . I can get you . . ." he drawled out, choking on his blood.

A smirk spread across my face and I shook my head. "You chill the fuck out. We'll continue this shit later. One."

I closed the door and locked it behind me as I whistled. I knew he'd scream, but it wouldn't matter; no one would hear a thing.

It was another hour before I headed back to my condo. I cleaned up before I left the drop house. I dressed in all black again and discarded the evidence of my demented talents. I was still in a dark mood when I stepped into my crib and saw Angel on top of my brother. I was already seeing red. What replaced it was something worse, something darker. I wasn't into putting my hands on broads, but in this moment, all I saw was her fucking my brother again.

Like the bitch was a fucking pedophile nympho? After everything, the game was just what it was? All the drugs and shit pumped in her, after what she had said, she now was accepting the bullshit and fucking my kid brother? That shit wasn't about to go down on my watch, in my fucking home at that, so I rushed her and fucked her up. I snatched her by her fucking hair and smacked her as hard as I could without breaking her fucking jaw. She gave me a good fight back, but I wasn't even caring about it. The more she fought back, the angrier I became. Like what the fuck in her psyche made her think it was okay to do that to a boy? A kid?

I grabbed her by her throat as she lashed out at me, hitting me with everything she had: closed fists, slaps, scratches and kicks. I could hear myself calling her every whore and bitch I thought her to be. My hands connected to her face and body over and over. Everything had been put on replay for me and all I wanted was to break that bitch's neck.

It was like Micah's voice was in my head and I could hear his laughter as I stood in the hallway of my condo. Bitch played me up the middle and now my kid brother was in front of me defending her sick shit.

"Get out my way, Drew!" I hissed out, nostrils flaring, chest rising up and down in fury.

He held me back as best he could, shouting at me to chill. "It ain't even like that."

"It ain't like what, Drew? Angel fucking you again, touching you again, huh?" I shouted out. It felt like my soul was peeling from my flesh in agony at the thought.

"Naw, but you sure is fucking her right? I get it though; a ho for everyone right?" Drew snidely responded.

My head tilted to the side at what he said and it had me backing down. "Fuck you mean, nigga?"

"You heard me, nigga," he said in the same tone as me.

We stood glaring at each other like twins. I was taller and well built but Drew was growing up just as strong and stocky as me.

"Oh shit, so you on some broken heart bullshit huh? You get your dick wet for the first time, when you fucking shouldn't have, and now you in love? Why the fuck you here anyway, li'l dude?"

Drew's anger flashed across his face and I saw his fist come my way. I ducked and body blocked him before glaring at Angel who came running out.

"Enzo! Shawn, please stop. It's not what you're thinking. I wasn't doing . . ." Angel pleaded, trying to get through to me, but all I heard was air.

The pain in her eyes, the fear, and look of abandonment couldn't even get to me in that moment. I was in blackout mode and there was no coming out of it.

"Back up off us. I ain't got shit to do with you no more," I growled out.

Drew struggled as I held him over my shoulder moving down the hall, until I made it down to the parking lot. Sirens were everywhere and I didn't want to draw attention to us. I'd seen them when I came in, but didn't need the attention so I kept it moving.

"Get the fuck in the car, Drew," I ordered, dropping him down near my ride. He glared at me, but he knew to get in that shit just like I said.

I got in behind him then pulled off. We made our way out of the garage. I thought we would have to go through some shit, but luckily the cop they had guarding the exit was a Nightwings fan. For a picture and an autograph, he let me through with no problems. Once we were out of harm's way, I could see Drew straining hard to see what was going on.

"Looking for something?" I asked as we drove away.

"Yeah: a fuck you." Drew grumbled and sat back.

"You know what, fuck you too. Don't start being a fuck up, because that only makes shit worse for you and this fam, nigga. So you killing people now?" I asked, keeping my eyes on the road.

"How you fucking know what I'm doing or not?" Drew spat out then abruptly shifted up to look at me. "You fucking her!"

"Check it, one, you left a fucking body down with a sloppy kill in the area where Angel parks her ride. I was coming in when I saw that, nigga. What you did was sloppy as fuck. And I know it was you because Angel is too chicken

shit to kill anybody. Nobody else knows who
Kruger is around here so that only leaves you.
I'm not here to clean up after you, nigga. If you
going to be in your dick and start killing niggas
you need to be smart with that shit. You can't
just be killing niggas for fun."

"I ain't kill that nigga for fun. He was trying to
get Angel."

"And you were feeling like you were invinci-
ble I guess?" Drew glared at me. I kept talking.
"And me and Angel fucked, so you mad?" I said
in spite.

Drew swung forward catching my jaw, it had
me swerving the car and pulling over to connect
my fist in his face. We went at each other, in the
car, just like that before stopping and glaring at
each other, breathing hard in anger.

I licked my lips and shook my head. "Why are
you coming at me like you stupid?"

"Why you leave us hanging?" Drew countered.

My eyes closed before I pulled off again. "I
had to do some shit I ain't want to do for this
family and now it looks like you doing sloppy
stupid shit; why?"

"Because," was all Drew said.

"You need to get Angel out of you because she
ain't yours to keep, or have. She's her own, and
what y'all did wasn't lovemaking, or fucking. It

was straight-up rape. You need to understand that," I said looking at Drew.

"Why you fuck her then?" he countered again, and I almost punched him in his throat.

"Look, this is me and you. Ain't nothing separating us because we got love and we got blood, period. Loyalty is to you and my fam. Me and her fucked because we just did. I know you feeling her, but she ain't going to get with a thirteen-year-old. That shit just ain't going to happen."

"Yeah, but you don't know—"

I interrupted him. "She's not going to get down like that period and it ain't just 'cause I said so; it's factual. You shoulda had your dick wet by some girl your age, a shorty who was feeling you and you was feeling her and it was agreed on between you two, period. Ain't nothing you did cool. Nothing. But check it: her heart is, io'no. But look, she'll be your friend but don't expect shit else but that, it just can't and won't work."

"How do you know?"

"You see how she avoids you like the plague now? That means she ain't seeing you the way you see her. You can't be with her. You can't fuck her."

"But you two can?" he asked.

Staring at my baby brother, I was trying to get to his mental and help him understand the situation. What he'd done was really fucking with me on many levels. It had me going over many things in my mind with my link to Angel. She and I had a history, one where we survived fucking around with that nigga Dame. Both of us survived that shit with cuts, bruises, and battle wounds to count. Trying to leave that life behind hadn't been as easy as we thought it would be. The fact that my brother just went balls in the paint for Angel had me thinking hard. It had me realizing just how similar he and I were.

Shit, it wasn't that far back when Angel was dropped back into my life that I'd promised I would look after her, and I'd kept my word. It wasn't easy for me to sit there while watching my brother change through the seeds of pain and fucking insanity that now were placed into his spirit. Damn, I knew what that was like. I had tried to protect him from it, but here we were. Wasn't nothing I could do about it but try to help him through it.

Which was why I sat there working up the words to get my brother back on an even plane. I wanted to help him see that what went down between him and Angel was some fucked-up sick and twisted shit used as a means of manipulation.

After coming down from my anger, that pain that lived in my mind and soul like a second person, I realized what was really going on. Angel fought hard with me to make me see it, going so deep to remind me about how Dame was, and how he groomed females. Now my baby brother was a result of the game this nigga was playing, and we all were being forced to do shit that none of us ever wanted. It hurt to the core of who I was, and only added to the levels of insanity that was eating at me.

My baby brother was me, and I was him. Two devils growing into monsters. I had to save some of his light as much as I could. I had to and I would do whatever to make sure he never turned into me, or worse.

I could see hurt in his eyes but I could see an understanding. "Man, I don't even know what we're doing. We ain't doing shit. We fucked. I needed pussy, she needed dick, and we both agreed to that together. You'll understand that one day."

Drew sat quietly in thought. I shook my head and took the car to where I had Micah. I didn't say nothing but told him to get out.

"What's this place? Why the hell you got me here, big bro?" Drew asked.

His questions were pissing me the fuck off, but I keep it pushing. "If you want to be a fucking man, you need to act like it. If you gonna be a fucking killa you need to be smart about it. I can't stop you from doing what you gonna do, nigga, but you will listen and you will do things smart, like a man and not like a kid whose heart broke. Micah fucked us all up. He took from you, so I'm taking from him."

Drew watched me in confusion, following me through the house. I led him downstairs then opened the door.

"Micah! Wassup, nigga, or down I should say. You looking mad pale, my man, and a little thirsty. Let me help you with that."

I had Drew stand back and I walked in, adjusted the chains around Micah so he could shift from his downward hanging position, to standing up and facing us. I could tell he wanted to say something but couldn't, which had me smiling. Walking forward, I took a large glass, filled it with warm water from the tap, and held it up so he could drink. I watched him struggle to get to the rim and I felt my brother's eyes on us.

In that moment I was the devil, and I whipped out a towel, dropped it over Micah's face, watched him kick and struggle to breathe. The worse of it came when I turned that big glass of water over and let it stream down over his face. Micah's screams became louder as he began to drown in my waterboarding tactic. I let that go on for about a couple of minutes before stepping back and tilting my head for Drew to step all the way in.

A stillness came over my little brother before he walked in. I moved to close the door behind us. This began his first lesson in my way of war.

I sat him down, schooled him on what I learned E.N.G.A. meant, and then began to let him get whatever anger, pain, and madness that was growing into him out on Micah. I could see he liked a lot of what he did, but I took him to the side and gave him real talk on what we were. We were killers, but we weren't murderers. Our kills will be nothing like those who come for us, but the pain, the insanity, they definitely were going to get. He listened to me for hours before I was finished. I didn't know what he was thinking after all we had done. I couldn't read my little brother in the moment. He was like me for sure. We were both deep in thought, getting high off the tortuous acts we had committed. Neither of us would ever admit it though. It made me wonder just what Micah had awakened in me. My *tía* was on my mind heavy, so after I locked the drop house down, I told Drew we were out.

"Let's go see *Tía*," I quietly said watching the darkness of the sky.

Chapter 19

Shy

My coughs ripped through my body, causing my chest to burn from the roughness of the release. I never in my life felt as weak as I was feeling right now. Life was coming full circle, and crashing into us like waves at a beach. There was nothing I could do anymore to stop what was happening and it only put a fear in me that I was trained not to have. I glanced around my bed at the two young men in my life who had given me a joy like no other. It brought tears to my eyes at how much love they had for me, how much support they were giving me. That's why it made it harder for me to do what I knew had to be done.

"*Tía,* you need to rest. I know you're doing better and I'm happy about that but you need to rest," came from Enzo. His hazel eyes were dark in concern. There was only one time in my life where they turned a dark coal that put a fear in my soul that had me quickly trying to soothe that demon out of him. It hurt that I was about to bring it back out of him.

There was something going on between him and Drew, and it wasn't just because I had heard them talking in hushed tones outside of my room, but it was because I could read their body language clearly. I could always see when they were fighting, because they were so close, and right now, the tension was thick. I had blown up Shawn's cell phone asking him if he knew where Drew was. Drew had been on some emotional brooding shit, to the point that him and me had got into it and he stormed out.

Micah had hurt my boy, broke and changed his soul. I could see it was tainting his mental. Proof of that was in the change in his eyes. My hand moved to my remote control and I turned off the news reporting of a shooting at Shawn's condo complex. Reporters were saying they had no leads, but I already knew in my heart one or both of the young men before me were involved.

Coughing, I shook my head and sat up. "Come here. I want to hold both of your hands."

"Yes, ma'am." Both of my boys complied.

I studied Drew's face. His experience had aged him some. His carefree eyes held that of a quiet wisdom, too, which also made my heart sad. I reached up to run my hand over his curls, watching a smile flash on his face as he sat to the left of me.

"Okay. I'll make this brief. We all know I'm dying and it hurts my heart to say that but it is what it is. This family is breaking and I refuse to let it be destroyed when I pass. You two need to keep your bond of loyalty and trust between each other strong, no matter what may come your way or what you two may beef about; and I know your twenty-first birthday is coming up Shawn, but I want all anger and negative between us all to have settled by then because we have things to handle with the enemy."

Shawn bowed his head and squeezed my hand tight. "Ain't no negativity happening between us, *Tía,* and naw, your death? That's not what's happening okay? You got new doctors, new medicine. Better help than before. You're not dying; and me and Drew, we're good. We're just dealing with some shit you don't need to worry about right now."

"Yeah, *Tía,* we'll be a'ight. No worries, and no stress between us, on our word. I'm just worried about you. I'm not feeling what you said, because you are getting better," Drew said trying to reassure me with added hope.

They were lying and they could tell I knew it, but I wasn't going to even press it right now. I was going to let them both have that right now. From what I had seen on the news, this life of chaos was going to get worse. It was time things came to the light from the right person. I didn't want to leave my boys. I wanted to stay and pro-tect them for however long that I could and it warmed my heart that they both had that faith in my recovery and me.

"I'm sorry my heart . . . Let me say that bet-ter. I've been sick for so long that I learned that with this life you have to live as best as you can. I hope I put that in you, because I just want to say thank you for giving me your love and letting me love you this long. I have a story I have to tell you both and if it makes you both not love me, I understand. If you two hate me for it all, I get it and won't take nothing from you because of it. I . . . I just want you two to know I did the best that I could and I'll take with me this love you two have given me now and be content with that."

Drew slid a little closer to me, handing me a cup of water as I tried to get my thoughts together. "*Tía,* man, whatever it is, we always love you. You don't have to say nothing, we good."

I shook my head and handed him my cup back. "No, but I love you for that support. You two need to know this because after what happened to you both, I see that I can't keep my story quiet anymore. You both need it to not only protect yourselves but to understand the real meaning behind E.N.G.A. and go after those who come between you two."

Shawn's watching eyes began to darken. I could see he was trying to figure out what I was saying and it made me nervous.

"I need you two to promise to listen to my story and not leave before I can finish it please," I pleaded.

Both Shawn and Drew glanced at each other and I reached out to cup their faces and gaze into their eyes. They both took after me, but I also saw an equal balance of the man I hated for so very long in them at the same time. It made some interesting hybrid of the two of us. Two boys with the looks of angels but the roughness of a warrior all in the mix. Women were going to curse at their creation and find pleasure in it all at the same time. I could only pray that the rest of my DNA overrode their father's, and that any demons in them they would be able to control and use for their own means in good ways.

"Shawn. Andrew. Promise me. No punk shit," I demanded.

This time they both nodded. "Yes, ma'am, we promise."

Licking my dry lips, I lay back and gave a sigh closing my eyes, reminiscing. "Okay, then I can speak the full truth now. Some of this I shared with Drew already, but here is the full story. I was seventeen when I came to Atlanta from DC. I got into Spelman early to be with my cousin: your godmother, and our best friend." A smile spread across my face in the memory as I spoke.

"My parents used to send me to New York to visit my grandparents in Harlem every summer, especially when your . . . your mother Sade was doing her thing overseas in college. It's where me, my cousin Nicky, and Tee-Tee, grew up and ran the streets. Tee-Tee lived in Brooklyn. We would meet up at the train to do our thing. We'd sneak to Manhattan and go to the shops and steal the newest guap that we could find and take it back and be flossin' like we bought it. It was always small stuff that the parents couldn't figure out, but we did it anyway."

Pausing, I took another sip of water and thanked Shawn for handing it to me that time. "Anyway. We were our own clique. The baddest bitches on the street, especially because we sometimes ran after the baddest niggas on the street, Tee-Tee's big brother Cozy Black and his best friend, who was like a brother to him, Battle. Man, Cozy, and Battle were, back then, those were the niggas every *chica* wanted and needed. But we were the ones who got chill with them, especially when Tee introduced Nicky to Cozy Black."

I made sure they both were following me and I paused to see if they were. "Remember what I taught you both, to listen to the messages between the lines. Hear what people are saying as they give you knowledge?"

"Yes, ma'am, we're listening," Shawn reassured me.

Nodding, I sighed and continued. "Okay, we all were thick as thieves. For a moment there, Cozy and I hooked up, but he was feeling Nicky so we chilled on that, though he had her too. Nicky and I had a closeness like sisters even though we were cousins. So whatever I had, she had, and the same was for me. I'd go visit our grandparents' and her parents' homeland of Nigeria and just kick it hard; so would Tee-Tee. So understand that there was no beef ever between us when messing with Cozy. He was into his own world with Battle anyway, suave fucker that he is . . . was. They both were."

"*Tía*, take your meds, here," Shawn calmly stated, handing me my pills to take and leaning back against the bed with me to listen.

It was like he was my little boy again, him and Drew, and they were listening to me tell them about Africa, and our black history and reading them their favorite comics. This was something I would take with me until the end.

"So, when it was time for us to go to college, we made a promise to get in at the same school and not break up and we did. Everyone was happy about it. We headed down there, and this was like in the mid-nineties. Atlanta was still hot, still poppin' on a level you all don't even understand, feel me. We had so much fun. Freaknik had just been told to end, but it was still pockets of it going on. The girls and I were heading to one such party. We were dressed alike, looking too cute. Cozy Black had come to the campus to visit as an international student. By then, he had changed his name to Phenom."

I watched both boys sit up abruptly and look at me. I held my hand up to quiet them. "Listen, please, you know how my meds get me and I may fall asleep soon so listen. I said that wrong; he not only changed his street name from Cozy to Phenom, but he changed his real name as well. We all grew up on some spiritual principles that were a mishmash of C.O.G.I.C. values, with that of Buddhism, Ifá Orisa teachings, NGE United principles, which has Islamic beliefs in it, and we studied *The Art of War,* with other Asian strategic principles, hard. This was all because of our grandparents. But, anyway, he and Battle both changed their names once they started embracing the teachings, all after we had to leave NYC from bullshit we all got into. I loved visiting NYC but you can't get me to go back."

Licking my lips I glanced at him again. "Battle kept his name but we fell into using his new changed name, Jamir. Anyway, we all were heading out to the party. Battle and Phenom had gave us the nickname African Queens and we were down for that hard. When we got to the spot, we had a good time. Music jumpin' making all us big-booty girls pop it."

A soft laughter came from me and I patted both boys' hands. "Anyway, that night, me, Nicky, and Phenom went and hooked up for some fun. He had asked, and 'cause of some deal the two had, we all just did us. It was fun. I decided to catch back up to Battle and Tee-Tee, which was bad, because I ran into this tall dude on my way back to them. He had some other guys with him and they surrounded me; he kept talking slick, saying things like, I was watching you watch me. Said I was pretty for a redbone. He wanted to play in my long, thick hair and see if I was a screamer because he liked screamers. I stood there feeling sick, that this old nigga was talking like he was to me. I felt disrespected because every man in my family taught us women that we were queens and this nigga had me feeling like the lowest piece of shit alive."

Tears started rimming my eyes and I exhaled slowly and continued. "I told him that was nice and shit but I wasn't into old Al B. Sure!—looking niggas, with gray lint-lined dicks. Old dusty wrinkle nuts niggas who look like they wear more eyeliner than I do and I bounced."

Flashes of that night replayed in my mind. I saw myself pushing past greasy, thirsty motherfuckers who kept grabbing at my ass, tits, and pussy, with malicious grins on their faces as they laughed. Several razor blades whipped from my bangles. I cut each nigga who had nerve to touch me, and I ran.

"I remembered him laughing hard, saying we would meet again. I didn't believe it, but we did. The Queens and I worked in the community a lot for our sorority, so we were chillin' in the Trap when I ran into that nigga with the coal black eyes. He was leaning against a black Benz, in all white from head to toe. It was like he was eating me and stabbing me at the same time until he drove away."

Both Shawn and Drew made me comfortable in the bed. "Nicky and Tee-Tee had seen him watching me. So I told them that that was the guy who had tried to grab up on me."

My mind tinkered back as I remembered our conversation:

"Iya? That's that mothafucka that got greasy wit' you mama?" Tee-Tee asked with tone dripping from her lips. She stood next to me watching a man who was starting to scare me in a way I wasn't used to. Tee-Tee placed a hand on her ample coochie-cutter clad hip, and pushed her pretty, thick braids over her shoulder. We wore matching outfits, except my shorts were longer and just showing my thick thighs and accenting my white cami.

No words were coming from me because I was to frightened to even admit that nucca was punking me out. It was Nicky's soft and airy, slightly accented voice that drew my attention. She gave a slight giggle, but her words were all malice. "Yeah, that's that oshara nigga: that brand new nigga. He is about to see his death very soon."

I glanced at Nicky. She was sporting braids too but she had them braided up into a bun on the top of her head. She wore a set of Timbs with overall Dickey shorts that seemed to showcase her badass shape even in the bagginess of her clothes. Worry had me fisting my hands around my hung ankh necklace, but I wanted this nigga to leave me alone and I did not know any other way to do besides getting buck.

"Nicky, what you thinking to do?" I quickly asked.

A pretty smile spread across my cousin's pretty face as she addressed me. "That nigga is nothing but a gbege man; a trouble man. How do we deal with niggas doing runs on us? We twist it back into our favor, mamas, you know that."

We all nodded in understanding and I glanced back his way narrowing my eyes then flipping him off as he pulled away. "He made a mistake he will one day understand. Iku ya j'esin. Death is preferable to ignominy."

Nicky smiled at my words and Tee-Tee smacked on her gum with a laugh. She rested her elbow on my shoulder speaking up as she played with my huge afro puff ponytail. "Ya, big noi kore. A big mistake, but not yours. His ignominy will be his death and bring his ayewo, misfortune. Remember, feign disorder, and crush him. Sun Tzu."

Those words became our motto. Later that day, we took to the Trap. It wasn't hard finding his spot, because everyone made sure to know of a place they never wanted to go to. We found that nigga's ride and we took metal bats with wire wrapped around them to his Benz. Any car that was around we smashed it up. Shattered glass was everywhere. Tee-Tee scraped the painting off every car she could find, then both Nicky and me sucked out the gas in a few, letting it leak on the ground, then set that shit on fire.

One of Lu's men came out right when we were leaving and I flipped the nailed-up bat in my hand, swinging it upward to snap his neck back then smash his face in. Nicky's boot followed when his large frame hit the dirt, breaking his neck in the process and we all left out before being caught as Tee-Tee let out birdcalls for everyone in the Trap to hear. That night was the birth of the African Queens. Something I'd always remember fondly.

Coming back to reality, I could tell Shawn and Drew had questions and I needed to know what was on their mind. "Talk to me, honeys; what do you want to know?" I asked.

Shawn glanced at Drew, and then spoke up. "You telling me, you know that dude Phenom? That you two were close and . . . Wait, the African Queens. You started that shit? But . . ."

I nodded and sighed. "Very close; and yes, we did. Anika is my cousin, honey, and Tee-Tee . . ." My head bowed and I licked my lips. "Tee-Tee is and was . . . Trigga's mother, Fatima."

Shawn's shock echoed through the whole room. "What!"

"Please, listen; just sit and listen, please. May I continue? It's more; you don't even understand."

He said nothing to me and kept pacing, so I continued. "Anyway, that nigga kept stalking me after learning my routine. It was only when I was heading home to my dorm that it got crazy. See back then, downtown wasn't as clean as it is now. I mean Spelmen, Morehouse, all that area sat right in the hood. We could sling if we wanted and still make time for the books, it was that crazy. Well, I was coming back from having worked all night, when he found me on the Promenade. He basically followed me and told me that in order to work in his city, to live in his city, that I needed to introduce myself to the King of the South, Lu Orlando. Said that he was done with the games and that it was time to pay my dues. He said he wanted me because I was slick mouth and ignored him. Said he liked that, and it was a bonus I was pretty. Said he could use me to be his top bitch. That's when I ran."

The memories flooded me hard. It was like I was there again, fighting for my life and fighting against an evil I had only experienced in my nightmares.

"I couldn't understand why he was working so hard to get me, but I soon found out after he snatched me. He took me to an old house close to the campus where he raped me multiple times. Told me I had some good tight pussy. Said I would make him some good money. Told me he knew when he was in Harlem, talking business with my grandfather, that I'd be something sweet. A chill like nothing else went through me. I knew my grandpops was an old gangsta and that he'd meet with many wannabe thugs from around the nation, who were pushing up to be big bosses like him, but I didn't remember this nigga. I never remembered the nigga with a face of an angel but the dark eyes of the devil; his name fit him perfect, Lucifer."

My hand slid to my stomach as I continued, "I fought hard. Took the lessons I learned from my family to survive and fought back. I know the only reason I was able to get free was because he liked the chase. I knew I couldn't tell anyone because we all had heard of Lu in the streets. He was that nigga everyone ran from and didn't cross. You do what he says or you die and I did not want any of my friends and family to find out, so I kept quiet. I was so young and stupid."

Sighing, I wiped at my eyes. "I held the teachings of my grandmother and mother to heart in that moment. Words they shared with us girls before coming to the A. One I taught you two well. Ifa says, 'if one chooses to keep quiet when there is a problem, the entire problem will stay permanently with one.'" While I said those words, Drew chimed in saying it with me, with Shawn finishing it.

A light, sad smile spread across my face as I continued, "I practiced that religiously up until now. I became a gatekeeper of all of our secrets. Anyway, back then, I made sure to be in places he couldn't find me, but that never worked. I only was able to keep from being snatched again because I was around people, but that only lasted for so long. The second time he got me was when I went to DC for a wake for my grandparents.

"We weren't going to NYC for it, so we had it at my parents'. Lu walked in as if he owned the place and paid his dues. The moment I saw him, I knew I wasn't going to get away from him and I didn't. He cornered me when I was speaking to an old friend of my grandfather's in the hallway. He snatched me up. Told me to lead him to a quiet spot, and he raped me again. This time he used his belt and wrapped it around my throat to quiet me from screaming. He went at me for hours before anyone noticed I was gone. He left me a mess, and it was Anika who found me. Back then, we weren't the African Queens you know today. I have to say Lu shaped us into that, especially when I found out I was pregnant. She and Fatima helped me hide. I couldn't go far, so I went to Macon. I thought I was safe. I couldn't afford an abortion and I didn't want one. So, several months after my eighteenth birthday, I gave birth to a beautiful baby boy. That little boy was my life, my world and I loved him regardless of the circumstances of his birth. Shawn, please . . ."

As I was talking, Shawn had stopped his pacing; the moment I said those words, his fist went flying into the wall of my bedroom. I scrambled in the bed, and Drew even backed away in confusion just watching me. I screamed for Shawn to stop and he did, turning to look at me with red eyes.

"No fucking way! You lying . . . You are fucking lying!" he shouted.

I held both hands up as tears spilled down my face. My lungs felt compressed, burning, clogged, and tired. I shook my head no in anguish. It was Drew who came to my side and it was Drew who got Shawn to calm down enough for me to rest back in the bed and continue.

"Enzo," Drew shouted, but I cut into anything he had to say just to get this out.

"I'm so sorry. I . . . I did what I had to keep you from him. He . . . he still stalked me. Found me in Macon, this time with Sade. She had come to visit you and I when I saw his car parked across the street of my apartment. I had thought Anika, Fatima, and I had found a safe spot but we didn't. I had survived a full year with you and that nigga kept finding me. Sade took you to the store so I could sleep. As I was sleeping, he kicked the door into my place and found his way to me. You know what happens next."

By this time, I was breathing hard and trying to stay clear-minded. "He was pissed that I had left. Told me he'd find me and that he was bored with the pussy he already had and he needed my screams. I used to scream so much for him, after a while I stopped. When my sister came back, that nigga was naked in my kitchen making a sandwich and smoking weed. It was then that he saw you. She told me she covered your face and it was she who started the lie. She said you were hers and that she was visiting. Long story short, at that time, he didn't give a damn about her. Told her he had two spawns of his own he had to care for."

My lips trembled and I knew I was working on borrowed time. "He . . . he left us and I made a plan with my sister to keep you safe. She moved you away with her to Kennesaw, and I stayed in Macon until moving back to Atlanta. Anika helped me with that too and I didn't hear from Lu for the longest of times. I thought I was safe again because the time had passed. I picked up finishing school and got my nursing degree. Sade would bring you to me to visit on the regular and I would visit her. She was a good woman then, my best friend always, my loving big sister. I never was really aware of the changes in her then. I never knew until reading her diary later, after she'd died, that Lu had found you two in Kennesaw much earlier than I had believed.

"In her diary, I learned she had made a deal with him to leave me alone, but eventually that got too much for her, and I found out, when she came and when I saw his name tattooed on her back. I tried to get you back, Shawn, but . . . we both agreed that maybe going to another state was safer for you and her, so she took you to Chicago. She was doing great, except she didn't finish her international law degree, and became a Realtor. You lived the rest. My sister started deteriorating and I never knew because I was busy fighting Lu off of me, after he found me again. Every attack was worse. He locked me up in my own attic one time because he was mad that he didn't bust a nut." I muttered the last part in memory.

I bowed my head in shame, and continue talking to my hands. "He treated me like an animal but also made me act like a wife. It got worse when I was working with Tee-Tee, I mean Fatima, and Jamir in cleaning up the streets of Atlanta. In between visiting you whenever I could, I worked hard to find ways to leave Atlanta. By then Tee-Tee had married Battle and they had Trigga and my godniece Assata. Eventually, Lu left me alone again and I found out that I was pregnant again, this time with another precious piece of my heart, who I named Andrew after my dad."

This was when Drew stood up and ran his hands over his head.

"Drew, I kept you as long as I could. I knew Lu was still having me watched, so I made sure to hide my pregnancy. I went to Chicago to give birth, and then stayed around you for three months after you were born, and then Sade kept you so we didn't cause suspicion. Then after, I'd ship my milk up to you. At that time, I still didn't know he had found her."

As I spoke, I could feel my pills kicking in. "I . . . I couldn't tell you two any of this because of the pain, because how do you tell two young men, who you love to your soul, that their father is the man who bred the very man the Trap feared. I tried to keep you both out of the streets because of this. I tried to keep you, Shawn, from his touch but still, you found your way in your brother's hands. In Dante's hands. I tried. I killed niggas to protect you two. I dug many graves in the streets of Atlanta under the African Queens moniker. When Fatima was killed by Lu's hand, I knew this shit was only going to get worse. Lu had the A on lock. People were afraid of their own shadows. Anika and I began to plan. Eventually that plan included Phenom and the rest is what it is, but I tried."

Shawn's booming voice echoed in the silence of the room. His eyes now coal black, the demons in him were alive. "No! Fuck the tried. You sat here, you fucking sat here, and never told me, us, the truth. You have no motherfucking idea what I went through, *Tía*. Nah, that ain't even it huh? When Mom would lock herself away, it would be days we didn't eat. I fucking had to run the streets and get us food. Had to change Drew's dirty diapers that he used to be sitting in for hours. You don't fucking know! Naw, no, you fucking knew and you kept us there."

My hands cupped my aching face. Hot tears fell and my body began to shake. "I had to keep you away from him. I wish I had known earlier. We had no one to go to. Our grandparents were dead, my mom and pops had ended up dying two years before Drew's birth. We had nothing but our minds and plans to keep you secret and I'd do that shit again if I had to, but I'd do it better where he couldn't find you."

"You fucking telling me all this shit that the African Queen got now, you didn't have then to get help huh? Naw."

"Shawn! We were empire building then. Kids in college trying to figure out that the games our parents play will fall onto the children. It happened to me, and now it's happening to you and Drew. This is why I always told you parts of my story, in hopes that one day you all would understand me. I'm so sorry."

"You kept us from you. You are our fucking mom and you kept that from us. That shit is wrong. Fuck the rest. Fuck that nigga Dame, that nigga Dante, and they fucking daddy. I don't want shit to do with them. Never did, never will. Fuck those bitch-ass niggas! That shit in this, your part, is wrong as fuck," Shawn spat out.

I watch him walked out, slamming doors on the way. I glanced at Drew. He was hurt and angry. The way his hands fisted and his eyes darkened let me know, but it was the quiet way he just stood there then walked out on me that hurt me hard. I sat in my karma, sat in my pain, and I lay down trying to find the snatches of love I had only momentarily had only hours ago.

Something I remembered Zora Neale Hurston saying ran deep in my soul: "If you are silent about your pain, they'll kill you and say you enjoyed it."

This is my truth and the truth hurts, but there it was for me. All I could do was pray on it, pray on my sons, and have faith.

E.N.G.A. Which makes this a new chapter, in a new game for us all.

Epilogue

Micah

Three weeks later

"Don't you think you're getting in too deep, Micah?"

I looked up into the eyes of the woman who had become more than a friend to me on many occasions. She had been the one woman I could go to no matter how fucked up of a situation I'd gotten myself into. I'd been undercover in this operation so long that sometimes I did lose myself. I'd forgotten what was real and what wasn't a long time ago.

I came into the FBI an eager kid ready to take on whatever task was handed to me so I could rise in the ranks and I did. But it all came with a price. The first member of DOA I put in prison cost my partner her life. She had gone in so deep that by the time she realized her time was near, it was too late. After she put Lu Orlando in prison, we'd thought we were well on our way to shutting down one of the major underworld bosses in the South. We were wrong.

The history of DOA went all the way back to the Harlem Renaissance days. Lu's pops and grandpops were legends back in New York until a woman came between Moses Ekejindu and Caltrone Orlando. Since then, the two families had made the United States and abroad their playground. The blood feud between the two families left bodies from border to border in their wake.

"I ain't fucking in deep enough. If I was I'd have Dame and Dante Orlando behind bars instead of in the fucking ground," I barked out at the woman.

"How many more bodies do you need behind bars? You've locked up countless people," she argued.

"And I still don't have the ones I want."

"Who else is there? The main two you want are dead."

"DOA goes a long way, Candace. Not to mention, I'm still looking for Moses Ekejindu's great grandson. Every time I think I know who he is, his face changes," I told the woman who didn't know how close she was to the case herself.

Candace stood and stripped the latex gloves she had on off. My bloody clothes lay scattered over her front room. Dr. Candace Lewis had been in my pockets since I'd first laid eyes on her. When two of Dame's girls had tried to run away from him, it was me who had to walk into her doctor's office to ensure that there wouldn't be any problems for us afterward.

"That doesn't explain why you're after this Shawn Banks kid so tough."

"It's best if I get to him before he realizes who he is," I said as I struggled to slowly get up from the sofa she had stitched me up on. It had been three weeks and my wounds still needed tending to like they had just happened.

Her chocolate face turned to me. "What does that mean?" The woman before me was shaped like she was made for the gods, but because I knew all of her dirty little secrets, she would never be more than a woman I used until I was tired of her. Any woman who would put their own flesh and blood out on the street was scum to me. But the pussy was good and she was resourceful. She kept the Bounce Girls treated monthly with Pap smears and such, at least the ones who handled my extra business on the side.

From the outside looking in, no one would know that I worked for the Feds. I'd taken my undercover moniker to the extreme and had no plans to turn the heat down anytime soon.

"That means that I want him to make a mistake so he can end up behind bars like his father. I never want a boy as ruthless as Enzo to know his full potential. Never. I'd kill the son of a bitch first. It took the Feds years to clean the street of Lu Orlando's rule and thanks to some ragtag misfits from the hood, his two sons are dead now too. But that means nothing. You hear me? Nothing compared to how far the DOA organization really goes. If that boy ever found out who he was"—I shook my head, or at least tried to—"or if the big players in that organization figured out that Lu still had a son out there, we'd be back at square one. We can't afford that," I rambled on.

"How do you even know that this boy is who you think he is? Do you have any proof that he is the son of this man?" she asked.

"Candace, I know what I'm talking about and that is all you need to know. When you've been infiltrating a faction as long as we have in DOA, you know shit. This boy is dangerous and needs to be off the street and if I could get that little one, his brother, off the street too, that would be all worth it. I want to wash the fucking world of any Orlando still on US soil."

I was talking more so to myself than I was to her. I thought back to five days I'd been left in the basement after Enzo had tortured me. There was no doubt in my mind that he would have killed me had I not found a way to untie myself. I'd seen a lot of shit that Dame had done to people in the basement when it came to torture, but none took the cake like when I'd seen Enzo torture people. I never thought I'd find myself on the receiving end of that shit. The look in that boy's eyes said that he was his father's son in that moment. With as evil as Dame and Dante were, I was willing to bet money and my life that Enzo would be worse.

I hobbled over to look in the mirror at the side of my face. The place on my face where he had peeled the skin from my eyelids all the way down to the right side of my neck was decorated in white gauzes. My vision was blurry in my right eye from the injuries to it. The burns to my back would take months to heal. It hurt like hell for me to piss because of the burned hanger that had been inserted into my dick. As I looked in the mirror, I barely recognized myself.

"You still in contact with your daughter?" I asked Candace.

She sighed and looked at me like I'd annoyed her with the question. "I made contact that one time and that was only because I'd happened to see her when she was out."

"Contact her again."

"Why?"

"Because I know for a fact that Enzo is close with Jackson Hawks. If we get to Hawks, we can get to Shawn, and the only way to get to Hawks is through your daughter. So can you do that for me?"

I had already made contact with Dominique. As long as I had her on the inside, everything was good, but I needed shit to be great. I needed more than one ace in the hole for me to be satisfied. Dom had been in Dame's pocket for a long time. At first I had wanted to tell the young girl to run as far away from that nigga as I could, but Dom had her own agenda. Once it was revealed, I knew her days would be numbered. So the next best thing for me was Candace.

Candace folded her arms across her chest and cut her eyes at me. "What's in this for me?" She confused me at times. For as beautiful as she was, there was an evil interior that would trade her own daughter to death for her own selfish reasons.

I had to ask, "Don't you even want to see her?"

She didn't answer. "Why?"

"She's your daughter."

"Your point? What's in this for me?"

I inwardly shook my head and hobbled back over to the bloodstained sofa. I picked up two Vicodin, popped them, and then chased them with bourbon whiskey. I knew what I was about to do was foul, but fuck it if I cared.

"I'll give you what you want," I lied to her.

Candace placed her hands on her hips and casted a skeptical look at me.

I held my hands up. "I'm serious. When this is all said and done, it'll just be me and you. I'll be done with this whole thing and I'll give you the life you want."

"And all I have to do is get Gina to talk to you?"

I shook my head. "No, I need for her to do more than talk. I need for her to get Jackson Hawks somewhere so I can get to him."

"I hope you come prepared. That's a big nigga."

I nodded once. "I know how big he is. I worked in Dame's world for years. Remember when he brought all of those misfits in. Get Gina to talk to you and get her to bring Hawks with her."

"She won't be hurt?" she asked.

That had me tilting my head to the side. "Thought you didn't care one way or the other."

"Answer me," she demanded.

I shook my head with a lie in my heart. I'd kill anybody to further my agenda. Every last person I had in on this shit was expendable, including Candace. "Look, I just want to talk to them. I ain't trying to kill either one of them."

"And once you get this Shawn kid, you'll be done?"

"Yes, I promise."

Candace smiled and walked over to sit next to me. She ran a delicate hand over the disheveled waves and scars in my head. "Then lets finish getting you all healed up so you can get on your job," she crooned.

The pills mixed with the bourbon were beginning to make my head light and the fact that I knew what was on her mind made my mood even better. The higher I stayed off the meds, the less pain I felt. I needed to sit back and regroup. That nigga damn near killed me. I was closer to death than I'd ever been. In fact my body felt as if I'd been embalmed. I really felt like a zombie walking. That was until I felt Candace wrap her plush lips around the head of my dick. I'd had a hot metal coat hanger stuck up my dick hole, so the fact that there was a little pain as it hardened didn't surprise me. However, Candace's mouth felt so good wrapped around my head, I could ignore the pain for the moment.

My head fell back and I exhaled loudly. She would never know I used to fuck her daughter, just like she would never see her death was imminent. She knew too much and for that reason, killing her would be easy . . . after she helped me with my agenda.